"Take it off!" one of the women yelled

Despite the humiliation Trace felt, the thought of Phoebe being jealous cheered him up a bit.

In time with the music, he opened the buttons of his shirt. The crowd practically groaned as one. God, he loved these women. Their yelps were going to drive Phoebe crazy.

Holding Phoebe's gaze, he kept his pelvis moving with the beat. He pictured her hands in place of his own and let that erotic image fill his eyes with hunger.

Trace watched the rapid rise and fall of her chest. Damn, he wanted her. He let his shirt fall to the ground, and the women screamed and whooped.

Adrenaline surged through his blood in spite of how stupid he felt dancing around the room like a gigolo. He gripped the front of his pants and let the anticipation build. From the corner of his eye he saw Phoebe staring. Purposely, Trace waited until their eyes met. Then he pulled.

Dear Reader,

I've always found it wildly attractive when a man knows how to dance. Bring me to a wedding reception or a New Year's Eve party, and my gaze is automatically drawn to the fellow who's effortlessly moving his body in rhythm with the beat. If the guy happens to be particularly talented at shaking his tail feathers, well, then, be still my beating heart. On these occasions, when I finally drag my eyes away and remember where I am, I inevitably discover that I'm not the only woman in the room gasping for breath. And this got me thinking....

Her Private Dancer is my first book and takes place in my home state of sunny Florida. I love romance and have been an avid reader for many years, but I've finally discovered something that I love even more—writing funny, steamy stories with quirky heroines and heart-pounding heroes. I hope you agree. Let me know what you think. You can write to me at P.O. Box 410787, Melbourne, FL 32941-0787. You can also send your e-mail to camidalton@earthlink.net or visit my Web site at www.camidalton.com.

Happy reading,

Cami Dalton

CAMI DALTON

HER PRIVATE DANCER

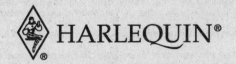

TORONTO • NEW YORK • LONDON
AMSTERDAM • PARIS • SYDNEY • HAMBURG
STOCKHOLM • ATHENS • TOKYO • MILAN • MADRID
PRAGUE • WARSAW • BUDAPEST • AUCKLAND

To Brenda Chin and Leslie Kelly for acts of friendship and kindness too numerous to mention. Thanks for getting me here. You guys are the best.

ISBN 0-373-69172-6

HER PRIVATE DANCER

_____Prologue_____

TRACE MCGRAW FORCED his mouth into a smile as he tilted his spandex-covered pelvis toward the elderly woman, who bore a striking resemblance to Mrs. Rosenthal, his grandmother's eighty-nine-year-old roommate at the Happy Vale Assisted Living Center. No sir, his second night on the job wasn't turning out to be any less embarrassing than his first. Especially, with Mrs. Rosenthal's twin staring at his package and all but licking her chops.

The look-alike briefly turned to the woman next to her and shouted over the wailing country-western song, "Ooh-wee. Get a gander of this one, Marge. Is that a gun in your drawers, cowboy," she crowed to Trace, "or are you just happy to see me?" The old woman nudged her friend with her elbow then laughed mischievously.

Colored lights flicked wildly around the room while a haze of smoke hovered above the all-female audience. The din of their cheers and whoops of approval almost drowned out the bass beat pounding from the speakers like a dozen tribal drums. Trace surmised that unfortunately, the friend, Marge, had still been able to hear since she removed a five-dollar bill from her purse and said, "I don't know, Delores. I think we're gonna need a better look." Then she wiggled her eyebrows.

After his first performance last night on board the _Mirage_, a casino ship out of Miami where twice a week the women of south Florida ruled the high seas, Trace knew what to expect. Even still, he wasn't quite prepared for the speed and dexterity with which good old Delores moved. Before he could even blink, Delores had snatched up the money and started reaching for his costume.

Trace bit back a curse, but held his pose, not moving so much as a tassel on his fringed chaps. The fringed chaps that blatantly highlighted the bulge in his black briefs. Not easy considering the look in Delores's eyes, but Trace couldn't blow his cover now no matter how much he wanted to slap his hands over his groin and run back to the dressing room. Or jump off the ship. That would be fine, too, three-mile swim back to shore and all.

Five nights a week, the *Mirage* left port for international waters where the ship threw open its casino doors then aimlessly wandered the Atlantic for a few scheduled hours of gambling, drinking and watching Vegas-style reviews. Glitzy productions complete with showgirls. During the regular cruises, that is. On the Ladies Only nights, the entertainment distinctly veered into dangerous territory. At least for Trace McGraw, newest member of the dance troupe, the Ladies' Knights. Miami's answer to Chippendales.

He almost sneered at the apropos comparison, but somehow kept his stupid smile plastered in place. *Damn, he hated this cover. And this story. And his editor, Manny....*

Trace cast a quick glance at the other male dancers on the floor, and wondered if they'd ever felt the same bone-deep humiliation he was experiencing. Obviously not, if the guy dressed as Tonto and gyrating away with some woman's hand down his thong was anyone to go by. Disgusted with just how far down his career had actually plummeted, Trace mentally hurried Delores along and shifted his stance to counter the floor's subtle pitch and roll.

All things considered, though, he should probably look on the bright side. At least he didn't have to get completely naked. Wearing this damn butt floss was definitely torture enough without being forced to show the full monty. Of course, his suede vest alone, worn open and shirtless, was sufficient to have him blushing like the proverbial virgin in a whorehouse—not to overdo the whole western theme here. The ten-gallon hat, chaps and thong were merely a bonus.

Delores finally finished slipping the bill into the spandex at his hip when Marge piped up, saying, "My turn. You're not in any rush, are you, cowboy?"

"Of course not, ma'am," Trace answered, hiding his grimace along with another healthy sigh, while Marge searched for more cash.

It wasn't easy to pinpoint the exact moment that had led to this, but if he had to make a guess, he figured it was Christmas, fifth grade. The year his sister Gwen had given him the sound track to *Saturday Night Fever*. The same year Pittsburgh had its worst blizzard in history and the snow had fallen so hard he couldn't go sledding or even build a damn snowman. The infamous year he'd caught disco fever.

Bored out of his mind, he remembered splashing on some Aqua Velva—another pitiful example of what the females in his family considered a Christmas present—and dancing around his room like John Travolta Jr. in training for the *Solid Gold* olympics. If Gwen had just given him the sports-magazine subscription with the free football phone as he'd asked, he wouldn't be in this mess. Because if he'd never learned to dance, when his editor, Manny, had spotted him at a colleague's wedding reception six weeks ago, Trace would've been just like every other rhythmless white guy in the place who froze in panic when the music started.

The waistband of Trace's skimpy underwear snapped back into place like a rubber band and Trace snapped back to the present.

"Well. You're a big one, aren't you?" Delores glanced at her friend. "Did you see him, Marge?"

Marge rolled her eyes. "I'm old, not blind." Turning to Trace she said, "So what do they call you, big guy?"

"Probably Big Guy," Delores crowed, smacking her knee, and they both laughed uproariously.

Trace shook his head, and in spite of himself felt a grin tugging at his mouth. The frisky pair reminded him of the two old men from *The Muppet Show*. Watching them, he chuckled softly.

If any of his friends from the *Herald* could see him now he'd never live it down. Trace had been well on his way to becoming one of the paper's top investigative reporters when he'd gotten fired. Unfairly, in his opinion, as well as that of every other hapless male who'd ever been cornered by the boss's oversexed daughter, Jeanine. Now, thanks to his ex-editor and the vindictive Jeanine, Trace was lucky to even have his job at the *Daily Intruder*, which was saying a lot since he was presently employed in journalism hell.

Undercover as one of the dancers, Trace was investigating a tip Manny had gotten about male prostitutes on board the *Mirage*, and the middle-class suburban housewives who solicited them. Apparently a growing problem Manny felt would send the *Daily Intruder*'s circulation skyrocketing. Obviously Manny was an idiot. An idiot who knew his readership and who'd threatened to fire Trace if he refused the story.

As much as Trace hated the assignment, he found himself reluctant to give up the finer things in life like food and shelter. And after his first night on the job, he had a hunch there was a much bigger story taking place on the decks of the *Mirage*.

It was a well-known fact the *Mirage* was owned by the supposedly retired ex-Mafia boss Angelo Venzara. Or Mr. V., as he was called by his employees. But last night when Trace had gotten lost and wandered near the hold, he'd seen enough to have him reassessing Venzara's supposedly reformed status. Specifically, the two armed thugs who'd been carrying an unmarked crate toward Angelo Venzara's private area of the ship.

A couple of calls to some of Trace's old sources confirmed that things onboard might not be all they seemed. In the past few months, the *Mirage* had made a number of hastily scheduled launches during its off-hours. And been spotted loading unmarked cargo during one of the cruise's island stops in the Bahamas. Even without his journalistic instincts cranking up to full alert, Trace had come across enough evidence to know that Mr. V. was up to something. And with his much-hated cover already established, Trace was going to find out. Because if he was right, it was a chance to get his career back, and that was worth anything. Even doing the electric slide in his skivvies.

A group of young lovelies a few feet away tried to catch his attention, banging their drink glasses on the table top and waving money from their hands like little flags. Trace laughed softly. Maybe he needed to get a better attitude. He had to admit that whatever this cover cost his pride it was more than made up for in horny women. After all, what red-blooded male wouldn't enjoy all these screaming females anxious for a chance to get him naked?

He tipped the brim of his hat to the two feisty seniors. "Thank you, ladies. It's been a pleasure," he said, genuinely smiling this time.

"I'll say!" Delores sent him a wink.

Chuckling, he turned to leave, but before he'd made it more than half a step, he felt a hard smack across his semi-bare ass. His eyes widened.

"Great chaps!"

"Even greater buns!" His frisky friends hooted with laughter.

Trace sighed and shook his head. Then again, maybe his attitude had been just fine all along, not to mention a whole lot safer.

"WHAT DO YOU MEAN, you don't know when you're coming back?" Phoebe Devereaux said into the phone. "How long can you just hang out in the Caribbean when you don't have any money?" Phoebe managed to keep her voice one level below shouting. If she lost her temper now, she'd never get the whole story out of her little sister.

"I mean, I don't know when it'll be cool for me to come back. I told you, that cop, Alvarez, is going to be majorly pissed off when he finds out I skipped town. I keep telling him that Mr. V. is legit, but Alvarez won't chill out," Tiffany said. "And money's not a problem. My boyfriend Tony's going with me."

Phoebe cradled the phone to her shoulder and massaged her throbbing temples. Since they were kids, Tiffany had been getting into trouble. Always the faithful big sister, Phoebe had rescued her from too many scrapes to count. Most of which, from the moment Tiffany had hit puberty, included a man. The no-good, love-'em-and-leave-'em bad-boy type that was Tiff's favorite.

Phoebe shook her head, her gaze finding the open window across from her. The sound of the neighbor's lawn mower floated inside her cozy little kitchen while a soft breeze ruffled the curtains. What had started out as a fairly perfect day lazing around at home, Tiffany had managed to destroy in less than five minutes. No surprise there, really, considering the source.

"Okay," Phoebe finally said, plunking her glass of iced tea

down onto the countertop and pushing it away. At the moment, she was a little too tempted to round up the one and only bottle of liquor in her house and spike the heck out of it. "I want you to start over at the beginning, and this time don't leave out a single thing."

"Oh, all right." Tiffany heaved a sigh worthy of the stage. "But then I really have to leave, so pay attention this time."

Phoebe didn't respond. She was too busy grinding her teeth.

"Like I said before, there's going to be a big meeting on the *Mirage* next Saturday night. Some guys who used to work with Tony's uncle, Mr. V., are coming over from Vegas and New York and the whole ship is gonna be closed off for customers that night. Nothing illegal is going on, I'm sure, no matter what Alvarez says, but even still, the whole thing is pretty hush-hush. Me and a few of the girls happened to know about the private cruise because Mr. V. himself asked us to work special for the party. Hang out for dinner and drinks then do a shorter version of our show. And well—" Tiffany hesitated "—the cops want me to listen in on the meeting. They've tried before to get one of their own people on board, but Mr. V. likes things private and he hates cops. I mean really hates cops. His men can spot a plant a mile away."

"But why you? Why not one of the other showgirls?"

"W-e-l-l," Tiffany hedged, "the police have some stuff on me. If I do what they ask, they'll cut a deal with me and forget about pressing charges. But if I don't come through, I could do time."

"Do time! Are you trying to say you might go to jail?" Phoebe wasn't being naive. Tiffany's antics had always more than crossed over the lines of propriety, and the men she hooked up with were blue collar at best, spiked collar at worst. She also took particular glee in trying to shock their dysfunctional parents into an early grave, though, as of yet, hadn't been successful. Phoebe understood why her little sister did these things and in part felt responsible. But Tiffany wasn't a criminal. She just liked to date them.

Tiffany snorted. "It's so stupid, because they'll never be able to make anything stick, Tony promised. Besides, Tony says Mr. V. has gone straight since he retired and that the cops will drop everything once they figure out he's on the up-and-up."

"Well, if Tony promised then I'm sure you're fine." Phoebe rolled her eyes. "But just so I know, what exactly do the police think they have?"

Tiffany hesitated. "Okay. But don't freak out. A couple of times I went with Tony when he had to make a delivery for his uncle. Nothing major, I promise. A fake passport, I think. Maybe a couple of handguns, but only once. I swear."

"Guns." Phoebe sputtered the word. "You're dating an arms dealer?"

"He's not an arms dealer. Cripes, you exaggerate everything," Tiffany grumbled. "He was only doing a favor for his uncle. You make it sound so serious."

"It *is* serious. By the way, Tony's family sounds great. I think I saw an episode about them on *The Sopranos*." She squeezed her eyes shut and pinched the bridge of her nose.

Once again Phoebe found herself forced into the role of Tiffany's savior. Something she'd already sworn she'd done for the last time. Yet, even though Tiffany shouldn't have ridden shotgun with her gangster boyfriend, Phoebe couldn't bear to think of her little sister in a prison cell. Which meant that she had to get to Miami today if she wanted to stop Tiffany from making the biggest mistake of her life.

Spying the phone book, Phoebe grabbed it off the shelf and started flipping the pages. "All right, Tiffany, you're going to listen to me and do exactly what I tell you. First off, break up with that mobster—"

"He's not a mobster!"

"Of course not. He commits crimes and everyone in his family has names like Scarface or Luigi the Choker. What was I thinking?" Phoebe recognized her mother's biting sarcasm in her words and immediately softened her voice. "I know you care about him, Tiff, but he's no good for you." Phoebe hesitated then forced herself to go on. "After you break up, go straight to the cops and tell them you'll do whatever they say. I'll call the airline right now. I'll try to get a flight out tonight. It's only six or seven hours from San Francisco to Miami, so I should be there by tomorrow morning. But get ready because when this is all done we're packing you up and I'm bringing you home."

"Are you insane? I'd rather let the cops put me in jail than live back under the same roof with Mom and Dad. Besides, San Francisco isn't home. Miami is. Heck, we grew up here. Just because you chose to buckle under Mom's nagging and move out west after you left New York City doesn't mean I'm stupid enough to be on the same side of the country as our parents. Not that they'd want me there, anyway."

Phoebe winced. Truthfully, the thought of living with her parents sent chills up and down her own spine. Being within a thirty-minute drive was bad enough. But she wasn't the one who'd ruined her life and couldn't be trusted. Tiffany had done this to herself and it was about time good old Mom and Dad helped share the burden of keeping up with their crazy, younger daughter. Though they'd never bothered to concern themselves in the past. But Phoebe would fix that, too. Somehow...

"And I'm not breaking up with Tony," her little sister continued. "Even though the police have no reason to harass Mr. V., he admitted that some of his uncle's associates may be a little on the shady side. Tony doesn't want me around that kind of stuff, especially now that I'm—" Tiffany broke off then finally said, "Well, I'll get into that later, but he's quitting the family business for now. And I'm leaving Miami. Only a person with a death wish would spy on Mr. V. and I'm not that stupid. If you want to help the police so much, you work at the *Mirage*. Hey—" Tiffany dragged out the word "—wait a second...I think I just came up with an idea."

Phoebe recognized that particular sound in her sister's voice and it made the little hairs at the back of her neck stand on end. "Whatever you're plotting, forget it."

"I really think this can work. Listen, we're both dancers, right?"

Phoebe practically choked. "I'm a ballet teacher. You're a showgirl. Big difference."

"Meaning, I have a good time and get laid more than once a year?"

"Why sell yourself short?" Phoebe snorted. "You could probably get it every hour dancing at that stupid place." Though truthfully, she didn't really disapprove of Tiffany's job as much as she'd just sounded. There were scores of serious dancers who worked on cruise ships. At casinos, as well, for that matter. Still, there was a mile of difference between a tutu and a thong. Yet, in spite of the ridiculousness of Tiffany's suggestion, Phoebe actually tried to envision herself in one. A thong, that is, and immediately the image came into focus.

She bit her lip and squeezed her eyes shut. Secretly, she'd always wished she could be more like her little sister. Less inhibited. Daring. Confident enough to embrace life and take what she wanted. See an attractive man and go for it—wait a second. The *attractive man* part of her internal ramblings brought her up short. Back in college, she'd learned her lesson about embracing life and attractive men the hard way, hadn't she? So what on earth was wrong with her? The one and only time Phoebe had ignored her head and followed her libido instead, she'd ended up losing her heart. She didn't want to go through that again, did she? Sure, Tiffany had more fun. Just too much of it. Without any thought of the consequences.

"Stop bitching. You're just jealous because I'm happy and like what I do," Tiffany said, hitting the nail smack-dab on the head. "Just hear me out. If you got a job on board the *Mirage* then you could listen in on Mr. V.'s meeting. It's perfect." Her little sister's voice rose with enthusiasm. "Officer Alvarez won't care who gets the information as long as someone does."

Phoebe's mouth fell open. "I thought you said only a person with a death wish would spy on this Mr. V. person."

Tiffany made a scoffing sound. "I was exaggerating. All right, Mr. V.'s pretty anal about his privacy, but other than that he's very sweet. Now, his bodyguard, Sonny, can be a little creepy at times, but as long as you don't let him catch you, you'll be fine. Come on, Phoebe, help me out here. It's not like you're doing anything else. You don't even have a job."

Phoebe made a face and stuck her tongue out at the phone. It wasn't the words themselves that pierced so much, but the sentiment behind them. As if her life only existed to make Tiffany's easier. "Forget it, Tiffany. It will never happen. And for your information, I still have my job. My knee is fine now. I should be back at the studio any day." Phoebe wasn't about to admit that she'd put off giving the prestigious ballet academy where she worked an actual return date. Before Phoebe had reinjured her knee a couple of months ago, she'd already begun to lose interest in her classes.

With the big 3-0 bearing down on her with all the surety of a SCUD missile, Phoebe found herself more than just a little tired of teaching moody teenagers the finer points of the Vaganova method. Especially when said teenagers were constantly harassing Phoebe to ditch the classics and teach them more fun stuff like *Who Let the Swans Out?* Call her selfish, but there had to be more to life than this.

Then again, if her knee hadn't given out seven years ago, Phoebe would already have a real life. She scowled down at her leg. The New York City Ballet had been sympathetic yet adamant when they'd let her go from the company. A principal dancer with a bum knee wasn't in their repertoire.

"Come on, Phoebes," Tiffany wheedled, using the nickname she'd given Phoebe when they were kids. "Just think about how pissed off Mom will be when she finds out you danced as a showgirl."

"Tiffany, I'm a little old to be enticed into one of your harebrained schemes simply to annoy our mother."

"No, you're not. Besides, you're going to take my place on the *Mirage* because you love me and want to help me. Sending Mom over the edge is just a happy coincidence."

The corner of Phoebe's mouth curved upward. Sometimes she didn't know why she bothered trying. Winning an argument with Tiffany was impossible, and for a brief moment, Phoebe actually allowed herself to consider Tiffany's request. It wasn't as if Phoebe couldn't do any form of dance. The stress of dancing in toe shoes was the actual culprit that aggravated her weakened knee. Unfortunately, ballet was all she'd been taught. Her mother, Madeline Devereaux, had never allowed anything else.

Phoebe frowned. Maybe Tiffany was right and pissing off their mother was motivation enough.

While Tiffany blathered on in the background, Phoebe pictured herself in one of her sister's outrageous getups and, not surprisingly, a frisson of excitement pulsed low in her belly. She pressed her hand to her stomach. Her imagination went to town and she could almost see her body undulating to a throbbing beat under a row of hot stage lights. She licked her lips and envisioned a gorgeous man in the audience, all his senses focused on her while she swayed her hips and... doggonit! How did Tiffany plant these crazy ideas in her brain?

Phoebe narrowed her eyes and slammed the phone book shut. Fantasizing about being a sexy showgirl and actually trying to be one were two different things. No matter how enticing the prospect seemed, if she ever actually had to go onstage and perform half-naked like that, she'd probably have the worst panic attack of her life.

Tiffany must have sensed a negative answer coming her way because she jumped in before Phoebe could speak, and said, "I know the *Mirage* isn't exactly your kind of place, Phoebe, but you've got nothing to lose. Face the facts, you're in a rut, and now's your chance to get out of it. Listen, there's more to life than what you're living. It's time to decide what you want and go for it. Take me, for example. I look at life like sex. You can either lie back and get screwed or climb on top and ride the hell out of it. That's my motto."

Phoebe almost dropped the phone. After a minute of pure speechlessness, she cleared her throat then said, "How beautiful. Truly touching, and I mean that. You should cross-stitch it on a pillow." She wiped her hand over her face then shook her head. "Unfortunately, I don't view infiltrating the Mafia the same as *riding the hell out of life.* Look, Tiffany, I think it's about time you swung down from the, er, *saddle,* so to speak, and learned to clean up one of your own messes. I'll come to Miami and stand by your side." Phoebe's voice rose as she picked up steam. "But there is no way I'm going to dance on that ship in a sequined bikini so you can sun yourself on some darn beach. So, save your breath. There's not a single thing you can say that will make me change my mind."

Tiffany remained silent until Phoebe felt she'd scream. Finally, her little sister spoke. "Phoebe, I know you think I'm being a jerk, but, honest, it's not me I'm trying to protect."

Phoebe slumped against the wall and rubbed the back of her neck. "Tiffany, what are you trying to tell me?"

Her sister then spoke the two words guaranteed to change Phoebe's mind. "I'm pregnant."

PHOEBE'S ANKLES wobbled precariously in her three-and-a-half inch high heels and she cursed under her breath. It wasn't easy to run in screw-me shoes while balancing a tray of deviled eggs and a gift-wrapped Crock-Pot, but it had taken her forty minutes longer to navigate through the Miami traffic than she'd planned and she couldn't mess this up by being late.

One of the showgirls, Candy, was getting married and Phoebe had been invited to the bachelorette party. Oddly enough, after only three days, she seemed to be fitting in better with the showgirls than she ever had at her previous jobs. Probably because she was Tiffany's sister. And probably because, for the first time in her life, she was the worst dancer of the bunch.

Phoebe grinned and thought to herself, "I'm a showgirl." There were times when the absurdity of it almost made her laugh out loud. So far, she was enjoying herself, too. She'd only been in town a couple of days but things were going remarkably well. Exactly as she'd planned.

Thanks to Tiffany's grossly exaggerated reference, the *Mirage* had hired Phoebe on the spot. Of course, not surprisingly, she hadn't been asked yet to join Mr. V. on his Mafia Reunion Cruise next Saturday, but she wasn't alarmed. It was one thing for Mr. V. to make Phoebe a showgirl on the spur of the moment. Another for him to welcome her right in with open arms to witness his illegal activities. Besides, she still had plenty of time. Well, a week to be exact, but her first performance was in two nights and Phoebe knew that Mr. V. and his right-hand man, Sonny were waiting to see how she held up onstage.

She'd also spoken with Officer Carlos Alvarez. Though he'd been understandably angered at Tiffany's impromptu honeymoon, he'd agreed to present Phoebe's offer to his captain. Which reminded her that she had an appointment with Alvarez in the morning to discuss the specifics of the case. They were meeting at Tiff's condo, where Phoebe was staying. As a precaution, Alvarez had told her not to risk coming down to the police station a second time. Though the detective doubted Phoebe was being watched, he'd told her not to underestimate Sonny Martorelli.

She fought back a chill, the thought of being watched at any time in her future enough to make Phoebe want to pirouette herself right around and onto the first plane back to San Francisco. But she'd come too far to wimp out now. Besides, she had no reason to be nervous. She was an intelligent, capable woman. She could do this. Actually wanted to do this. And not just for Tiffany.

Phoebe had come to Miami as much for herself as to protect her new little niece or nephew from any potential harm. She'd allowed Tiffany to believe that it was her pregnancy that had changed Phoebe's mind, and in a way it had. But it was more the reality of Tiff getting married suddenly and starting a family that had really knocked Phoebe's world off kilter. Her whole life Phoebe had played it safe, and yet Tiffany was the one with a husband and a new baby on the way. In three months Phoebe would be thirty years old and had nothing to show for it. The men she dated were boring. Her job was boring. Her life was boring. She was in a rut. Tiffany had been right. *Go figure.*

Well, no more. Phoebe had made a decision. For once, she would take control of her future. She'd always wanted to be more like her little sister and now she could. Performing on the *Mirage* was a chance to spread her wings. Try a new form of dance. Experience some excitement. Some danger.

Phoebe almost stumbled at this and her chest grew tight. All right, she thought, and steadied her breathing. So she wasn't completely sold on the danger part. But she liked ev-

erything else. Phoebe frowned again. And maybe comparing
the bumps and grinds executed onstage at the *Mirage* to a
dance form might be a bit liberal, but she was tired of playing it safe. Always being responsible. Always thinking
things through. Tiffany hadn't, and look at her. Granted, the
whole Mafia thing was a drawback, but maybe Tony and Tiffany were right and the police were wrong.

Phoebe had met Mr. V. when she'd first arrived, and the
Godfather he wasn't. Oddly enough, finally seeing Tony's
uncle had been a bit of letdown. A short, round little man,
Mr. V. had seemed to be more interested in talking to Phoebe
about his special tomatoes than her new job on the *Mirage*.
He'd asked if she liked Italian food and offered to make her
a spaghetti feast with his own homemade sauce once she'd
settled in. Heck, it had been kinda hard to remain scared of a
guy who'd talked about tomato sauce for ten minutes running and wanted to know whether she personally preferred
bay leaves or cilantro in her marinara.

Remembering the funny conversation, Phoebe grinned
and already felt better. Now was not the time to let one of her
panic attacks sneak up on her. Though her primary reason
for attending Candy's bachelorette party was to get a foot in
with the other dancers, she couldn't let the technicalities of
her mission distract her from her own private goals. Important private goals. To grab life by the balls and wring every
last drop from them. After all, she thought with a grin, why
should Tiffany be the only one with a fun motto?

Finally coming to a stop, Phoebe stood before the long row
of apartments and squinted, trying to make out the number
over the entrance. It was so dang dark out here she could
barely see a thing. The one and only street lamp in the entire
complex stood beside the last building where a half dozen or
so balloons were tied to the door. Bingo, she thought in relief,
and took off toward it.

As she hobbled along the sidewalk, she wondered fleetingly whether the sense of camaraderie she felt with the showgirls would last and was surprised at how much she hoped it would. Growing up, Phoebe had always been painfully self-conscious around her peers and—oh, all right, so she'd been more like a tongue-tied mess, though she'd tried hard to relax and be herself, which had only made matters worse.

Add this in with the combination of Phoebe's success in dance, her top placement grade point average, and a mother who'd never let her do anything that even remotely resembled fun—including wasting time with boyfriends or, heck, even regular friends—and the other kids had all come to the conclusion that Phoebe was one stuck-up prima donna. Throw in a few panic attacks for fun, and it was easy to see why she hadn't exactly been voted the most popular person in her school. Looking back on it, she was lucky they hadn't thrown rocks at her in the streets.

However, with age and enough therapy to help even the most screwed-up of Hollywood starlets, Phoebe had overcome the worst of her introversion. Yet, there were still times when she fought the odd twinges of anxiety. Oh, like, say, whenever she let herself think about all the different ways that she could fail in the next few hours being the perfect example. Phoebe grimaced, eyeing the tastefully wrapped present in her arms. Somehow, she doubted giving Candy a Crock-Pot would convince the showgirls that she lived life on the edge. The deviled eggs didn't exactly say bad to the bone either.

Darn it. Already she was doing this wrong and the realization made her breath hitch. But before Phoebe could get herself more worked up, one of her ridiculous heels caught in the pavement and she tripped forward. The Crock-Pot and eggs flew from her arms and for a brief moment her body seemed to fly along, too.

As if in slow motion she pictured herself landing on her

bad knee, injuring it permanently, all of her plans for Tiffany and herself ruined, but there was nothing she could do to stop herself. Until her body mercifully slammed into rock-solid man. Not about to question her good fortune, Phoebe clung tight.

"WHAT THE—oof!" The air whooshed from Trace's lungs as the crazy woman careened into him.

"Help," she squeaked.

Trace managed to get out a quick "Whoa, careful," while he staggered backward from the force of her momentum. Instinctively, he brought up his arms to catch her, then decided this might not have been such a good idea.

Her long, wriggling body molded perfectly to his and he suddenly found his hands filled with her well-rounded bottom. A tingling feeling, almost like an itch, spread through his palms, yet Trace forced himself to ignore the writhing bounty in his hands and reminded his overactive hormones that after the fiasco with Jeanine, he'd sworn off women for good. At least he thought he had. It all seemed pretty vague to him right now with this particular woman's legs clamped tightly on his thighs and her high, firm breasts pressed into his chest, prodding his skin like two hot brands and making him remember how much he enjoyed being prodded by two hot brands. Especially, when those brands were moving and jiggling around with the rest of her.

Suddenly the bachelorette party he was on his way to perform at seemed rife with possibilities. A concept that made him question his sanity, but he couldn't afford to waste another second on his wayward thoughts. Not if he wanted to get rid of the human suction cup in his arms before they both went down for the count.

"Hey, hold still," he warned, scowling. He tried to catch his balance and adjust his footing but this somehow only made everything worse because she squeaked and shock-ingly started to climb him like a monkey up a tree. He cursed, wondering what the hell was the matter with her and opened his mouth to ask, except a yelp came out instead. She'd stabbed the back of his leg with what had to be one of the most wicked high heels in creation, and his knees buckled forward.

Trace tripped off the sidewalk and they went down hard. Or rather she did. His face landed on something soft and plump, well, actually two somethings soft and plump—oh, all right, technically right smack-dab *between* two somethings soft and plump—and if he wasn't mistaken, her knee was shoved up under his armpit.

"I can't breathe. Get up, please." The voice beneath him sounded strangled.

You and me both, lady, he wanted to say, but couldn't since speaking required air and there was none left in his lungs. He tried to move. However, turning his face wasn't an option either. Not with her long, dark hair tangled around his head as if someone had thrown a net over him, and for a few very long seconds Trace feared he was going to suffocate with his face mashed tightly to her breasts.

All in all, he supposed there were worse ways to go.

The woman squeaked. "I mean it—get up." Her pelvis pushed against his, trying to buck him off. Their limbs were so jumbled it must have looked as if they were playing a bizarre, X-rated game of Twister.

"Ptthew." He finally worked his head to the side and spit out the strands of hair filling his mouth. "Stop moving," Trace barked, the words harsher than he meant to sound as he gasped for breath. She didn't listen, but then the way his night was going, this shouldn't surprise him. Great, he thought in disgust. His groin tightened, responding like any normal red-blooded male would if holding a writhing female and contorted into a position that a Cirque du Soleil performer would envy, and he could feel himself swelling up to a regular blue-steeler. Her feminine cleft perfectly aligned with his growing arousal. He understood the woman's alarm, but all this moving around only made his problem worse.

"Please," he panted, "just stop moving. I'm stuck." Knowing if he pulled up too hard or fast he'd rip half the hair from her head, he tried to keep his upper body still as he wriggled his hand out from underneath her luscious bottom. They were so close he could feel her muscles tighten through the fabric of her clothing. Her body suddenly went rigid.

Hell, she must've just noticed his killer hard-on.

"You've got two seconds before I start screaming." Her words, if not her tone, should have been enough to deflate the near phenomenon taking place in his pants. They weren't.

Compelled to defend himself, Trace pointed out, "Hey, I know you're upset, but if you remember, you're the one who ran into me."

She huffed. "I'm sorry! It's dark and I didn't see you. I'm not trying to be rude but you're lying on top of me like a dead fish. Well, mostly dead," she muttered. "And you keep poking me."

Heat crept up his neck. For all the appreciation she was showing, he should just yank her bald and let her live with the consequences.

The woman started wiggling again. "Ow, it really hurts."

Trace made a strangled noise. "I don't know if you're aware of this, but moving around underneath a man is not the way to get his body to stop 'poking' you."

She immediately stilled. "Um, I was talking about that pin or whatever it is you have on your shirt. It's pok—uh, digging into my chest."

Trace winced. "Sorry," he mumbled and tried to shift his weight with little success. He'd forgotten about his stupid costume and the fake police badge. In the last week he'd been a cowboy, a construction worker, an Indian and now a cop. Why the hell women got turned on by seeing him dress up like one of the Village People was beyond him. "If you just give me a minute here, I'm caught in your hair," he said, his jaw clenched as he carefully started to untangle the silky mass from what seemed like every possible spot of attachment on his body.

Why me? he wondered. As if being felled by this wiggling wacko wasn't bad enough, in less than half an hour he'd be dancing at Candy's bachelorette party. Last week when Barbie and Candy had asked him to perform, Trace had figured this would be a good chance to find out what the showgirls knew about the *Mirage*'s secret cargo, as well as the private cruise he'd recently overheard a couple of Mr. V.'s men discussing. Especially since Mr. V.'s niece, Angie Venzara, would be at the party tonight, too. But the reality of stripping down to the ridiculous triangle of spandex and string, that even now was chafing the hell out of him, and doing it in such intimate surroundings, had Trace rethinking his master plan. He wished his costume came with a gun so he could just shoot himself now and be done with it. Damn, his life sucked.

Trace sighed. "Okay, I think that's it." Determined to be free before he embarrassed himself even more, he tried to stand and immediately identified the final obstacle. He cleared his throat. "I never thought I'd say this to a woman, but you're going to have to unclench your leg from my back. If you want me to stop poking you, that is," he added dryly.

The woman gasped. "Oh, I d-didn't realize," she stammered, her voice turning sheepish.

The pressure on his ribs eased and Trace carefully pushed onto his hands and knees. Out of breath and panting, he kneeled over her, their faces only inches apart. He blinked, looking straight into her cool, gray eyes. No, not just gray.

They were silver. Reflecting the light. Unforgettable—like the haunting notes of a long-ago melody.

The light from the street lamp pooled around them and he could just make out her face. The woman's eyes widened. Her thick dark lashes fanned out to her eyebrows. "Trace?"

He held his breath. Her skin was porcelain smooth, her mouth lush, full and red like a wet berry. She was beautiful. Amazing. He'd only known one other face so perfect.

His heart kicked into a pounding rhythm. "Phoebe? Phoebe Devereaux?"

The only woman he'd ever loved smiled up at him hesitantly. That she'd broken his heart nine years ago hardly seemed important.

2

"DAMN." Trace's chest clutched painfully. Well, at least he now understood his physical reaction to her on the ground. His mind might not have known who it was, but his body sure as hell had.

She shifted and winced. The change in her expression broke his spell and he realized that he was still kneeling over her. Awkwardly he rose to his feet.

"Sorry," he said, and as she sat forward, Trace backed up a step to give her room. Desperate to tear his eyes away from her, he glanced around the darkened yard. "You dropped some of your stuff. Let me help you."

He turned his back to Phoebe and started toward the cluster of palm trees a few feet away. He needed a moment to regroup here, and muttering a curse, adjusted himself inside his pants. Trace scowled and with some difficulty leaned over and picked up the dented present from the grass. He couldn't believe it. Phoebe Devereaux. His college sweetheart.

Trace took a deep breath and combed his fingers through his hair. Well, more like his college obsession, really. Nine years ago, they'd both attended the University of Miami. The first time he'd seen her in the school bookstore he'd felt all but struck by lightning. One look had been enough for him to fall and fall hard. Unfortunately, she'd needed a good hundred or so more, but by their senior year when she'd finally come around, he'd never been happier. For a brief time anyway. Before she'd dumped his ass.

Trace's hand shook as he fumbled with the crumpled white bow, trying to set it back on top. *Get a grip, McGraw.* He willed his racing pulse to return to normal. It's only Phoebe. No big deal. *Yeah, right.* Trace released the ribbon and watched it fall dejectedly on its side. Too bad his hard-on refused to have the same reaction.

Shaking his head, he walked back to Phoebe and set the wrapped box down next to her. "Wow—" He broke off and cleared his throat. "Phoebe Devereaux. It's been a long time." After the major kiss-off she'd given him back in college, Trace knew he should walk away. Give her a brief greeting then turn around and never look back. But he couldn't. He wanted to know everything. Soak up each detail of the past nine years of her life in a moment. Well, crap. He might as well just rip out his heart now and hand it to her on a silver platter. It'd save them both a lot of hassle.

"Yeah, a long time…" Her voice trailed off as she stared at him.

Trace shook his head, and in spite of the roiling sensation in his gut, felt a smile tugging at his lips. Apparently some things never changed. Phoebe sat gazing up at him as if he were a tasty dessert she couldn't wait to devour. Of course, if this played out anything like it usually had in the past, rapidly following on its heels would be her expression of self-loathing and disgust, so he didn't bother getting too flattered. Why she'd always done this was beyond him. Hell, just the thought of Phoebe had always affected him the same way and it didn't make him want to run out and commit hara-kiri.

Since she didn't seem to be in any hurry to stop staring at him, Trace decided to return the favor, and what he saw caused his mouth to curve into an unholy grin.

Her sundress lay hiked up around her waist, revealing a tiny scrap of lace he supposed passed for panties. Though he'd always been a sucker for her long sable hair, it looked a little ragged at the moment with bits of grass sticking out and a rather large leaf tangled at the side. On top of that, one of her shoes must have flown south during their tumble, because only a single, lethal-looking high heel graced her arched foot.

It was enough to make a man drool. She was the sexiest thing he'd ever seen and color-coordinated to boot. Shoes, dress and underwear all in a glaring shade of pink that he could honestly say was his new favorite color. He wondered what she'd do if he told her that he could see London, France and every little bit of her underpants. *Little* definitely being the key word here.

Unfortunately, though not unexpectedly, Phoebe seemed to catch herself making calf eyes and pulled up short, retreating behind a stone wall of composure with a dash of indifference thrown in for good measure, in case he hadn't taken the hint. Trace narrowed his eyes. It had been nine years. He was a full-grown man. Her denial of their attraction shouldn't matter. Yet, he felt as if he were back on campus following her around like a puppy dog begging for a date because he was so damn crazy about her he couldn't stay away.

The same old frustrations from the past, the ones demanding he force a response from her, raged through his body. He was not the only one affected here. Before he walked away, Phoebe Devereaux was going to admit what she had only once in the past, and then ruined by never speaking to him again. That she wanted him and wanted him bad. Though, Trace decided with a smile, he might not make her say it in those exact words.

He knew from personal experience the only way past Phoebe's reserve involved annoying the heck out of her until she got screaming mad, and then *man, oh, man,* would he get a response. Despite the turmoil twisting his insides, he felt a surprising spark of excitement. Damn, this was going to be fun....

Trace crossed his arms and purposely put on his most cocky expression, which just so happened to be the one that had always riled her up the most. "Not that I mind the view, but maybe you should pull down your dress. Unless, of course, you want to pick up where we left off now that you know it's me." It was almost too easy, he thought wickedly.

Phoebe's forehead wrinkled and she glanced down at herself. A strangled noise rushed past her lips before she scrambled to her feet, the whole while brushing down the front of her dress. "Oh, please," she finally said, with a dramatic look heavenward. "As if I would ever want to pick up anything with you." Her voice was a little too shaky to achieve the disdainful tone Trace knew she was going for.

"Hey—" he raised his hands "—you were the one wiggling around down there like you were doing the horizontal lambada. Not me." He shook his head. "No sir, no matter how I begged, nothing could keep you still."

She stiffened, bringing his attention back to the long, firm limbs he'd so intimately held only moments before. The same ones he remembered from nine years ago and had felt like heaven wrapped around his waist, around his back, his shoulders, his neck....

Aw, hell. His pants were never going to lie flat.

"Poor Trace. I see you're still delusional. How sad." She sniffed and turned away, clearly dismissing him as she presumably began to search for her missing shoe.

Trace scowled. Like hell would she blow him off that easily. "While you, it seems, have changed quite a bit. If memory serves correctly, you never used to wear underpants. Not that I'm complaining. They're quite nice. You have excellent taste."

She whipped her head back around to gape at him, her mouth hanging open.

Score one for the home team. He'd stunned Phoebe Devereaux silent. Now to really piss her off. "Why, Phoebe, I can think of only one other time I made you speechless. And here, I'm not even touching you...." He shook his head but couldn't contain the wide smile that spread across his face at the direct hit.

Of course, she didn't stay silent for long. In his experience, she never had. Not with him anyway. It had always been a source of amazement to him that the same painfully shy woman who could barely make small talk with the other students, became a screaming virago at the least of his taunts. The dichotomy of her behavior had been the biggest turn-on of his life. It had gotten to the point that by his senior year, she'd say one mean or argumentative thing and his favorite body part would pop up like one of those plastic thermometers on a turkey. For a while there, he'd been afraid that he'd never be able to get an erection without having a whopping argument first.

Phoebe narrowed her eyes. "Crude egomaniacs tend to have that effect on me. Now, if you'll excuse me." She started to lift her cute little nose in the air, but he spoke before she could turn away again.

"You don't have to explain, Phoebe. I know exactly how I affect you." He purposely made his voice low and suggestive. "But, I was thinking about our night together. You remember, Phoebe, right? The night when we—"

"It was nothing." She actually growled and he could just make out the telltale flush on her cheeks.

"Bull." Not one of the most original comebacks but he was riding the edge here and deserved a little slack.

She waved her hand. "We had some fun. Well, at least you did, anyway. It wasn't a big deal."

Trace merely crossed his arms and raised his eyebrow. Why argue something so patently false? Besides, if he opened his mouth, he might do something stupid. Like tell her exactly how much that night had meant to him.

She rolled her eyes then pretended great interest in her fingernails which, in this light, he knew doggone well she could barely see. "All right," she said grudgingly, "it was pleasant."

His other eyebrow joined the first and they both crept higher.

Phoebe clenched her jaw and fisted her hands at her sides. "Fine, I really enjoyed myself."

Since she was doing so good on her own, Trace still said nothing, and she bit out, "Okay. I had as much fun as you, if not more. The heavens moved, the earth shook." She smiled sweetly. "But if you recall, I got over it." While steam all but poured from his ears, she shrugged, no longer meeting his eyes. "I can't believe you're making such a big deal over this. For that matter, I'm shocked you even remember."

He cursed. "Oh, I remember all right...." As if he could forget.

Twenty-one years old and in love for the first time in his life, Trace had held her in his arms and watched her come.

He'd slid into the hot, delicate flesh between her legs until her beautiful thighs had begun to quiver on either side of his hips and she'd exploded in release. Though she'd never told him, Trace had known that she was a virgin. Phoebe had willingly given him a gift no other would have, and at that moment, he'd felt as if it had been his first time, too. There was no way in hell he'd let her brush off that night as unimportant. On a physical level alone it had been one for the history books even if she had completely rejected him the next day.

Phoebe scoffed. "Oh, please. If you remember anything about me or that night it's because I was just another conquest. One of many for you, I'm sure, but still true."

Jerked back to the present, he stared at Phoebe, her protest like a blow to his solar plexus. Irrationally, anger burned through his veins, every bit as strong today as if it were only moments ago when she'd looked at him scornfully and refused to speak with him. Refused to answer his phone calls. Refused to offer even the most basic of explanations for the violent change in her attitude.

Too far gone to care what the hell he said. Trace retorted, "So I guess you shoot off like a firework for every man that buys you dinner?" He shook his head, feigning disbelief. "Huh. Somehow I had you figured differently."

Phoebe sputtered for several seconds then finally managed to say, "We had one lousy date and things went too far. Stop acting as if we shared some great night of passion."

"Lousy, huh? So you're saying it was my poor taste in restaurants? You begged and moaned for more but called it quits on us because I couldn't afford to take you someplace fancy?" He made a tsking sound. "And you call me the shallow one."

"I can't believe this." She shook her head, her expression incredulous. "You're mad. Mr. On-the-Make McGraw is pissed off because a woman actually exists who wasn't interested in going to bed with him a second time."

All right, now he was mad. Phoebe loved to throw the womanizer card in his face. So women liked him? Big whoop. He'd asked Phoebe out every week for four years and she'd said no. What was he supposed to do? Become a monk while he waited? As it was, when he'd finally worn her down, he'd been so damn happy and relieved she'd said yes, whatever little awareness he'd ever had of another female had literally fled his brain. Her accusations made no more sense today than they had nine years ago.

He narrowed his eyes at her. "Hell yes, it was a shock. One night you were so hot I thought my skin was gonna burn to a crisp, and the next, I'm worried about frostbite."

She pulled back her shoulders and lifted her chin. "Let's get some facts straight here. I was not hot and I never moaned."

"It's nothing to be embarrassed about. You can't help it if you're a moaner," he said placatingly.

"If I moaned it was because you disgust me."

"Phoebe...Phoebe." He shook his head. "Really, it's okay. You don't need to make excuses. I thought it was cute when you made those deep, throaty sounds. Loud, but cute. Especially when you got that breathy little catch right before you were about to co—"

She broke in, "I hope you die. Slowly and painfully." Phoebe dragged out each word. "And I'm there to watch it."

Head up, chin thrust forward, her eyes flashed dangerously. Her chest rose and fell with each of her labored breaths. She was amazing and, in spite of everything, he'd never wanted her more.

Trace almost barked out a laugh. There had to be something wrong with a man who found pure contrariness on this massive a level arousing. A dose of Spanish fly poured down his gullet. But damn if he didn't feel as if he'd just swallowed a whole bottle.

PHOEBE GULPED for air. Trace McGraw was the most aggravating, annoying, frustrating, handsome and sexy man she'd ever known. The bane of her college years. The object of her most erotic sexual fantasies. The man responsible for her one and only orgasm. And, after nine years, he stood before her determined she relive it. Maybe if she'd ever had another one she wouldn't be reacting to his barbs like the poster child for PMS.

And did he have to look like something out of Greek mythology, too? A god come to life to depress the heck out of the mortals? Even with it this dark outside, she could see him well enough to know she'd be in big trouble if it weren't this dark outside. Her palms had grown damp just from glancing at him—*oh, all right,* staring at him—and she wiped her hands on the skirt of her dress.

The man looked near-perfect. His almost black hair was a bit too long and fell in the kind of artless disarray women spent hours in front of the mirror trying to achieve. Though she wasn't quite able to see the exact shade of his eyes, she knew from experience they were big, and astonishingly blue, and, at only the slightest glimpse of their brooding intensity, could make anything with ovaries want to rip off her clothes and drop spread-eagle to the ground. It brought new meaning to the phrase *stop, drop and roll*. Except with Phoebe. With her it had always been panic, overreact and run. Well, all but that one time. Unfortunately, she didn't feel much like running now, either.

Phoebe scowled and tried to ignore the almost magnetic tug his six-foot-two form exerted over her own shivering mass. What the heck was wrong with her? Since when did she let an insignificant thing like a square and masculine jaw snare her interest? Or deep-set bedroom eyes? Or a flawless nose, more narrow than not, that led to a mouth with lips just plump enough to make her picture them shiny and wet, and wonder if they'd taste as good as she remembered...?

Phoebe realized the direction of her thoughts and could have kicked herself. Jeesh. She should be running and fast. That night may have been earth-shattering for her, however it was just one of many for Trace. *True*, said an insidious voice in her head. *But that was a long time ago, and since you're a new and liberated woman only interested in your next good time, there's always the chance that if you ask real nice, he might be willing to shatter the earth for you again.*

Phoebe flinched and told the sex-starved portion of her brain to shut the hell up. Then she looked into Trace's beautiful frowning face and her pulse leaped and her own nearly shriveled-on-the-vine ovaries all but quivered. Jerking herself back to reality, she tried her hardest to appear bored with him and the entire discussion. The last thing her pride needed was for him to realize how much he still affected her. Or how much the memory of his betrayal still hurt.

"Listen," she said, waving her hand, "all that stuff happened a long time ago. I don't even know why we're arguing." There. That sounded pretty good.

He stilled for a moment then slowly shook his head and took a step closer. The scent of pine and something intrinsically Trace wafted through the humid air, tickling her nose and bringing with it a rush of memories. Sexual memories. Amazingly graphic and sexual memories. You're pathetic, she told herself, and it was all she could do not to walk over to that tree there behind him and knock herself unconscious.

"You don't?" he asked.

He was too close, but Phoebe couldn't have backed up to save her life. She dug her fingernails into her palms and forced herself to laugh. "Not really, no. Heck, we were practically kids." Any second her nose was going to grow into a great sequoia.

The real problem was that Phoebe remembered too much. Like how he'd replaced her with another woman less than twenty-four hours after she'd left his bed. Phoebe had been at ballet practice that next day and hadn't been able to meet with Trace. Except she'd finished early and, like a lovesick fool, had headed straight for Trace's apartment hoping to surprise him. Unfortunately, she'd been the one surprised. By the beautiful girl with him at his front door.

Stunned, Phoebe had only been able to stand silently and watch the stupid goodbye kiss that the busty redhead had planted on Trace—ridiculously childish in her opinion since the floozy's lips had been tightly puckered and she'd even made a big smoochy noise, for heaven's sake. Of course, Trace, the creep, had been amused, laughing affectionately then pulling the young woman back into his arms for a warm hug before waving her off.

Why the image still made her chest ache, Phoebe refused to analyze, and helplessly, she stared at Trace.

The corner of his mouth curved up, but there was no humor in his expression. Then he leaned down and his breath feathered her ear, the sensation enough to stop her lungs from working. "I don't believe you," he whispered. "You remember exactly how good it was between us. You're lying, Phoebe, and I know why. Because you're just as hot for me now as you were back in college and for some reason that really ticks you off."

Phoebe took a step back from him, her movements jerky. She lifted her chin. "How charmingly put. And untrue. Besides, there are more important things than physical attraction." Though at the moment she couldn't think of a single one.

"Really? Name one."

Rats. He *would* zero in on that particular problem. "Okay," she said, then licked her lips again. "Um, mutual interests."

His smile widened. He moved toward her, closing the space she'd put between them. "Believe me, sweetheart, the interest here is definitely mutual." His hand stroked down her bare arm. The little hairs on her skin rose in his wake.

"Yes, well—" she cleared her throat "—I seem to recall that your interest had a much shorter shelf life than mine." She took another step away but he kept pace, all but stalking her.

Trace shook his head and lifted his thumb to her bottom lip. "Now, that's where you've always been wrong, Phoebe." He gave an exaggerated sigh. "But I guess since you're still not ready to believe me, I'll just have to prove it." He lowered his mouth and Phoebe panicked. If he kissed her, she couldn't be held responsible for her actions. Specifically, throwing herself at him and howling at the moon.

"No, no," she said, still backing up. "That's okay. Let's just call a truce here and agree to disagree."

Trace grinned. "Nah. I'd rather be right."

"No." Her eyes going wide, she stumbled backward when pain shot through her bare foot. "Ouch!" she wailed, bending down.

In less than a heartbeat, Trace knelt at her side. "What happened?" he asked. "Are you okay?" Then he curled those devastating fingers of his around her ankle and a charge raced up her leg as if she'd become a live wire. Instantaneous electricity.

Phoebe scowled. "I'm fine," she said, though her voice wobbled. Next the words "I don't need your help" somehow came out of her mouth when what she really wanted to say was, "Please, if you have an ounce of mercy, don't touch me."

"Hush." He gently turned her foot. A small line of blood ran from her pinkie toe. "Hey, you've really hurt yourself," he said, his voice gruff. "You're bleeding."

Oh, why couldn't the creep be consistent? One minute he was the ex-boyfriend from hell and the next all sensitivity. Of course, she shouldn't have been surprised. Trace had always played by his own rules. In other words, he didn't mind driving her nuts, but if she ever needed anything he was first in line and always came through.

Except at the end when he'd turned out to be a two-timing pig just as she'd always feared. *Then again,* the sexually deprived voice chimed back in and said, *maybe it's about time to let all those pesky little bygones be bygones. After all, nobody's perfect, he was too young to know how much he hurt you, yada yada yada. Think of whatever excuse it'll take for you to have wild monkey sex with him at the earliest possible opportunity—as a matter of fact, right here and now seems to be available.*

"I'm fine," she blurted. "I'm sure it's nothing."

"You're not fine. You have a cut," he said, and before she could argue, he stood and scooped her into his arms in one motion.

Phoebe's stomach rolled and she braced her hand on his chest. His muscles were hard and lean beneath her fingers. His shoulders wide and—she noticed where her thoughts were going. No! Absolutely not. No wild monkey sex. She didn't care how good he felt. Or smelled. Or sounded. Or whatever other freakishly attractive characteristics the man possessed that made her want to copulate with him on the spot.

Trace set her down on the steps leading into the apartment building and when he spoke, he sounded angry. "This is my fault. I should have found your shoe right away instead of letting you walk around like this in the dark." He pulled her foot onto his lap.

Distance seemed to be the key here, and she somewhat gently tried to kick his hand loose. "How's it your fault?" she complained. "I could've looked for my own darn shoe. Besides, I'm the one who ran into you." Trace tightened his hold until she stilled. Other than that, he ignored her. Phoebe sighed and finally gave in. If the man wanted to turn heroic, far be it from her to interfere. The sheer pleasure of his touch also weighed heavily in his favor, but she hated to admit to herself such a major personal weakness.

Forcing herself to look away from him, since drooling was a very real possibility, she noticed something glinting from his shirt.

"Is that the thing that kept poking me?" she asked.

He started to jerk her foot away from his groin, then caught himself. His cheeks turning red, he frowned up at her. "What are you talking about?"

Fighting a grin, she pointed to his chest and was about to clarify her question, when she realized he was wearing a badge. And a dark blue uniform. Phoebe made a startled sound then shook her head. "Oh, my gosh, you're a police officer. I can't believe it."

He made a strange face. "Me neither," he answered on a sigh.

She stared, unsure how to respond. Trace McGraw...a police officer? Her mind fundamentally rejected the idea. Though law enforcement was certainly a noble profession, he'd been a wonderful journalist. For Trace to have given up his writing, even if it was to become a cop, just didn't seem right. Actually it seemed wrong, and made Phoebe sad in a way she hadn't even felt at her own ruined ambitions. "Why? I thought you were going to become a reporter. You were so good."

Traced snorted. "And how would you know?" he asked, not bothering to lift his head.

Without thinking, she said, "Because I used to read your column in the school paper, of course." Phoebe smiled and leaned back on her hands. "I was always excited when the next edition came out. I couldn't wait to see what you were going to write about next." She stopped and shrugged. "But even if I'd only read one issue, it would have been enough to recognize your talent."

"Oh, really?" He looked up, a cocky grin spread across his mouth.

Heat crept over her cheeks. Oh, that was nice. She sounded like an adolescent girl waiting for the next issue of *Tiger Beat* to hit the stands. "Well, it wasn't just me. Everyone did. You were constantly uncovering some injustice around campus," she said, lifting her chin. "Like the time you wrote about that lecherous professor who tried to seduce most of his female students into earning extra credits in his bed." Phoebe shuddered. "By the way, your story couldn't have come at a better time for me. I was registered to take his class as soon as we got back from Christmas break."

Trace's smile slipped away. "I know."

Phoebe paused again, brought up short. "You knew?" she asked. "But how? What do you mean?"

He shrugged. "I read your schedule. It slipped out of your purse in the library."

Phoebe raised her eyebrows and Trace sighed. "It's not like you didn't know I made a habit of doing my homework in the library at the same time as you. Anyway, when I saw Professor Eiken's name on your list, I just about sh—" He broke off, not finishing the crude expression. "I hadn't really heard much about him until then, but one of my friends was dating a girl who'd been all but raped by the man a week or two before." Trace's jaw had hardened and he suddenly seemed to stare at Phoebe as if, well, it didn't make sense, but he stared at her possessively. As if she were his to protect so that's what he'd done. But that couldn't be right.

Trace McGraw was not possessive over women. There were too darn many of them, for one thing. And for another, he didn't need to be. She doubted that there'd ever been a single female in his entire life who'd willingly left his side without having to be physically shoved along first. Phoebe looked away and rubbed her forehead. Obviously, she'd misread Trace's expression and he must still get angry when he thought about all the problems that article had created for him. Even after all this time, she could understand why he'd be upset.

With only a semester to go before graduation, Trace had exposed one of the most powerful faculty members on staff and the ensuing scandal had been huge. Professor Eiken had tried to have Trace expelled and almost succeeded. The man had even started a lawsuit against Trace and the university, but dropped it when a shocking number of abuse claims started pouring in.

And Trace had gone through all of that to keep her safe? Phoebe's pulse fluttered. She was shocked and, well... amazingly flattered. He'd written that article for her. She had no doubt he'd been concerned for the other girls as well, but still...he'd been so generous. And he'd never even

told her. Phoebe paused and bit her lip. These were not exactly the actions of a man who'd only been trying to get her
into bed. The risk he'd taken spoke of a level of caring that
she'd never given Trace credit for. But if he'd cared so much
then why had he cheated on her?

Phoebe glanced away, unsure what to believe. Instead she
asked, "So why didn't you stay with it? Reporting, I mean."

Trace shot her a look. "I did," he said after a minute, rubbing the back of his neck. "But let's just say it didn't exactly
turn out as I expected." At Phoebe's silence, he grudgingly
added, "I got fired. It's a long story and I'd rather not go into
it right now." He shrugged. "Listen, that platter you were
carrying must have broken when you fell. I think you
stepped on some glass. There's not enough light for me to
take it out down here."

"Oh," Phoebe said, suddenly self-conscious. "That's
okay," she smiled. "I can do it myself once I get upstairs."

"Not likely," he snorted. Then he scooped her back into
his arms and stood. "Relax. It's my job to serve and protect."
Trace smiled, his teeth a white slash against his bronze skin.
"And that's exactly what I plan to do."

"ARE YOU SURE this is the right place?" Trace asked with a
scowl.

Though he'd spoken loudly, Phoebe had just been able to
hear him over the music and feminine laughter floating from
behind Barbie's front door into the hallway. He was standing
rigid, staring at the shiny brass numbers and holding Phoebe
against his chest. And the more Trace stared and listened, the
tenser he grew until his fingers were all but squeezing her
legs and side.

Phoebe's lips twitched and she nodded. "Yep, 701. This is
it."

A spark flared in his eyes but he quickly lowered them and
she almost snickered. Obviously, he couldn't believe Phoebe

was going to a party that made *Animal House* sound genteel. Grinning smugly, Phoebe reached out to knock on the door but he stepped back.

"You know what? We forgot your present. We better go back down before somebody steals it. It'll be gone. I'm a cop. I know these things." He began to turn toward the elevator.

"Wait," she protested, putting her hand on his chest, which made them both freeze for a moment and look down at her hand and his chest. Slowly, she slid her fingers away. "It'll be fine. Believe me. Anybody who wants that Crock-Pot or the smooshed deviled eggs can have them."

"You mean, that present you brought is a Crock-Pot?"

"Yes. Why?"

He paused for a minute then shook his head and laughed. "It's stupid, really. For a second, I thought you might have gotten the wrong address or something. You know—" Trace shrugged "—right building, wrong party." Strangely, he sounded relieved and his expression had brightened significantly. "Listen, why don't I get you inside then run down and grab that gift for your friend?" He grinned down at her. "No happy homemaker should be without a Crock-Pot."

Phoebe wrinkled her nose. "Which is exactly why we can leave it downstairs. I doubt Candy would ever use it," she said, and Trace flinched then almost dropped her.

She clutched at his arms. "Oh, gosh. I'm sorry." Heat crept over her cheeks. "Thanks, but really, you can put me down now. I have to be heavy."

"You're not heavy. How did you say you got invited to this party?" he asked without missing a beat.

On the elevator ride upstairs, Phoebe noticed Trace seemed intent on poking and prodding into each and every detail of her life since they'd last seen each other. Unfortunately, there hadn't been much to tell—or much that she'd been willing to tell. After all, her life seemed to her unfathomably boring and pitiful—especially when she shared it with the ex-boyfriend she hoped to turn bitter with regret for having let her slip away. So, all too soon, Phoebe had found herself explaining her return to Miami. Call it pride, vanity or sheer humiliation, but she hadn't told him about her new job on the *Mirage* as a showgirl.

Somehow, going from prima ballerina to showgirl seemed sort of shallow and pathetic after he'd chosen to become a cop when his own pursuits in journalism hadn't been successful. Instead Phoebe had stammered her way through an awkward lie about a lagging dance production she was helping to get back on its feet. Then she'd told him about her new friends and the bridal shower tonight.

She should've just said she was in town on vacation, but against her better judgment she'd wanted him to believe her return was more permanent. Just in case. It was a ridiculous waste of time that could only lead to trouble, yet the discovery that all those years ago Trace's feelings for her might have been stronger than she'd believed made her chest go all hot and fluttery. Not to mention the ball of warmth that spread through her lower regions whenever she even happened to glance at him. Jeesh, it was all she could do not to throw herself down on the ground and toss her skirt back over her head. Phoebe almost laughed. Tiffany would be so proud.

Trace turned his head toward her, his gaze snaring hers. "Well?"

All thought fled her brain the moment their eyes met. "Well, what?" she asked like a total dolt.

"The party?"

She tried to sound normal, but it took all her concentration just to breathe properly, his lips barely inches from her own. "Yes. I'm going to a party."

The muscles in his neck and shoulders tensed under her arms. "Did you say you worked with the women at the party? Danced with them?"

"Um, I think so." Phoebe gave up trying to focus on his questions. His eyebrows were lowered. Funny how she'd never noticed they were a shade lighter than his hair and perfectly arched. Perfectly perfect. A sigh welled in her chest.

"And this friend is getting married?"

Little sparklers flared to life down low in Phoebe's body every time his lips formed a word, and she nodded. Anything to keep those supple lines of flesh moving.

"Phoebes—earth to Phoebe?" His silky voice speaking her name was an act of God. He shook his head, his fantabulous mouth grinning sinfully.

Sin... Yes. She wanted sinning. Lots of sinning.

He chuckled softly. "You know you're killing me, don't you? Here..." He gave her a hard kiss, his lips firm and warm, but he pulled back aeons too soon. "Now, pay attention, kitten, and if you're good we'll try that again." His eyes darkened. "Only longer. Much longer." Trace stared at her mouth for a moment before he shook his head and lowered his eyebrows determinedly. "I want you to tell me who invited you here."

The longer version definitely sounded good but she couldn't remember what she had to do to get it. Something about listening. Or answering. Oh, why hadn't she just sucked face with him when she'd had the chance?

"Phoebe—" He shook her.

Couldn't he tell that she was having a major hormonal breakthrough here? Phoebe sounded cross but didn't care and said, "I told you in the elevator. Some of my new friends at work invited me. If you must have specifics, I think Barbie was the one who officially asked."

His lips parted and a startled huff of air escaped. She inhaled his sweet breath. She couldn't take it a second longer, and just when he opened his mouth to say, "Barbie! Good Chr—" Phoebe cupped his face with her hands and yanked him to her, cutting off his words. Blood pounded in her veins. Oceans roared in her ears. Phoebe couldn't believe it. All on her own she'd reached out and kissed him. She was an animal!

Fortunately, it didn't take much to refocus him, because as soon as they connected, Trace made a muffled grunt then jumped into the fray. He licked into her mouth, and with the first warm swipe of his tongue she could swear that goose bumps rose on every square inch of her skin. Then he moaned, the sound pained and rough. The noise vibrated her lips and started a quivering sensation arrowing straight to the tips of her breasts.

Unbelievably, he still held her, and she shifted in his arms, tilted her hips until she'd twisted and they were stomach to stomach. It was like rolling over into a fire. Ready to incinerate on the spot, Phoebe began to rub her nipples against the pressure of his chest when, with a jarring return to reality, the apartment door next to them jerked open.

Trace wrenched his mouth free and Phoebe almost wailed. Much slower to recover, she finally followed his line of vision to the doorway. One of the showgirls, Barbie—the hostess for Candy's party—stood just inside.

"Well, it's about time," Barbie said, before turning her head and yelling over her shoulder to the women inside the apartment, "Hey everybody, get your money out. Tiffany's big sister found the stripper! It's show time!"

3

TRACE FROZE. He wanted to move, but couldn't. If only to clap his hand over top of Barbie's blabbering mouth. It was like watching a car accident he couldn't prevent. In slow motion.

Phoebe cocked her head, her expression clearly confused. "Stripper?"

Barbie chuckled and shook her head. "As if you didn't know. And I thought Tiffany was the wild sister."

Phoebe frowned and looked toward him.

He refused to meet Phoebe's gaze—not easy since he was still holding her, and her face was only inches from his own. Barbie said, "Come on in." The buxom showgirl smiled and waved for him to follow, but his feet felt as if they'd been trapped in hardened cement. "Good thing you finally got here. The girls were getting a little rowdy. But I'm sure they'll be much happier now that the 'Sea Stud' is here." She stopped and ran her gaze over him from head to toe.

Trace cringed and thought, damn Barbie and her big mouth, anyway. Of all the demeaning things he'd been through in the last couple of weeks, the stupid nickname the customers on the ship had come up with had to be the worst. Unfortunately, the *Mirage* had been only too happy to cash in on the situation and had started hanging posters of him in costume from the neck down all over the ship. And while he was mostly glad they hadn't used his face, he was also disgusted to realize that some small part of himself balked at the idea of being just a body. As if he were a piece of meat.

"Sea Stud?" Phoebe's voice came out a squeak. "You mean that guy in all those posters on the *Mirage?*"

Barbie nodded. "You didn't know that was Trace?"

Phoebe merely shook her head, though he could feel her body go stiff as a poker in his arms.

Trace's mind churned. How the hell was he supposed to get himself out of this one? And how much truth should he tell her? That he wasn't even a male stripper but really a reporter for a tabloid rag because he'd lost his job at the *Herald?*

He could just picture himself trying to explain that particular fall from grace. *You see, Phoebe, it's like this. I got fired from the* Herald *because I wouldn't sleep with the boss's daughter in the supply closet during the annual work Christmas party. Unfortunately, I'd imbibed a little too much yuletide cheer, and between the alcohol and the shock of being dragged into the dark little room on my way back from the john, Jeanine had my pants open and zipper down before I could wrestle her off me. Now wait, this is the really funny part. Jeanine's dad, my editor, walked in on us and she blamed the whole thing on me. Not only did he fire me on the spot, he started a smear campaign that pretty much killed any chances of me getting hired by the sort of newspaper a person would read outside of a line at the grocery store.* Frankly, Phoebe believing he was a male stripper was less embarrassing.

Phoebe swallowed. "So, that's your body in those posters." Her cheeks turned rosy. "Uh, it's a good shot. Nice abs."

Those same abs tightened, but for the moment Trace was saved from having to give an explanation when the bride-to-be, Candy, walked into the small foyer. She placed her hands on her hips. "Hey, what's the holdup?" Candy asked.

"Yeah, you two." Barbie reached out and grabbed his sleeve, which left him with no choice but to let her pull him inside.

"Wait a minute." Candy winked at Phoebe. "If anyone

should be carried over the threshold it's me. I'm the one getting married."

"Candy's right," Phoebe said. She pushed against his chest. "You can put me down now."

Automatically he tightened his hold. "Sorry, ladies. No can do. Phoebe's hurt." Hurt and nuts if she thought he'd give her up that easily. Not after that lip lock she'd just given him back in the hallway. For her, that kiss was nothing short of a proposition and it was one he intended to take her up on.

Trace ignored Phoebe's huffy exhale and shook his head at the other two women. "She stepped on some glass outside and can't walk. If one of you would tell me where the bathroom is, I'll carry her there. Oh, and I'll need some tweezers. Maybe some first-aid stuff, too."

"Oh, brother," Phoebe mumbled as she crossed her arms over her chest. She turned her face away from him and studied the wall.

"Are you okay?" Candy asked her, stepping closer. "I hope it's not bad."

"I'm fine, really, but thank you. It's just a cut. He refuses to listen." Phoebe jerked her thumb toward him.

"Are you sure?" Barbie asked. "Right now your dancing's not so great, kid. The last thing you need is an injury." She lowered her voice, "Especially if you're still hoping to get in on the extra money Saturday night."

Wait a second, Trace thought, frowning. In the midst of worrying about his own lies, he seemed to have forgotten that Phoebe had told a few humdingers of her own. A sinking feeling settled in his stomach, like when an informant took back everything he'd said only an hour before the paper went to bed, and his heart pounded. How the hell did she know Barbie and Candy? And what the hell was she doing on the *Mirage?* "What the hell are you guys talking about?" he interrupted, his voice overly loud, but apparently this didn't matter since none of them listened to him anyway.

Candy nodded to Phoebe as if he hadn't spoken. "You've got the right equipment—you just need to learn how to use it better." Candy quirked her mouth. "A lot better. No offence, Devereaux."

Phoebe laughed, sounding genuinely amused at the insult. "None taken." Then she hesitated. "But you think I'll be good eventually, right? I mean, I'm not a lost cause or anything?"

The two women shared a look then Barbie said, "You'll have to work your fanny off before Tuesday, but me and the girls can help you."

Phoebe beamed. "I was hoping you'd say that. Thanks. You guys are the best."

Barbie and Candy laughed. "Hey, you're Tiffany's big sister. We're all family on the *Mirage*."

The muscles over Trace's ribs tightened until he could barely breathe. "Hey," he interrupted again, giving Phoebe a quick shake. He was going to get her attention this time no matter what, except now that Trace had it, he couldn't speak because the thoughts swirling inside his head were so ridiculous he felt like an idiot to even ask. "You're gonna think I'm crazy, but, well, you're not—I mean, this is so stupid, because there's no way—" He stumbled over his words while Phoebe's eyes glittered with a certain malicious satisfaction that made his stomach clench. "Tell me you're not a showgirl on the *Mirage*...."

Phoebe lifted her pert nose in the air, her lips curving smugly. "Sorry, Stud of the Sea. No can do—"

"Sea Stud," Barbie and Candy corrected in unison.

Phoebe rolled her eyes. "Whatever." She flicked her finger under his chin. "Looks like you and I'll be working together. I can't wait to see you do your little routine. Who knows? Maybe I can even pick up a few pointers."

"HERE WE GO, kids." Barbie flipped on the light then stepped aside for him to enter the bathroom. "You can set her down then I'll show you where the stereo is. You brought a tape for your music, right?''

Phoebe patted him on the shoulder. "Trace is a professional. Of course he brought his tape."

Heat crept over his face. "I'll check out the sound system in a minute. She's going to need some help—"

"No, I don't," Phoebe cut him off, then fiercely whispered into his ear, "Put me down."

Trace dumped her cute butt onto the rim of the tub, his lips twisting at her muffled grunt, then closed the door in Barbie's startled face. He turned the lock, not about to let anything or anyone interrupt him.

"Well, okay," Barbie's muffled voice spoke from the other side. "But hurry it up. The crowd is getting restless. Especially Angie."

Trace winced. He'd mostly agreed to dance at this little shindig because of Venzara's niece, Angie. Rumor had it she used the male dancers on the *Mirage* like her own personal stud service. Not that Trace was interested in joining her stable, but at this point he'd date the stage manager, Phil, if it meant getting enough information so he could write a real story. Trace sighed. At the moment, Angie was the least of his worries.

He turned around and faced Phoebe. There was really no place to go in the small room, so he leaned back against the door and crossed his arms. She was smoothing down her hair, looking into the mirror above the sink from her perch on the tub. She pretended to ignore him, but he'd caught her sneaking glances his way more than once. Pursing his mouth, he stewed over the load of garbage she'd fed him in the elevator. Lagging dance production, his ass. He'd pictured her helping some struggling inner-city troupe, charitably promoting the arts. Not shimmying around a casino ship in feathers and heels.

"You lied," he said flatly.

She jumped at his voice then dropped her arms. "I thought that was my line, *Officer McGraw*."

Trace narrowed his eyes. "Touché. But then that shouldn't be much of a surprise to you since you've always accused me of being a liar."

She lifted her chin. "Only to juggle all of your women. I should have realized the habit would leak into other areas of your life."

"Then what's your excuse?"

She looked away and busied herself with her skirt, pressing out the wrinkles. "I told you the truth. The *Mirage*, er, needed my expertise and I agreed to help with choreography and things like that, as well as, um, giving the girls a few pointers on technique."

"That's not what it sounded like when you were talking out there to Candy and Barbie. In fact, it seemed like, if anything, *you* needed *their* help."

"I guess you misunderstood. Could you hand me the supplies from the medicine cabinet? We better be getting out there." She gave him a cool smile. "It seems your adoring fans are pretty anxious to see you." She raked him with her gaze, narrowing in on the fly of his pants before shrugging her delicate shoulders. "As I said before, I barely remember our time together in college. I guess I'll just have to wait and see what all the fuss is about."

He leisurely stroked his thumb over the handcuffs dangling from his belt. "You're lying again, kitten. Don't push me. Unless you want to play a round of bad cop captures naughty showgirl." But just referring to Phoebe as a showgirl was too much for him, and he clenched his jaw until the bone all but throbbed, then blurted, "Since when are you a dancer on the *Mirage*?"

She raised her eyebrows to a haughty angle. "Not as long

as you, I'm sure, oh great Stud of the Sea. I only started a few days ago.''

"Sea Stud," he mumbled.

She tucked a fall of silky hair behind her ear. "I'm sorry. What was that?"

He gritted his teeth. "Sea Stud. You keep saying, Stud of the Sea. It makes me sound like some kind of sick cartoon logo for a weird brand of tuna."

She rolled her eyes. "Oh, right. *Sea Stud* is much more dignified."

Trace took a deep breath and forced himself to let it out slowly. "Never mind. Let's talk about something more important. Like why you're a showgirl."

"Why are you a stripper?"

He felt pretty confident one of the blood vessels near his temple was going to burst if she didn't answer him soon. "You first."

Trace had no doubt that Phoebe was purposely goading him. She peeked from beneath her lashes and said, "You mean something along the lines of, you'll show me yours if I show you mine?"

Trace swore under his breath. The thought of her showing him anything was enough to make his hands shake. "Thanks, but a few answers will be just fine for now. I'll show you whatever you want afterward."

She snorted, switching tracks. "I'm sure I won't be interested."

He gave her a look that said he knew better. "I could prove you wrong, but I'll wait. Hell, I might not even have to. Who knows when you'll get the urge to plant one on me again. You've gotten pretty aggressive in the last nine years, Phoebes."

Her back shot ramrod straight at his taunt. Of course, he probably shouldn't have gone so far, since it was his fondest hope that she'd plant one on him again and soon.

Face flushed, she said, "You're right. I have changed. Which is exactly why I'm now at the *Mirage*." Then Phoebe cocked her head, her expression becoming baffled. "I don't know why you're carrying on like this. I am a professional dancer, you know."

Yes, but there were professionals, and then there were professionals. Trace conjured up an image of Phoebe wearing nothing but the tiny scraps of fabric the *Mirage* passed off as a costume while she kicked and pranced in front of a roomful of drunks from the casino. He clenched his fists, his voice almost a growl when he said, "Because you do not belong on that damn ship."

Phoebe lifted her chin. "Well, I disagree. I think it's perfect."

Trace barked out a laugh. "If you like being pawed by a bunch of soused gamblers, I guess. "He ran his hand over his jaw. "You've got a strange idea of perfect, kitten."

Phoebe hesitated then shook her head. "You're exaggerating. I've already talked with the girls. It's not that bad." She shrugged then held out her hands palms up, her smile almost sheepish. "Besides, I'm actually looking forward to performing like that. In front of the men, I mean. All that testosterone-driven attention is kind of exciting."

Trace grew dizzy and could only stare. What the hell was going on here? This was not the same woman he'd known nine years ago. This Phoebe was far more aggressive and there was an awareness in her eyes. A light of speculation. Sexual interest. His heart pounded and a responsive tug of arousal coiled low in his stomach. Cripes, he'd barely been able to control himself around the repressed Phoebe. He'd go insane around the new and improved version. Then Trace remembered her exact wording and he frowned, wondering if he'd even have the chance. She'd sounded pretty excited when she'd talked about the male customers. Plural. Hell, it made the back of his eyes hot just thinking of her with some lamebrained jerk on the make. Never mind multiple lame-brained jerks.

He finally choked out, "Since when? Back in college you could hardly talk to a man let alone bump and grind in front of one."

She lifted her head and looked at him down the length of her nose. Not easy considering she sat three feet lower than him. "I'm a showgirl not a stripper, remember? That's what *you* do. So, if anyone around here is doing the bump and grind, it isn't me."

Next she'd accuse him of dancing with a pole. His body grew taut and he took a step toward her. "I do not bump and grind," he bit out then hesitated. "Much," he added, then scowled. The pain-in-the-butt woman had the nerve to laugh, so he turned away to keep from killing her. He planted his hands on either side of the sink and let his head hang down.

Phoebe taunted, "Why shouldn't I enjoy the men? Isn't that why you do it, Trace? All those women worshiping your body?"

"Hardly." He snorted. "Some of us actually have to work to put food on the table, kitten. Not everyone has rich parents to help them."

She huffed, "I'll have you know I've paid my own way since college."

"Well then, right there you're doing better than I did."

Phoebe tapped the toe of her one high heel against the tile floor, clicking out a rapid beat. "I'm not going to feel guilty because my parents had money. Believe me, it came with plenty of strings attached. I'm still trying to cut my way through them."

Trace stared at Phoebe in the mirror. From what he knew of her parents, this tidbit didn't surprise him. He straightened then rubbed his hands over his face. "Listen, I'm not trying to be a prick, but there are a lot of things happening on that ship you do not want to be around." When he finally looked at her again, he couldn't help but notice her reaction. She'd gone still and her eyes were alert in a way they hadn't been before.

"What exactly are you talking about?" she asked, as if she was choosing her words carefully.

Trace paused, himself. If he didn't know better, he'd think Phoebe was fully aware of what was going on with Angelo Venzara. But he did. Know better, that is. Yet his instincts were on red alert and wouldn't quit. But why? He turned to face her, leaning his hips against the sink and crossing his arms in front of his chest.

"Everything," he answered slowly, studying her response, though for once her expression gave nothing away. Finally, Trace sighed and scratched the back of his neck. "Nothing. It doesn't matter." Suddenly tired, he just wanted to end this and for Phoebe to be safe. Meaning not ogled by strange men on the *Mirage* or anywhere near Mr. V. and his shady employees. Especially Sonny Martorelli. Just the thought of her even knowing about the man had Trace breaking out in a cold sweat.

Exasperated, he said, "I just don't get it. I've seen you dance, kitten. You're an amazing ballerina, but a showgirl? I don't know how you even got hired in the first place." The minute the words left his mouth he knew he'd made a huge tactical error. "What I meant to say was, the women on the ship—the way they dance—I just can't see you—wait." He held up his hand. "That's not what I meant either. Let me start again. Because you're a classically trained dancer, you can't—" He broke off, struggling for a diplomatic way to explain she was too damn good, inside and out, to be anywhere near the *Mirage* and that the mere thought of her at risk would drive him insane. But after living with five sisters, he knew she'd consider it as much of an insult to be referred to as too classy or wholesome than to be called a tramp.

Phoebe had apparently deciphered her own explanation from his silence. Glaring, she stood then limped past him. She swung open the medicine cabinet and grabbed the things she needed for her foot. "Listen, none of this matters. I'm anxious to get started and I know what I'm getting into. My sister was a dancer on the *Mirage* for two years. It's why I took the job."

She sounded sincere on both counts, which was definitely a shockaroo. "Sister...? Wait a second. Are we talking about that teenage Lolita who used to come and visit you in college?"

Phoebe smirked and reached over for the tweezers she'd placed on the counter. "Put the moves on you, did she?" She chuckled. "Doesn't surprise me. I swear she has some sort of radar, so that she can just glance at a building and tell if there's a good-looking guy inside." She grinned fondly then leaned over to look at her toe.

Trace tugged on his ear. "Tiffany's her name? She was, uh, friendly all right. You introduced us at the rec center on campus. When you left us alone for a minute, she offered to teach me a few things I'm not even sure are anatomically possible. I'd forgotten about her. Though how I don't know. One tends to remember the Amy Fischers in life."

Phoebe stopped what she was doing and pursed her lips. "I understand the sentiment, but she is my sister and I love her. So knock it off. Besides, she's calmed down a lot. Sort of," she muttered under her breath. "She just got married a couple of days ago to a nice man." Phoebe seemed to have trouble saying this last part.

"You're kidding?" He whistled softly. *"May the force be with him."*

This made Phoebe laugh. "Somehow I think Tony Venzara can handle her. And if not, I'm sure Tony Jr. will settle her down the rest of the way."

Trace stilled. "Who'd you say the lucky guy was?"

Her mouth flattened. "Tony Venzara. His uncle owns the *Mirage*. The pair is on their honeymoon right now."

His mind churned over the information as she plucked the shard of glass free from her toe without a wince. She tossed it in the trash then grabbed a cotton ball, dabbing at the drop of blood welling from the tiny cut. He watched it all, though barely registered her actions. "So that's why Candy said you were almost family with the Venzaras. Your sister married into them and you're taking her place in the show."

Trace stared as she applied the small bandage. Internally, a battle raged. Five minutes ago he didn't even want Phoebe anywhere near the *Mirage* and truthfully still didn't. But she'd soon be performing on the *Mirage* whether he liked it or not. And as Tony Venzara's new sister-in-law, Phoebe might unknowingly come across all sorts of useful information for his story.

The only tricky part would be picking Phoebe's brain without her catching on. Of course, it went without saying that Trace would have to make sure she stayed out of any danger. But he'd planned to keep an eye on her anyway. He didn't know when she'd become his responsibility, but she had. Not that he wanted anything permanent. He knew better. Besides, he wasn't the type of man she'd ever trust with her heart. Now, her body on the other hand, that was a different story....

Phoebe stood and dumped her shoe in the trash. "I guess I won't be needing that," she said ruefully. Then she smiled at him. "All right, I'm ready. Lead the way, O Sea Stud."

"Lead the way," he repeated grimly. "Does this mean you're going to watch while I, uh, give Candy her present?"

Her eyes flickered with heat and Trace swallowed hard. "Are you kidding?" she asked. "I wouldn't miss this for the world. You're not embarrassed for me to see you dance, are you?"

"Embarrassed?" He grunted. "Not likely." More like suicidal. "I just wasn't sure if you could handle it," he bluffed. He looked down at the floor, scuffing the carpet with his toe. Absently he stared at his boots. They were black and clunky, low-heeled. Between midcalf and ankle. The kind one of those biker guys who ride around on the back of a Harley would wear. Though Trace hated his costume, he had to admit the boots were sort of cool.

Phoebe made a scoffing noise at his last comment and said, "Oh, please. As you've repeatedly pointed out, I've already handled everything you've got to offer."

Trace quirked his eyebrow. "And you said you didn't remember anything about that night."

Phoebe shrugged. "Some things are vague, but mostly I lied." Her voice sounded cocky, but she licked her lips as if her mouth had suddenly gone dry. Everything in Trace's groin pulled tight. Phoebe might pretend she didn't care but he knew better. They weren't kids anymore. As an adult she had to know how unbelievable it had been between them that night back in college. Her kiss out in the hallway and the look in her eyes whenever she peeked at him from beneath her lashes proved it.

She was feeling the same overwhelming sexual pull as Trace, and once she saw how the women reacted when he stripped, she'd have a freaking cow. The thought made him feel marginally better, though not quite good enough. If Phoebe insisted on watching him dance, then he was going to make damn sure she had a lot more to think about than how stupid he looked with his thong stuffed full of money.

Trace brought his body in close to hers, purposely crowding her space. He leaned forward then pressed his lips to her ear. "I want you to know something." He let his breath wash over her skin and she swallowed loudly. "The whole time I'm dancing...I'll be thinking of you." Then he gave her a look impossible to misinterpret.

"Oh." Her lashes fluttered. "Well, that's, uh, very nice. Thank you, I think."

Grinning to himself, Trace took a step back, careful to keep his face blank as he opened the door. He'd definitely rattled her cage. "After you." He held out his arm for her to go first.

But as she went to pass him, Phoebe stopped and got in a shake or two of her own. "Hey, I was wondering, does this gig include you showing us, well, *everything?* Because some of the girls and I were debating about whether that guy in those posters on the *Mirage* stuffed his briefs. You know, with socks or something. I suppose I have a vague recollection of your, er—" she stumbled for a word then settled with "—*anatomy,* but nine years is a long time. And you know what they say. Everything in the past always seems bigger until you see it again. Though I guess we'll soon find out. Won't we, Sea Stud?"

Trace's jaw dropped and Phoebe tilted her head, her arms crossed over her chest. "Why, Trace, what's the matter?" she asked, a smile flirting at the corners of her mouth. She clucked her tongue. "Huh. I guess this time I stunned you silent. And here I'm not even touching you...." And with that she sauntered away.

4

PHOEBE ALL BUT BEAMED as she walked along the apartment's little hallway. For the first time in her life, she'd actually gotten in the parting shot with Trace McGraw. Oh my, was her new self turning out to be a lot more fun than she'd anticipated! However, there was definitely one gray cloud on her otherwise blue horizon. Trace was a male stripper, and the thought alone was enough to sour her expression.

Why on earth would a man with a college degree become an exotic dancer? It was one thing for her to want a wilder life, but Trace's had always been exciting enough, thank you very much. None of this made a darn lick of sense and Phoebe had a funny feeling there was something more going on. But what? She could understand why a man like him would lie about *not* being a stripper—hey, she herself had been less than anxious to cough up the details on the whole showgirl thing—but she had this niggling suspicion that he was lying about *being* one. That seemed weird, even for Trace.

Fairly disgruntled with the entire mess, Phoebe knew she wouldn't be getting her answers anytime soon and pushed the mystery aside. She was determined to get her bachelorette party experience under way and, straightening her shoulders, headed toward the growing volume of noise. Then she stepped into the living room and her eyes went wide.

Barbie's tiny apartment was filled to bursting with at least thirty spandex-clad, silicon-enhanced showgirls—as well as other assorted friends of the bride—who danced and drank with gusto. Glasses of what appeared to be every conceivable type and combination of liquor were being raised in a never-ending blur, the spectacle only to be outdone by the number of lighters being flicked at an even more astonishing rate. Thus the dense cloud of cigarette smoke hovering above the partygoers like a blanket of fog. A dangerous thing. With the amount of hair spray used to support their gravity-defying dos, one wrong move and over half these women would go up in flames.

Not to mention the showgirls', um, textile-challenged clothing. Before tonight, Phoebe would never have believed that a mere quarter yard of spandex could actually cover the essential components of the feminine form. *Cover*, of course, being a relative term. Phoebe bit her lip and glanced down at her own dress then back at the crowd. The silky, pink material had seemed so sexy on the hanger, but in this group she stood out like a sore thumb.

"Hey, kid." Barbie was standing next to Phoebe and holding out a tall frosty glass. "You look like you could use something cold and numbing. I know I sure as hell would after being locked up with that hunk." Grinning, she urged, "Go ahead, I make a mean piña colada."

Phoebe smirked. "Well, Trace can certainly drive a person to drink, that's for sure. Thanks." She'd never cared much for alcohol but desperate times called for desperate measures, and suddenly the idea of getting good and snockered seemed like a smart one. Phoebe took a sip. The perfect blend of icy pineapple and coconut slid down her throat straight to her empty stomach and she could barely taste the rum. Phoebe had just been handed the perfect drink.

"You're right. This stuff is great. Thanks," she said, lifting the glass to her mouth for another healthy swallow.

"Not a problem, but be careful," Barbie cautioned. "If

you're anything like your sister I'm sure you can handle it, but those babies are a lot stronger than they taste."

Phoebe ducked her chin, secretly tickled that Barbie thought she could keep up with Tiffany in anything, let alone the booze-swilling department. Smiling to herself, she took another sip. Then another.

"Hey, there you are." Daisy came up and gave Phoebe a quick hug. All the showgirls on the *Mirage* had names like this. Honey, Barbie, Daisy, Candy. The list went on. "I heard about what happened, you lucky dog." She looked around the crowded room where Candy and some of the others were clearing away the gifts and pushing back the furniture. "Where is the big stud? I thought he was going to start."

Barbie answered, "I made him wait in the bedroom until Candy finished with her presents. We weren't going to open them yet, but we needed something to do while he took care of Phoebe's boo-boo."

Daisy lit a cigarette. "Poor baby. Did he kiss it and make it all better?" she asked, then blew a thin stream of smoke into the air.

"You don't have to answer that," Barbie said, taking Phoebe's nearly empty glass, "though we wish you would." Laughing, she turned to the kitchen and told Phoebe, "I'll be right back with a refill."

Phoebe grinned and shook her head. Normally, their teasing would have had her dying of embarrassment by now, but for some reason it only seemed funny. For the first time, she noticed the song playing in the background. She started moving her hips in sync with the beat and thought, *what a fun party.* One song blended into the next, and before she knew it, she was as caught up in the crazy rhythm as everyone else in the room. Which was why she jumped when a pair of hands settled low on her hips from behind.

"Not bad, kitten, but if you want I'll be more than happy

to give you a private lesson." Trace's deep voice sent a shiver of awareness straight down Phoebe's spine.

Before Phoebe could answer, Barbie came up to her and handed back the newly filled glass. "Try going a bit slower this time," Barbie said with a wink, before turning to talk with Daisy.

Phoebe grinned at the showgirl then stepped away from Trace, his touch entirely too distracting. Then she figured, *hey, I'm at a party, why not live a little and flirt with the man?* Phoebe drummed up her own cocky smile, and said, "Thanks, but I think I know a bit more about dancing than you." She paused then daringly gave him a thorough once-over. Leaning in toward him, she lowered her voice and said, "But maybe, if you ask me real nice, I'll give you a private lesson...."

Trace narrowed his eyes. "You're drunk," he said flatly. Then he captured her wrist and lifted her drink.

"What are you doing?" she protested, trying to struggle free without spilling.

"Checking to see how big of a mistake you're making." He sniffed again then frowned. "Is this thing a virgin?" Trace directed his question to Barbie.

"If it is, then it's the only one in this whole apartment," Barbie retorted.

Both Trace and Phoebe stilled, and she had no doubt he was remembering how one person at this party had lost her virginity. His pupils widened and he said softly, "How could I forget?" Phoebe could swear her uterus actually jumped in response. However, just because her body was singing out the "Hallelujah Chorus" didn't mean her brain agreed.

Still annoyed that he'd all but said she'd have to be drunk to flirt with him, she scowled and reclaimed her wrist. "There's nothing wrong with my drink. It smells like fruit."

Trace frowned and pointed at her as if she were a child. "I

know, so be careful. Those are the worst kind. You'll be knocked flat before you even know what hit you."

The man obviously didn't understand the full scope of his amazing sex appeal, or her body's reaction to the thought of him stripping. Otherwise, he'd understand her need for alcohol. Also, he'd be crowing. Jeesh, just knowing that in the next five minutes she'd be seeing him naked had her breath coming in quick little jerks. Cripes. She was almost panting. A dead giveaway. Phoebe lifted the glass to her mouth. Trace frowned harder, but Barbie interrupted him before he could start in with another lecture.

"You ready?" their hostess asked.

"Sure," he answered, and Phoebe wondered if she was the only one to notice how reluctant he'd sounded. Then Trace leaned close and lowering his voice said, "Watch it with that stuff, and remember—I may be dancing for Candy...but I'll be thinking of you, kitten, the whole time." He winked and strode to the center of the room.

TRACE LOOKED AROUND. So...this was hell. He'd always known it was where he would end up. He just hadn't pictured having to strip in front of Phoebe when he got there. The only thing missing was Manny, his boss, with a pitchfork and horns.

Angie Venzara wiggled her fingers at him from her seat on the couch just a few feet away then blew him a kiss, her puffy lips slathered with lip gloss and pulled into what she probably thought was a sexy pout. It wasn't, but that didn't matter. Trace was supposed to be interested here, so he smiled back, then watched morbidly as the woman tucked a wad of bills between her half-melon breasts. She finished this up with a quick pat and a sultry wink. He did not even want to think about what he was supposed to do to get that money.

Meanwhile, the beautiful pain-in-the-butt woman he really wanted was in the back of the room slamming down the cocktails like a frat boy on spring break. And somehow through the whole thing, Phoebe still managed to look classy and refined. Maybe it was the angle she held her head. Or the long, sleek lines of her body compared to the other women's overblown curves. Regardless of the reason, in this group, she was about as inconspicuous as a swan amongst a barnyard of squawking hens. She didn't belong. So what the hell was she really doing hanging out with these women?

Barbie caught Trace's attention. She stood by the stereo and sent him a questioning look. Hell, it was now or never, and at his brief nod, the music started.

"All right, Sea Stud, take it off!" Angie yelled in her nasal whine, a voice to haunt his nightmares, yet one he realistically couldn't ignore. Even with the possibility that Phoebe might come across with some valuable information as Tony Venzara's sister-in-law, he needed to keep his options open with Angie. It made much more sense to secure Angie's interest tonight. Meaning he couldn't tone down his performance, or ignore her.... Phoebe would kill him, and the thought of her being jealous cheered him up a bit. Hey, with his ultimate humiliation only moments away, he'd take whatever small consolation he could get.

The bride-to-be, Candy, sat in a straight-backed chair in the center of the room. He knelt down next to her and dangled the handcuffs from his finger. "I take it you want the cuffs?" he asked.

Candy nodded. "Well, of course. I'm a dangerous woman, Officer. You may want to pat me down for weapons, too." She batted her long black lashes at him. "Please."

Trace laughed wearily and stood back up. "I kind of figured you'd say that." He had nothing against Candy personally, but damn this was embarrassing. Heat crept up his neck, but he took a deep breath and said loudly, "If you could please step around behind the chair, miss." He motioned with his hand for Candy to rise. "That's it. Now place your hands on the back of the chair, please."

Candy leaned forward and did as he asked then sent him a suggestive look over her shoulder. The position had pushed out her bottom. Grinning at Candy's harmless antics, he stepped up behind her and placed one of his low-heeled boots between her feet, lightly kicking them apart. He squatted down. Starting with her ankles, he ran his hands over her legs and slowly rose as he worked his way up her body. The other girls hooted and whistled, throwing out remarks.

Unable to stop himself, he glanced at Phoebe, hoping she wouldn't be too upset. He should've known better. Her studiously disinterested face read, *hurry up already and get on with it.* So she was bored, was she? Well, not for long if he had anything to say about it. Fighting a smile, he stood and pulled Candy upright. He snapped the cuffs onto her wrists and directed her back down into the seat.

He took a deep breath and then in time with the music, started with the top button of his shirt and slowly worked it open. The women whistled and cheered, but Trace ignored them, all his intensity focused on the bride. He especially ignored Phoebe, knowing how much it would drive her nuts. At this moment she was probably working herself up into a lather wondering whether he was really picturing her or not. Trace was and almost groaned.

Staring into Candy's eyes, he bumped his hips left then right. He ran his hands across his chest, then spread the sides of his shirt wide, showing off muscles he already knew the women liked. Sure enough, they squealed like a bunch of girls at a boy-band concert, and Trace almost laughed out loud.

He hitched his pelvis forward, letting the material of his pants strain across his groin and slowly skimmed his hands down his abdomen until his fingertips slipped under the waistband of his pants and rested inside. The crowd practically groaned as one. God, he loved these women. Their yelps were going to drive Phoebe crazy. A fair exchange considering he'd been pretty mind-whacked ever since she'd run him to ground out in the yard.

Trace turned his back on the roomful of man-hungry showgirls and dipped his shoulders, letting the fabric drop and catch at his elbows. Eyes closed, he arched his neck, throwing back his head while he pumped his hips against his hands. On count with the music, he pivoted back to the crowd. He opened his eyes, found Phoebe's gaze, and held it while he kept his pelvis moving with the beat. He pictured her hands in place of his own, saw her on her knees before him, and let the desire stirred up by that erotic image fill his eyes with hunger.

He watched the rise and fall of her chest move faster. He could see the muscles in her neck move as she swallowed awkwardly. His pulse roared in his ears, the moment stretching out between them. Damn, he wanted her. The drums pounded from the stereo. He thrust his arms to the side, then dropped them down. His shirt fell to the ground. The women screamed and whooped.

Adrenaline surged through his blood in spite of how stupid he felt dancing around the room like a gigolo. Excitement and energy pulsed from the crowd and he couldn't help but respond. They knew what came next. He gripped the front of his pants and let the anticipation build. From the corner of his eye he saw Phoebe, her gaze glued below his waist. Purposely, Trace waited until their eyes met. Then he pulled.

PHOEBE TRIED to swallow but couldn't. Saliva seemed to be the missing factor here, and hers had gone MIA about the same time as Trace's pants. Unfortunately, even with that ridiculous thong he wore, Phoebe could tell there was nothing wrong with her memory of Trace's male anatomy, vague though her actual glimpse of it may have been nine years ago.

Though they'd never spoken about her lack of previous experience, Phoebe was certain Trace had known she was a virgin on their infamous night. An incredibly aroused and freakishly excited virgin, but a shy one nonetheless. He'd seemed to sense this before they'd even touched, and had gone out of his way to soothe her fears. Dim lights, fluffy blankets, hours of foreplay during which he'd slowly removed her clothing one piece at a time had all transpired to conceal his intimate parts.

As a result, Phoebe's eyes had barely been able to surface from her sensual haze long enough to see Trace's face let alone take a nice long gander at his family jewels, and she'd convinced herself that nothing could have been that spectacular no matter how he'd felt. *Boy, had she been wrong.*

Well, at least the pesky sock question had been cleared up. Yes indeedy, Phoebe thought, and took another drink. Good Lord! And to think, at one time in life, the man had actually begged her for a date. Every weekend, no less. He should've just shown up at her dorm room sans pants and saved them both a lot of trouble. Or pulled her aside in the library and flashed her the goods. Phoebe felt pretty confident she'd have stopped resisting then and there and gone along quietly.

For the first time, Phoebe realized she wasn't the only one similarly affected. If she'd thought the women were loud and rowdy before he'd dropped trou, it was nothing compared to this.

"Oh my God!" One of the dancers pushed off the couch and sat up straight.

"Told you it wasn't a pair of socks," another shouted.

"Call Jimmy and tell him the wedding's off," Candy begged her friends.

"Tell him yourself. I'm busy staring," Daisy answered,

and she wasn't lying. Her eyes were trained on Trace's groin like a pair of lasers.

A woman with dark hair and a funny nose beckoned Trace over with a bill she'd pulled from her cleavage. Phoebe's jaw turned slack. The woman held a fifty in her hand, then took her good sweet time tucking it into his briefs. No wonder Trace was no longer a reporter. These nuts were making him rich.

Phoebe frowned and went to tap Daisy on the arm but missed. She squinted down at her hand and tried again. This time her limb obeyed and, smiling at her success, she said to Daisy, "Hey, who's she?"

"Ouch," Daisy turned and glared. "*Hey*, yourself," she said, rubbing the red spot on her shoulder.

"Who's the floozy with all the money?" Phoebe spoke precisely. When she wasn't careful, an odd slurring had crept into her speech.

Daisy cocked her head questioningly, so Phoebe pointed to Miss Moneybags. They both watched the woman pull out another fifty. She put the bill between her teeth then leaned toward Trace's crotch. Phoebe gasped and narrowed her eyes. For cripe's sake, was there a never-ending supply of cash down there? The woman was plucking fifties from between her boobs like tissues out of a box.

Phoebe frowned and reached for her purse. If she was lucky she might have thirty-five cents and some ones. Not exactly incentive for Trace to come and give her a lap dance, but maybe if she palmed them he wouldn't see how little he was getting. But her purse wasn't on her shoulder.

"Ahh," Daisy said, dragging out the word and reminding Phoebe she hadn't yet been given an answer. "That's Angie Venzara, Mr. V.'s niece and Tony's sister." Daisy paused for a second, a teasing light twinkling in her eyes. "Hmm. I wonder what that makes you two now that Tony and Tiff have tied the knot."

Phoebe scowled. "Not related."

Daisy chuckled. "Don't blame you for not claiming her as one of your new in-laws. Angie can be a pain in the butt, but she's basically harmless."

Phoebe didn't argue and thought, speaking of butts, if Angie reached for Trace's one more time, Phoebe was going to kill her.

At just that moment Trace's gaze snared her own. Phoebe yawned exaggeratedly then took her time patting her mouth. He laughed and shook his head, which for some reason made her feel juvenile. Thrilled to have amused him, Phoebe lifted her chin and pretended great interest in...well, hell, there was nothing else in the room a person would be interested in with Trace carrying on half-naked, a thong and a pair of biker boots the only things covering his astonishing body. She fingered the flower arrangement on the table at her side and leaned over to smell them only to discover they were fake and smelled like plastic.

Great, she thought in disgust. This was exactly the wild-woman persona she'd been hoping to convey. A mostly naked god strutted around the room and here she stood, like a true party animal, sniffing the plastic flowers. Well, no more. As soon as she got out her money she wanted a look-see of her own. She fumbled at her hip for her bag and then remembered she didn't have it on. But where was her purse? She'd brought it, hadn't she?

"Excuse me," she slurred, shoving her way through the squealing females. Phoebe rolled her eyes. The way they were carrying on, a person would think she wasn't the only one who'd seen all of four men naked, one of them being her grandfather the summer she was five and walked in on him in the bathroom. Wait a second. Phoebe bit her lip. She'd technically still only seen three, since she hadn't gotten a good look that night with Trace and right now he wore a thong. And bare butt cheeks didn't count no matter how nice those butt cheeks were. Rats!

Well, she'd fix that problem once she got her thirty-five cents.

Her search of the floor, underneath the end tables and behind the furniture for her purse led her to the front door. Where the heck was the darn thing? Maybe she'd dropped it outside. She had a vague recollection of losing something outside, but she didn't know what.

A pounding noise rattled her skull. Loudly. Phoebe cupped her head, and that's when she noticed the banging had grown louder. She peered at the front door. The wood practically shook inside the frame.

She finally figured out someone was trying to get inside and said, "Hold your horses." Quickly, she walked across the foyer, but the room tilted precariously with her movement. Groaning, she turned the handle and swung open the door.

Fully aware her mouth had dropped open but unable to do a thing about it, Phoebe stared up at two young blond Adonises dressed in police uniforms. Talk about Miami's finest. Yikes. But then the truth dawned on her and a slow smile spread across her lips. She'd already been taken in once tonight by Trace and wasn't about to fall for this fake cop act again. Real police officers did not look like these guys. And two this gorgeous wouldn't be traveling in pairs. The city wouldn't allow it. Women would be committing petty crimes all over Miami and then resisting arrest.

"May I help you boys?" Phoebe practically purred. If Trace thought Angie had friendly hands then just wait till he saw what Phoebe had in store for these two. He'd find out just how it felt to be the one watching for a change.

A look passed between the men before the first one spoke, "We're with the Miami-Dade Police Department—"

Phoebe interrupted and said, "Oh, I bet you are," then winked.

"Excuse me?" the second and slightly older Adonis asked. He was maybe twenty-five, tops.

Phoebe thought about how annoyed Trace would be and practically rubbed her hands together. Instead she said, "I'm sorry. I shouldn't have interrupted your little speech. Go ahead." And she waved her hand for them to continue. "Very authentic, by the way," she whispered.

They stiffened at her compliment, and Phoebe thought, *these guys are good.* Maybe they were aspiring actors or something, because they never broke out of character once.

Number two cleared his throat. "We received a noise complaint from another resident in the building. Is this your apartment, ma'am?"

"Ma'am?" Phoebe repeated then wrinkled her nose. "It's a nice touch but you make me sound like my grandmother. I think I'd prefer miss."

Adonis number one's cheeks flushed and number two shrugged. "She must be drunk."

Phoebe sniffed. "I'm not drunk." She tried to sound indignant, but then she hiccuped and ruined the whole effect. "Oh, never mind." She sighed then said, "I was just trying to be helpful. If I don't care for the whole ma'am thing, I can guarantee you the other girls won't. And that's bound to affect your tips, but you guys do what you want. Men always do."

Adonis number one all but choked and started to say something but Phoebe cut him off. "It doesn't matter. Come on in," she said, stepping back. "We'll find Barbie. Trace is almost finished, so I don't know if you're early or late. Were you three supposed to perform together?"

"Perform?" Adonis number two was looking at her as if she'd escaped from the loony bin.

Phoebe shook her head. Tweedle-Yum and Tweedle-

Yummier might be easy on the eyes but they'd definitely been shortchanged in the brains department.

"It's okay. Follow me, fellas. The girls are gonna die when they see you guys. You two are gorgeous." The first one blushed bright red and mumbled a thank-you, which seemed to embarrass him even more. The second one turned only a shade lighter but looked her over from head to toe. By the time he finished checking her out, he'd made up for the color difference. Phoebe laughed and thought to herself, *young guys are fun. I actually intimidate them.*

She hooked her finger through the closest Adonis's belt loop and pulled him in her wake. As they walked by Daisy, Phoebe stopped and asked, "Do you have any money?"

"What?" Daisy asked, still looking at Trace.

"Money," Phoebe yelled louder. "Do you have any money I can borrow?"

"Sure." Daisy reached into her vest pocket and pulled out a few bills. She leered and said, "So, you want a little peek at Trace, huh? I thought you could get that for free."

"It's not for Trace. It's for these two." Phoebe pointed behind herself.

Daisy's cocky smile stayed in place until she saw the two studs.

Adonis number one pulled Phoebe's hand free and said to Daisy, "Is this your apartment, ma'am?"

Daisy's mouth fell open, and Phoebe rolled her eyes and said behind her hand, "I told you to go with miss." Phoebe then plucked the money from Daisy's fingers and said, "I'm taking them to Barbie. She must've hired them for some kind of grand finale."

Daisy shook her head and grabbed for Phoebe's arm. "Holy crap, Phoebe, you don't understand—"

"Of course I do." Phoebe glanced at Trace, who'd stopped dancing and was staring at her and the new arrivals. She reached back for Adonis one's belt again and almost laughed aloud as Trace's jaw dropped. Then Barbie stepped into view and Phoebe said, "There's Barbie, come on." But she didn't need to go far because suddenly Barbie was on them.

"Hey," Phoebe said. "Your grand finales are here. Where do you want them to set up?"

Barbie frowned at her then looked at the men. "I live here. Is there some kind of trouble?"

Phoebe winked. "The only problem I see is for Trace and whether he can handle the competition. Something tells me these bad boys don't use any socks either." Phoebe reached out to pat the closest Adonis's chest, when a hand clamped down on her arm.

"Not a good idea, kitten," Trace said, pulling her away.

"Afraid these guys will look better out of uniform than you, Trace?"

Now Trace too was giving her a look that said, have aliens abducted your brain?

"No one here wants to see these men out of their uniforms, least of all me." Trace smiled at them but it came out more like a grimace.

"Ha! That's what you think." She jerked her arm free. "I, for one, can't wait to see them naked." She let her gaze run all over number two since he was closest. She reached out and patted his butt. "Nice buns," she said conversationally. "I bet they'll look every bit as delicious as they feel."

Trace groaned and Phoebe thought she might have gone a little bit overboard with that last part, but she lifted her chin and kept her hand firmly glued to number two's backside like a suction cup, brazening the moment out. Except, the moment kept dragging. That was when she noticed the music had stopped.

"What's wrong? Why'd the party stop?" She frowned and looked around. "Aren't we gonna watch these guys take their clothes off?"

Daisy groaned and Barbie smirked. Trace closed his eyes.

"Why not?" Phoebe tried to put the cocky edge back in her voice. "But they're strippers. It's what they do. Strip!"

Trace just shook his head no.

Number two reached back and peeled her hand off his butt. "Like we said, *ma'am*, we got a complaint about a disturbance of the peace. And though I'm mildly flattered you want to see me in the buff, my wife might have something to say about it."

"Wife...?"

"But I'll pass on what you said about the nice buns part. She'll get a kick out of that."

"Nice buns," she repeated weakly. Her gaze darted to Trace. The idiot just shook his head again, clearly amazed at the magnitude of her blunder. Everybody in the room seemed to be doing this. Shaking their heads or fighting laughter. Phoebe suddenly didn't feel so good. The fruit and alcohol churned in her stomach.

Barbie put her arm around Phoebe's shoulder. "Aren't *you* the dark horse?" She playfully nudged Phoebe's hip with her own. "You know, kid, I was worried about you, fitting in with us and all, but I can tell you'll do just fine. Hell, I don't even think Tiffany has ever copped a feel from a cop." Barbie chuckled and soon others were joining in. "We're gonna have some good times ahead with you on board the *Mirage*, kid. I just know it."

Phoebe looked at her new friend and smiled weakly. "Yeah, it'll be nothing but great times," she said. Then she handed Daisy back her money and passed out.

5

THE SHRILL RING of the telephone brought Phoebe from deep sleep to bone-jarring consciousness in an instant. Her lids flew open and she tried to sit up. She realized two things as she immediately flopped her body back onto her pillow and threw her arm over her eyes. One, she wasn't in her own bed in San Francisco, but in Tiffany's in Miami. Which meant that last night hadn't all been a bad dream. And two, she had the mother of all hangovers.

Another peal reverberated through her pounding head and she groaned, careful to keep her eyelids firmly shut this time against the bright sunlight as she fumbled for the bedside table. In her clumsiness she knocked the cordless receiver off the base and heard the next ring from somewhere down on the floor.

"Oh, crap," she said, her voice a meager croak. But the noisy rings were too painful to ignore and she slid from the covers. Squinting, she patted the cold tiles under her knees. Unfortunately, the only thing Phoebe could see were the dancing brown spots burned onto her retina. The stupid phone must've slid somewhere under the bed.

Lowering her chest, she reached beneath the dust ruffle. Phoebe stretched her arms as far as she could until her fingers brushed against smooth plastic.

"Gotcha," she said, then sat back on her heels, lifting the phone to her ear. "Hello," she said. "Hello?" But by now the ringing had stopped. She moaned and dropped her forehead into her palm. "I'm never drinking again," she muttered.

"Um, that's probably a good thing since that's not a phone you're trying to answer."

Phoebe screeched and turned so fast she fell to her bottom. The ice-cold tile practically numbed the flesh covering her lower cheeks and another realization hit her as she stared up into Trace's equally stunned face.

"I'm naked," she said.

He nodded, his eyes glazed. "As a jaybird."

She swallowed, and with a shaking hand pulled the blankets down from the bed and tried to cover herself. "What are you doing here?"

He stared at her, a funny expression on his face. "You couldn't drive so I brought you home. It was late. I didn't feel comfortable leaving you alone and decided to sleep on the couch."

"Oh, well, thank you. That was very nice of you." She licked her lips then asked casually, "And, um, my clothes?"

"I heard you go to the bathroom around four, but by the time I got to your room you were already back in bed." His voice sounded distracted, and he added, "I'd look for your clothes in there."

"Oh, good. Good." Phoebe cleared her throat. "Were you, uh, standing there long enough to see me reach for the phone?"

He closed his eyes and said, "God yes." Then he glanced at her hand. "Except that isn't a phone you're holding."

Confused, she looked down then shrieked. "It isn't mine," she yelled, throwing the purple, penis-shaped vibrator back under the bed. "It's Tiffany's!"

Trace rubbed his chest to the left of his breastbone. "You have no idea what that did to me, walking in here and seeing you like that. Naked and on your hands and knees, holding a vibrator." He actually trembled. His face filled with sexual heat, until finally he shook his head as if to clear it. Then he started to laugh.

Blushing this hard had to be lethal, Phoebe decided as her face turned hot enough to fry her skin. So why on earth wasn't she dead? Anger seemed like a reasonable response to her current situation, and she scowled and said, "Thanks for the ride, but next time just let the cops bring me home." Clutching the sheet, she tried to stand while at the same time preserve what was left of her modesty, though realistically, she had none left to speak of.

His laughter slowed down to the occasional chuckle. Shaking his head, he didn't even bother trying to hide his grin. "Sorry, but you scared the *real* cops off when you grabbed Mr. Young and Lethal's butt."

"Real cops..." Her eyes widened and she plopped back down to the floor.

Trace rubbed his jaw. "That's pretty much what you said last night. Right before you passed out."

She groaned and dropped her head onto her upraised knees. "You can go now."

"It's all coming back to you, huh?"

"Yes. Thank you. If you wouldn't mind closing the door on your way out, I'm going to kill myself."

Phoebe heard Trace's laughter and the soft tread of his bare feet as he walked toward her. "It wasn't that bad," he said, as he squatted down next to her, elbows on his knees.

She didn't bother lifting her head. "Yes, it was."

"All right, it was a little bad." He placed his hand on her back, rubbing in small delicious circles, and she had to bite her lip to keep from moaning aloud, it felt so good. "But it's not like you're the first person who's ever gotten drunk and done something they've regretted. Believe me," he said flatly.

She thought about what he said, but mostly thought about his warm fingers gently gliding up and down her vertebrae. A host of sensations rippled across her skin. She sighed and turned her head toward him, and was about to speak but found her eyes following the sculpted muscles in his arm.

Before, she hadn't really been paying attention to how he looked this morning, but focused more on the fact that he'd seen her hootchie rather than on his appearance. But now she noticed his chest was bare and his jaw darkened by a night's growth of beard. His rip-away pants were back on. They hung low on his narrow hips, bronze skin tantalizingly exposed everyplace else including his feet, which were big and long with a sprinkling of dark hairs on top. Aye-carumba. The man was beautiful.

When she finally made it back around to his face, he winked then grinned, and any coherent thought she may have possessed fled her brain. Darn, she hated it when he caught her gawking.

Needing to pull herself together, she frowned and looked away only to find herself staring at the pencil drawing of a nude couple hanging next to Tiffany's dresser, then blushed even more. Though she probably shouldn't be embarrassed since the darn thing was actually sort of tasteful. Most of Tiffany's pictures were like this. Sort of artsy-fartsy in a pornographic kind of way.

Realizing that Trace had actually been quite kind to her—laughing at her naked backside notwithstanding—she forced herself to speak honestly. "Thanks for taking care of me last night. Sticking around in case I needed you." She shrugged, fiddling with her sheet. "And for trying to make me feel better." Phoebe turned her head and met his gaze. "I remember you used to do this a lot back in college. Try to cheer me up when something went wrong. You must hate to see people sad."

He moved his hand to her forehead, running his thumb across her eyebrows and soothing away the lines of tension. "Not true," he said softly. "There are some people I hope are miserable every day of their godforsaken lives. But you, kitten, you should always be happy. Always." He kissed the tip of her nose.

"Why are you being so nice to me?" she whispered.

Amusement danced in his eyes and he whispered back, "I'm always nice to you."

Phoebe took hold of his wrist, stopping his fingers. "No," she said simply and shook her head.

"Aw hell, Phoebe." He looked away from her. "You have to know I'm attracted to you." He raked his free hand through his hair, then said, "I'll be thirty this year. That's a little too old to kick you in the shins or pull on your pigtails, but it pretty much adds up to about the same thing." Tapping her under the chin, he leaned close as if telling her a secret. "Didn't your mother ever tell you that little boys just grow up to be big ones?"

Phoebe sighed and let go of his arm then rested her chin back on her knees again. "My mother never told me anything about men. She pretends they don't exist. Especially my father."

"Ahh," he said, as if she'd just revealed some big insight into her psyche. Then he shrugged. "It's better than my mother. To this day she acts like my old man is going to come walking through her door at any moment. He'll have been gone twenty-eight years this May."

Phoebe nodded and said "Ahh" the same way he had. They looked at each other and smiled. "Are we actually having a moment here?" she asked. "We've had so few of them I'm just checking to make sure."

Trace leaned toward her. "Here's another tip. Try not to get too mushy or sentimental with a guy. It makes him nervous. Then he'll get up and run from the room or try to ruin the moment by doing something manly. Like burping the alphabet."

Phoebe nodded as if he'd imparted some great pearls of wisdom. "So where does that leave you?"

Trace clapped his hands and rubbed them together. "Since I've never been one to flaunt my masculinity, why don't I go and make us some coffee?"

Phoebe snorted, but before Trace stood he pressed his lips to her ear. She could feel the heat of his body, so close to her own, and swallowed hard. "Get ready, because I'm going to do that thing again when it's like I'm pulling your hair, but only the big-boy version." But the phone rang before he could make good on his threat, and Phoebe didn't know whether to wilt in relief or let out a snarl.

Blowing out a breath, Trace reached underneath the bedside table. If only the stupid thing had been as easy to find the first time. "I'll be back," he mouthed.

Watching him leave for the kitchen, she answered, "Hello?"

"Phoebe, is that you?" Tiffany asked. "You sound funny."

"Yeah, it's me," Phoebe answered, not in the mood to explain her grumpy disposition, and instead asked, "How's the honeymoon going?"

"As if you have to ask. Wonderful, of course, thanks to Tony, the best husband in the whole wide world. The real question is how's everything going with you?"

"Pretty good. Your friends say that I seem to have some raw talent, and with a lot of practice I might not be too bad." Phoebe laughed and Tiffany joined in with her. "Actually, Barbie and Candy are going to work with me tomorrow on the routines. That only gives me one day to perfect my *moves*, so we'll see. By the way, your friends are nice. I like them a lot."

"I don't know who you are, but put my sister on the phone right now. She's the skinny woman wandering around my apartment with the sour look on her face."

Phoebe chuckled and put her hand on the bed, pulling herself up to sit on the mattress. Then she leaned back against the headboard and adjusted the sheet around herself.

"You, Tiffany, are a brat. I don't know why I put up with you."

"Because you love me and are the best thing that's ever happened to me. Until Tony, that is." Tiffany sighed. "I know how much you've done for me, Phoebes." Her little sister's voice became soft. "But I promise, this is the last time. I'm going to be a mom pretty soon and I want to be a good one. To do all the things for this baby our parents should've done for us."

"I know, sweetie. And you will. You'll be the best."

"I don't know about that, but I'm going to try. And Tony's gonna be great, too. He loves me, Phoebe. He really does. And he loves this baby. For the first time in my life I'm finally part of a family." Tiffany laughed self-consciously.

Though Phoebe was thrilled for her little sister, a lump swelled in her throat. When would she have what Tiffany had found? "I'm happy for you, Tiff," she said, her voice breaking. "Really happy for you."

Tiffany sniffled. "Thanks." Then she grumbled, "Damn hormones. This baby has turned me into a freakin' watering pot." Tiffany stopped and blew her nose. "Jeesh, would you listen to the two of us? It's like we're in some weird episode of *The Twilight Zone.*"

Phoebe rubbed the back of her hand over her eyes and gave a watery laugh. "All episodes of *The Twilight Zone* were weird. That was the point of the show. And what do you mean?"

"Well, besides the fact that I've suddenly turned into June Cleaver, let's start with you not being the best dancer on the continent and enjoying it. And making friends with women of questionable backgrounds. Of course, the fact that Mommy Dearest is safely across the country and out of guilt-and-inadequacy range might have something to do with it."

"Give me a break, Tiff." Phoebe crossed her fingers behind

her back. "Mother's opinions have no bearing on my behavior and haven't for years."

"You've been an adult our whole lives, and by the way, you can take your hand out from behind your back and uncross your fingers, you big dork," Tiffany said as an aside, then got right back to the heart of the topic. "It's not right. You knew that if you behaved well enough and jumped through all Mom's hoops, she wouldn't sink her claws into me. And for the most part it's worked. Unfortunately, a little too well, but it's not your fault Mom doesn't have enough love left over to trickle down past her oldest daughter. Heck, even that's a little iffy. Frankly, the jury's still out on whether she can stand you, either."

"Well, it's been nice talking to you. The stroll down memory lane was a blast. Let's not do this again sometime." Phoebe was never in the mood to delve into their dysfunctional childhood and certainly not with a hangover, but Tiffany wouldn't be deterred.

"I'm just saying that you deserve to have some fun. You sound different since you left San Francisco. Which is good. I know you've always felt guilty because of how Mom treated us differently and all, but I swear, Phoebe, I got the better end of the deal. I had a life and I had you. But what did you get? A mother who's never pleased no matter how hard you try? A career you hate? Some of the most boring boyfriends Mom could possibly find?"

"Hey." Phoebe started to protest.

"Oh, come on. I bet not one of those nerds ever rocked your world, did they?"

Phoebe sputtered. "W-well...*rocked* would be a strong word, but they were very nice men. Stable and committed. I never once had to worry about one of them carousing around." Then Phoebe paused. Why on earth was she defending the boyfriends of the living dead?

"Carouse?" Tiffany snorted. "I think you have to have a

pulse to carouse. None of them did. Listen, I'm not talking about falling in love here. I'm talking about going a little wild. Mixing it up. Having some fun. Getting laid."

"I agree."

"I mean, come on, Phoebe—wait a second, what did you say?"

Phoebe laughed, loving the fact that for once Tiffany was the one in shock. "I said, I agree."

"You actually think I'm right?"

"Yep. I'd already come to the same decision. That's part of why I came to Miami. I'm not a total pushover no matter what you think."

Tiffany squealed so loud, Phoebe had to hold the phone away from her ear. "This is great. I can't believe you're actually going to take my advice."

"I'm not taking your advice—I'm following my own. I made some decisions about a lot of things and I'm sticking to them, so there."

"It's about damn time." Tiffany's voice turned philo-sophic. "I always wondered what you had against orgasms."

Phoebe groaned. "In case I haven't mentioned it, you are the most annoying little sister in the entire world. And I was never against orgasms. In theory, anyway." Her last boy-friend, Mark, had been a kind, attractive man and she'd gen-uinely liked him. Not love. Not lust. But a nice, safe like. Phoebe just hadn't felt any great sense of passion with him, and his attention in bed had somehow made her feel more embarrassed than aroused. Now, with Trace, on the other hand...badda-bing, badda-boom, and Phoebe had taken off like a Roman candle.

"You just need to learn how, is all." Tiffany said. "Buy a *Cosmo* and take a peek into that box under my bed. The girls threw me a shower and got me some interesting battery-operated companions. I, of course, don't need them with

Tony the stud-muffin at my beck and call, so take whatever you want."

"You have no idea what a relief it is to hear that your purple friend that lives under the bed has never been used." Phoebe made a face. "I accidentally touched it."

"I think you can use the purple one underwater, too."

Phoebe pulled the pillow over her head. "And on that bizarre and embarrassing note, I'll say goodbye."

But Tiffany wasn't done, and a tone of surprise entered her voice. "I can't believe how perfect everything is turning out. Me and Tony and the baby are doing great, and you're whooping it up in Miami. Now you just need to work Mr. V.'s party and prove he isn't committing the crime of the century and we can all be together." Then she giggled and said, "I'm not that far along, but this baby makes me want to start nesting. I just can't wait to get home and change the small bedroom into a nursery. I think I'm going to paint it yellow, but I'm not sure."

Phoebe pushed the pillow aside and sat up. "Hold up there, Martha Stewart. You need to slow down. This isn't a done deal." Phoebe didn't even bother mentioning the difficulties in turning Tiffany's home of erotic art and memorabilia into a child-friendly atmosphere, and merely stuck with the problems that were keeping the crazy woman out of the country. "I still haven't been asked to dance Saturday night."

"I'm not worried. They'll ask you. If there's one thing you can do, Phoebe, it's dance. But that reminds me," Tiffany continued, "Tony and I were talking. You know he doesn't believe that his uncle is guilty, but he wanted me to tell you about this little island off the Bahamas Mr. V. bought about a year ago. He calls it something Italian. Isola Pomodoro, I think. Mr. V. used to talk about moving down there but never has. Tony thinks those unmarked crates the police are so worried about might be coming from the island. He doesn't know what's in them, but Mr. V. has been worrying about tropical storms brewing down in the Caribbean and stuff like that. Always wanting updates on the weather." Tiffany hesitated. "He might be growing something, Tony just doesn't know. If Mr. V. or Sonny doesn't ask you to take my place Saturday night, then you should be able to do some snooping around on your own. If I were you, I'd start with finding out about that island."

"No, if you were you, you'd run like hell and get me to do it. Tiffany, if your husband knows anything, he should go to the police. For heaven's sake, I'm not a private investigator."

"Tony can't rat his uncle out to the cops."

"Lovely. And I can. For a minute there I actually thought you were growing up."

"You're overreacting again. Even if Tony thinks his uncle is innocent, he can't help the police. It's against the Venzara code."

Phoebe growled. "You mean the kind of code a family that's Italian but isn't Mafia would have?"

Tiffany sputtered then said, "Exactly."

"I'm not buying it. And if Tony knows so much, why don't the police get him to do their dirty work instead of you? Sure, having a showgirl will be helpful at the party, but other than that, Tony would be a much better spy. He was, after all, the one who committed the crimes. You just accompanied him."

Tiffany went silent. Phoebe stilled and her stomach dropped. "Tiffany, what are you keeping from me now?"

"I didn't say anything before because I knew you'd only get more worked up, but...Tony didn't just tag along so he could keep me company. He sort of skipped town to avoid the cops, too, and I just kind of thought that maybe—"

"I know where you're going with this and I can't believe it." Anger didn't even begin to describe Phoebe's emotions, since there was a whole bunch of fear tangled up in there, too. She shook her head. "You actually expect me to keep both of your sorry butts out of jail, don't you? Great. Perfect. Let me just get my greatcoat and magnifying glass and I'm sure I'll have the mystery solved in no time." She rubbed her forehead and could barely catch her breath.

"It's not that big of a deal, Phoebe. Nothing has changed. Once the police figure out they're wrong about Mr. V., they'll drop the charges against both of us. When you talk to Alvarez, just tell him—"

Phoebe gasped, and said, "Talk to Alvarez, oh damn." She grabbed the alarm clock off the side table. "I forgot, he's supposed to come over this morning. He'll be here any minute. I've got to go." Phoebe hung up, feeling a small measure of satisfaction at cutting Tiffany off mid-rant, then hopped out of bed.

Ooh, she felt like dumping Tiffany in jail herself and then throwing away the key. How could her sister do this to her? As if Phoebe already wasn't under enough pressure, her new brother-in-law's freedom now rested on her shoulders, too. But that was Tiffany for you. If she could con Phoebe into one favor then why not two?

But in spite of her anger, she'd been taken aback by how happy Tiff was about Tony and the baby. Phoebe had never heard her little sister sound so excited or content, let alone enthusiastic, to put down roots. Jeesh, talk about *The Twilight Zone*. And Tiffany was wrong about their childhood. As domineering and controlling as their mother was, at least Phoebe had known that someone cared even if that interest was based on how well she excelled in ballet. Heaven knows their father had always been more committed to his law firm, or driving their mother crazy with his latest mistress, than to either of his daughters. Which left Tiffany flat out in the cold. She could have fallen off the face of the earth for all their parents would have noticed.

If Tiffany had somehow managed to find happiness then Phoebe knew she was going to do whatever it took to make sure her sister stayed that way. Even if that meant picking up the slack for Tony Venzara as well. Of course, she didn't have a clue as to how to pull this all off. It was one thing to listen in on a meeting and then pass along whatever she heard, but to investigate a possible Mafia organization... yeah right.

Scowling, Phoebe marched across the floor, then all but jumped out of her skin when she saw Trace. He stood inside the doorway, his eyes dark and intent. Oh, great, she thought, wondering how long he'd been there. Just what she needed right now on top of everything else. A stripper with the instincts of a bloodhound. If Trace was here when Alvarez arrived, he'd never leave.

Glancing at him beneath her lashes, she gave a quick little wave as she walked to the closet, the sheet wrapped around her like a toga. "Uh, hi," she said, louder than she'd meant. She cleared her throat, and said at a more normal volume, "I forgot you were still here. Here in the apartment. Since you were in the kitchen and all..." Her back to the room, Phoebe winced. Well, that was smooth. Jeesh, could she have sounded more nervous if she'd tried?

Thankfully, Trace merely grunted at her comment. Meanwhile, she grabbed Tiffany's robe and wiggled into it, keeping the sheet in place then letting it fall in a pool of fabric at her feet. There wasn't time to find anything else. She yanked the belt tight, and after a deep breath, turned to him.

Trace was studying her, a glass of water in his hand. "I brought you something for your headache." He handed her two white tablets. "The coffee will be ready in a minute."

"Oh, thanks," she said. She tried to smile but her face felt too tense to make the proper expression. She popped the pills onto her tongue and had just lifted her drink to her lips when Trace asked, "Who were you talking to? It sounded pretty bad."

Phoebe choked on her water, and after a violent coughing fit, which she tried to play off with a rather high-pitched laugh, she said, "Oh, that was Tiffany." Shrugging casually, she answered, "I'm always upset when I talk to my little sister."

She ignored the sense of urgency compelling her to shove Trace out of Tiffany's condo bodily, and took her time walking to the dresser then setting down her drink. She picked up her hairbrush. Mercifully, her hands didn't shake. A dead giveaway. She decided that the old saying about catching more flies with honey than vinegar and all that junk was applicable, and Phoebe attempted another smile. "Listen, I really appreciate all your help this morning, but I'm sort of in a hurry. I forgot that I had an appointment."

His expression serious, he moved closer. "Hey, kitten. Are you in some kind of trouble?"

Her pulse leaped. "No. No, not at all. Of course not. No." She snatched up the glass of water and took another gulp before she could blurt out what had to be at least her fifth or sixth lame denial. Then she looked away. "Why would I be in any trouble? I just forgot that someone Tiffany knows is coming by and she called to remind me." Phoebe began twisting her hair up into a bun, and jabbed the pins off the dresser into the knot to keep it in place.

Eyes narrowed, Trace crossed his arms, obviously making no effort to leave. "You're acting funny. Something's not right. What's going on, Phoebe?"

Again, she glanced at the clock while pushing in yet more pins. "What's with you and the questions? I thought you weren't a reporter anymore."

Trace smirked and pointed to her hair. "Unless you're planning on heading into a wind tunnel, I think you're done. And just because I'm not a reporter anymore doesn't mean I can't help."

Phoebe lifted her chin—hoping to appear as if she'd purposely been going for the porcupine-on-the-back-of-the-head look—then left the bedroom, Trace following doggedly on her heels. She sent him a patronizing smile over her shoulder. "Great. If I need anyone to take off their clothes and dance around the room I'll be sure to let you know."

"Hey—" he caught her arm, pulling her around to face him. Their eyes met, his snapping shards of blue "—I thought we were friends. Come on, I heard you on the phone with Tiffany. You're making me nervous, Phoebe."

Phoebe froze, her heart jolting into a crazy rhythm. "My private conversations are none of your business. And you and I are hardly friends," she retorted. Her hands trembled and she fisted them together. With everything at stake, no one could know her real reasons for being on the *Mirage*. Especially an ex-reporter who claimed to be a male stripper and whom she didn't trust further than she could grand jeté. And on top of that she could all but hear the minutes ticking away until Alvarez would be knocking on her door.

Trace took a step back as if she'd struck him. "We're not, huh? Why doesn't this surprise me? Phoebe the ice queen is back. But then, you love to play it hot and cold, don't you? What's your excuse this time, Phoebe? What horrible thing have I done?"

She *sooo* didn't want to be having this argument right now, but it was as if a part of her was detached, standing back, watching her spin out of control. Phoebe couldn't stop herself and she sneered, "Well, I haven't caught you having sex with a redhead in the last ten minutes, but I think listening in on a person's private conversation is pretty bad." Then she froze. *Ooh-wee*, would she love to be able to suck those words back into her mouth.

His face darkened. "Sex with a redhead? What the hell are you babbling about?"

Phoebe wanted to smack him and then smack herself. Her

and her big mouth. "Oh, never mind. Just leave." She waved her hand and began to turn away.

Then he said, "Not a chance. You started this," and backed her up against the wall outside the kitchen, keeping her there with his weight. "What redhead?"

She pushed on his bare chest but it was like trying to move granite. His skin burned her hands, making her palms tingle. In spite of everything, her breath quickened at the feel of his body so close and heavy and right against her own and she blurted, "Oh, all right. Everything else is going wrong, we might as well get into this now, too. I'm referring to the redhead I found leaving your apartment less than twenty-four hours after I was in your bed."

He tilted his head. "Are you talking about when we went out back in college?"

"Don't play dumb with me you, you—" She couldn't think of a name strong enough to call him and settled with "—jerk. You've only brought up that night every other sentence since we ran into each other outside Barbie's place." She punched him in the shoulder, hard, and he grabbed her wrists then pinned them to the wall at her sides.

"Hey, stop that and tell me what you think you saw."

"I don't *think* I saw anything," she retorted. All the anger and hurt she'd carted around for the past nine years poured out of her. "I'm sure you don't remember, but I couldn't be with you the night after our date because I had practice for one of the student shows. Except I got out early and decided to come by and surprise you."

"And...?" Trace prompted, when she said nothing else.

The words were almost hard to get out. "I saw you, Trace. I saw you with that woman."

"What woman?" He shook his head. "I don't know what you're talking about."

"Huh," she snorted. "Why doesn't that surprise me? I'm sure you had a hard time keeping us all straight, but I'm talking about the busty redhead who kissed you outside your front door. I saw you with her, Trace. You didn't even pull away when she gave you that loud, ridiculous kiss. You thought it was funny and laughed. You even hugged her. *Affectionately*," she emphasized.

He scowled and said incredulously, "And based on this foolproof evidence, you think I went to bed with this person?" He dropped her wrists and stepped back. "That's it?"

Phoebe crossed her arms and lifted her chin. "For old On-the-Make-McGraw, aka the Sea Stud? You betcha. As far as I'm concerned, that's plenty." Apparently she'd pressed a hot button, because he looked ready to explode, but since she felt ready to explode herself, this didn't overly concern her.

He pointed his finger at her and opened his mouth then paused. "Wait a second... I know who you're talking about. Damn." He shook his head and raked his fingers through his hair, making it rumple in funny angles. "Don't move," he commanded then turned and stalked into Tiffany's living room. Through the doorway, she saw him grab up his jacket and rifle through the pockets. He pulled out his wallet and came back.

Flipping to a picture inside, he said, "Do you mean this redhead?"

She glanced down. The woman's hair was longer than Phoebe remembered, but it was the floozy all right and she was still beautiful. Except there was a man with her and two little boys dressed in suits standing in front of the couple.

Phoebe curled her upper lip. "How sweet. You still carry her picture. It's nice to know I wasn't replaced by a fling. I guess a husband and children don't keep you two from staying in touch, though."

Trace's jaw tightened. "Shut up. As usual, you have no idea what the hell you're talking about. This is my sister Meg. She happened to be in town that night on a layover between flights and we spent a few hours together. I'd have asked you to join us but I thought you were busy."

"Your sister...? But, I thought your family lived in Pittsburgh."

"So? And this means none of them can fly on an airplane? Give me a break. If you'd ever spoken to me again, I could have explained. Here, look." Trace started going through the pictures in his wallet and Phoebe saw four more similar faces. "I have five sisters total, but you know that. However, just in case, take a good look. You might have seen me with one of them, too. Who knows?"

His eyes glittered with emotion and Phoebe put her hand to her stomach. "Oh, Trace." She paused and shook her head. "I...I don't know what to say. I thought..." She swallowed and tried to find the words to make it better, but what could she possibly say to make up for the way she'd ended their relationship? Back in college, she'd been so young and insecure and convinced she was right. And there were so many girls willing to take her place. Maybe if she'd had more experience with dating and boys she could have handled everything better. At least talked to him again.

"Well, now at least I understand why you hated my guts. I never could figure it out." His laugh sounded hollow. "I thought maybe I'd hurt you. I mean, I knew it was your first time and tried to be careful, but..." His voice trailed off.

Phoebe made a distressed noise then raised her fingers to her lips. "No. Not at all. Please don't think that." No matter how angry she'd been with Trace, never for a moment did he deserve to question the way he'd treated her physically. "You were wonderful and patient. You made everything perfect." She could feel her face growing hot and looked away, unable to meet the intensity of his gaze.

"Really?" He was quiet for a moment and finally, she risked a glance back. His expression had softened and he had a stupid, endearing grin on his face. He scratched his jaw. "Wonderful? And perfect, huh?"

Her face cranked hotter. To cover up her embarrassment she snorted and rolled her eyes. "As if you've never heard that before."

Trace lifted his eyebrows. "Oh, no. Let's not start that up again." He sighed and rubbed the back of his neck. "Listen, I never claimed to be a monk, Phoebe, but I'm not exactly the Don Juan of Greater Miami that you keep making me out to be."

Ha! she wanted to say, but held her tongue. It wasn't completely her fault she'd jumped to the wrong conclusion. Jeesh, women had flocked to him in droves. And Trace had never discouraged them. Had sex with them, yes. Discouraged them, no. Not according to the many satisfied females cruising the campus, and Phoebe retorted, "Of course not. He wasn't as successful as you."

Trace pulled back and frowned. "I don't know whether to be flattered or angry, but knock it off."

Phoebe scowled, trying not to be childish and petty yet failing miserably. "Oh, flattered, by all means. Why should I be the only one angry?"

"How about because you're the only one wrong?"

Phoebe opened her mouth to blast him then stopped. "Good point." She sighed heavily. In the silence, her eyes grew wet and she blinked rapidly. She *was* angry...at Tiffany for expecting the impossible, and Trace for being so darn handsome and right, and, well, mostly at herself for being so darn wrong and insecure. She sniffed noisily then stared down at her feet.

Suddenly she remembered that Alvarez was going to be here any minute and her heart almost fibrillated. "Oh my gosh, what time is it? Never mind, it doesn't matter. I can't explain, but I have so much to do before next Saturday, and I need you to leave. Please."

Trace gave her a funny look. "Leave? Right now, in the middle of this?" he asked, clearly flummoxed, but then his gaze sharpened. "Did you say next Saturday?" he asked. Phoebe nodded and tried to grab his shoulders so she could push him out the door, but he turned away before she could get a good hold and shrugged off her hands. A flush had crept up his neck and the muscles in his back were so tense he could have stood demonstration for an anatomy class. "Damn it...I knew you were somehow involved with Angelo Venzara. Christ, as if I don't have enough to worry about." He turned back around then lowered his face until they were only inches apart and she could feel his breath fan her eyelashes. He took hold of her arms, his fingers tightened painfully. "I don't know what you're doing, Phoebe, but you need to tell me everything. Now."

Phoebe's lips parted and she blinked. Her earlier suspicions that Trace was still hiding something from her roared to life. How the heck would a newly hired male stripper know anything about Angelo Venzara and Saturday night? "What are you talking about?" she asked tentatively, not about to reveal more than she needed.

"What am I talking about?" He narrowed his eyes, his gaze boring into hers. After a few seconds, he appeared to have come to a decision, and went back to his jacket to exchange his wallet for a thin little notepad. In front of her, he flipped it open and started reading aloud. "The *Mirage* started picking up unmarked crates from the Bahamas two months ago. No one knows what they're carrying and there are no records of those crates with Customs. Next Saturday night, Mr. V. and two other ex-Mafia bosses, Robert Renaldo and Lorenzo Delefluente, are getting together in person for the first time in fifteen years. So far the police haven't been able to place one of their own people on the ship. Should I go on?"

Phoebe shook her head, her eyes wide. "But how...how do you know so much?"

Trace snorted. "How do you think?"

She closed her eyes and whispered, "I knew you weren't really a stripper."

"And I knew you weren't really a showgirl," he said, his voice flat.

A knock sounded at the front door and she flinched. Trace looked into the foyer while Phoebe brought her fingers to her mouth. "Oh, no, Trace. You can't be here. You need to leave."

Trace slowly looked back at Phoebe, his eyes so dark she could hardly see the blue anymore. "Why?"

Phoebe swallowed and forced herself to meet his gaze. "You were very thorough but your information was wrong on one point. The police were able to place someone inside the *Mirage*." She shrugged and lifted her hands, palms up. "Me."

6

TRACE COULD ONLY GAPE at Phoebe. The knock on the door sounded louder and she looked up at him, her expression imploring. "Please, just do what I ask. Go wait in Tiffany's bedroom and I'll explain everything when Detective Alvarez leaves." She grabbed his hand and brought it to her chest. Her fingers squeezed his, her eyes pleaded, and Trace was almost ashamed to admit that even as angry and confused as he was, some small part of him registered the weight of her breasts against the back of his hand.

Oh, all right, a big part of him registered the weight of her breasts against the back of his hand, but she'd nestled his lucky appendage right there in her sweet cleavage. What the hell was a man supposed to do? And okay, so maybe he'd taken a quick peek at her tight little nipples puckered beneath her robe. And there was a slight possibility that he'd glanced at her plump mouth, red and moist and swollen from licking it over and over again, something he'd noticed she had a habit of doing whenever she was nervous.

But none of that mattered, because mostly, he sensed the desperation pouring off her in waves. He wanted to argue but said, "Fine. I'll make myself scarce, but I'll be right around the corner listening to every word you say."

"Just stay out of sight. I don't want Alvarez to know you're here." She ran to the other room then came back, shoving his boots and fake police jacket and shirt into his arms. Then she pushed at Trace's chest and he ducked around the corner, still within hearing distance.

His body felt numb and his mind raced as he listened to Phoebe greet the police detective. Why on earth would the cops use Phoebe Devereaux as their inside plant on the *Mirage*? Trace knew from overhearing Phoebe's phone call that Tiffany and her husband were in some sort of trouble and obviously responsible for Phoebe's current situation. But what sort of hold were they using on her, and why would she ever agree to something so colossally stupid as well as dangerous?

His stomach churned. He was so angry and scared for Phoebe he felt like killing her himself and saving Venzara's thugs the hassle of fitting her with a pair of concrete boots. Speaking of boots, Trace's own pair had almost shifted out of his arms when he wasn't paying attention, and as quietly as possible he tugged them on, leaving the rest of his things rolled together on the floor. If Trace was caught by this Alvarez person, he'd rather not be found impersonating a police officer. Wearing a rip-away uniform, no less.

Trace leaned back against the wall and waited while Phoebe exchanged pleasantries with the cop. Running over all the possible scenarios for her predicament, he happened to glance at the picture hanging across from him and grimaced. He wished Tiffany hadn't been quite so obvious in her choice of decor. It was hard enough not to pounce on Phoebe without the added passionate reminders everywhere he looked. And from what he'd seen during his brief stay, there wasn't a single damn room in the entire place that didn't scream sex. Sometimes subtly, sometimes not. This picture was a perfect example.

At first glimpse the print of swirling colors seemed innocent enough. Until he'd gotten a better look and the image of a couple entwined in a carnal act that required the flexibility of an Olympic gymnast had all but leaped out from behind the glass. Now he couldn't even glance at the darn thing without sweating. Or wincing. And mirrors. Lord, were there mirrors. Strategically placed on walls, tabletops, even bookshelves so a couple could see their reflection standing or sitting or doing whatever from just about every angle.

Trace sighed. Maybe Phoebe's sister just had funky taste in decorating and he was horny. He pulled himself away from his lustful fantasies involving Phoebe and the mirrors, and tried to concentrate on Phoebe and the cop. She was walking Alvarez into the living room now, her voice relatively calm as she offered the detective something to drink.

While Phoebe clanked around the small kitchen playing hostess, Trace replayed their argument in his mind. Hell if he wasn't still reeling from the truth of why Phoebe had turned on him like a she-devil nine years ago. Obviously, Phoebe didn't know Trace at all if she believed he was capable of nailing the first woman to cross his path the moment her back was turned. The irony of course being that he'd rather chop off his own arm than end up anything like his old man—a two-timing son of a bitch who'd screwed his way through most of the female population in their small town before he'd left his family one night to buy a pack of cigarettes and never returned.

After that, Trace's mom had worked herself ragged to clothe and feed her six children without so much as a phone call in twenty-eight years. As Trace had grown up, most of the town had predicted he'd become a chip off the old block. He hadn't, but that didn't seem to matter. An unimportant fact to the gossips who made up the majority of his neighbors. Being able to pass as his father's twin had only made it worse. They shared the same looks, same build, same cocky smile, and the same ungodly luck with women. Or so he'd been told. Trace wouldn't know firsthand since he'd been two years old when the bastard had taken off.

For the most, Trace let their assumptions roll off his back. The people that mattered trusted him. His mom and sisters, and most of his teachers in school. Fortunately, good grades overshadowed a multitude of rumored sins. Even though he'd held down a full-time job to help his mom, slinging midshift at the same steel mill where his father had worked, Trace had always known that being successful at school was his only hope of college and a chance to live someplace else, free from being compared to his damn father for the rest of his life.

Now, with Phoebe, on the other hand, it wasn't so easy to shrug off her unfair accusations. Well, mostly unfair. He did have ungodly luck with the fairer sex. And there had been a time or two or maybe even three when he'd been more than happy to take what was freely offered. But only with women who knew the score and whose only interests were in adding another notch to their garter belts. And never when he was involved in a relationship. Trace didn't cheat. Period.

He would also never purposely hurt Phoebe, and just the thought of her believing he had made him want to shake his head until everything made sense. How could she be everything he ever dreamed of one minute and then look at him as if he were horny pond scum the next? A walking hard-on with the sole drive to copulate at will then leave a trail of broken hearts in his wake? Perversely, when they'd been in college, her attitude had taunted him into living down to her worst expectations almost every time.

Trace winced, remembering the sensual binge he'd embarked on when Phoebe had stopped speaking to him. At the time, Trace had damn near glutted himself on women. Tall ones, short ones, curvy ones, he didn't care. He'd been an equal opportunity son of a bitch and the specifics hadn't mattered as long as they met two requirements. No long brown hair and no silver-gray eyes. The only good thing about the whole mess was that he hadn't managed to catch a disease.

But who the hell cared? he asked himself. So he'd been young and stupid. He wasn't anymore. What he felt now for

Phoebe was plain old lust, pure and simple. And the desire to finish what they'd started nine years ago. And the need to gorge himself on her delectable little body till neither one of them could move. But that was all. He'd have to be an idiot to fall in love with her again. Besides, he had a story to write and a career to repair. All that mattered was getting his career back and having sex with Phoebe. In that order. There, that sounded good.

So, why didn't he buy a single damn word of it?

Cursing himself six ways to Sunday, Trace heard Alvarez thank Phoebe and knew she was back in the living room. Jaw clenched, he glanced across the foyer then crept into the kitchen. He'd be able to hear better through the shutters over the bar connecting the two rooms. After years of investigative reporting where his job and occasionally his life depended on his presence going undetected, Trace hopped onto the counter silently and sat with his back to the wood slats. He pulled out his notebook ready to get the facts for the only thing that mattered. His story. And then sex with Phoebe.

So how come he still wasn't buying it?

The obvious answer popped into his mind and Trace flinched and thought, *Aw, hell....*

PHOEBE STARED DOWN into her mug. Like a mantra, one phrase kept running through her brain. Trace hadn't cheated on her and he was still a reporter.... Trace hadn't cheated on her and he was still a reporter.... And right now he was somewhere in this apartment listening to every word she and Detective Alvarez said.

She put down her cup and clasped her hands in her lap, while Alvarez used the cream and sugar for his coffee. As she waited, Phoebe couldn't help but return to her previous thoughts and decided to forget about the whole cheating issue for a moment because she'd been wrong. And while this mostly made her happy, it also depressed the heck out of her since she'd apparently acted like a complete boob. Instead, she focused on the issue that Trace was still a reporter. Well...if she looked on the bright side, at least Trace wasn't really a stripper.

Phoebe swallowed back a sigh, glancing at Alvarez beneath her lashes. While the detective blew on his coffee then took a sip, she tried to envision how furious he would be if he knew that she'd just blabbed her real reasons for being on the *Mirage* to a journalist. Some master of the operative world she was turning out to be. Forget torture. Just stick a hot guy in front of her and she'd spill her guts in ten seconds flat.

"I guess you're pretty anxious to find out what the captain had to say about your offer."

Phoebe started at the sound of the detective's voice. "Yes, you might say that." She licked her lips and offered him a tentative smile. Jeesh, she hardly knew how to act. Less casual. More formal. What exactly was the appropriate conduct for trying to bamboozle the police out of putting your nutty relatives in the slammer?

Alvarez smiled back. A nice-looking man, probably in his late thirties. Dark hair and dark eyes. Cuban, she'd guess, given his last name and the fact they were in Miami. He'd been polite to her when they'd spoken before, though she would have understood if he'd throttled her on the spot with all the havoc Tiffany and Tony running off had wreaked on the poor man's case.

"I hope you understand the situation," he continued. "I can't guarantee anything, but I did present your offer to my higher-ups."

Phoebe leaned forward. "And...?"

"Well, the situation's a little difficult. We're interested, all right, but—" he paused as if searching for the right wording "—we have to tread carefully."

Phoebe licked her lips, afraid to become too encouraged just yet. "Tread carefully?"

"Hmm." Alvarez made a sound of agreement then sighed. "Well, here's where it gets sticky. Officially, the police department can't request assistance like this from an innocent party. In other words, if we don't have anything on you, we can't ask you—" he paused with a grin "—or rather force you, to be a CI."

Phoebe frowned. "I hate to keep asking questions but what's a CI?"

"No, that's okay. It's a confidential informant. A person in the same situation as your sister. They've committed a crime that's not big enough to be our main concern in the case, but by making a deal to lower or drop their charges, we use them to gather information." He shrugged. "Every once in a while we'll let a civilian help us, usually because they've stumbled across something illegal at work. White-collar crimes. But not in dangerous situations if we can help it." He waved his hand. "Too much liability."

Here he stopped to look at Phoebe then shook his head. "But you want to spy on Angelo Venzara to keep your sister out of jail. That almost makes the department look as if we coerced you into taking your sister's place, when our goal was to make Tiffany listen in on the meeting not you." He let out a deep breath then rubbed his jaw. "But since we can't keep you from working at the *Mirage*...and well, you're already there, let's just say we're not going to turn away whatever you find out Saturday night."

Phoebe hesitated. "Oh, good, good, but I'm a little confused. Does that mean the charges against Tiffany will be dropped?"

"Off the record, since they were relatively minor in the scheme of things, the captain doesn't see why not if we're satisfied with what you bring to us."

Phoebe rubbed her forehead. "I guess that'll have to be enough for now."

Alvarez nodded, his expression serious. "I'll try to help, but I have to be careful. If I were to start telling you what to do, the department could be responsible if anything goes wrong since you'd be directly following my orders. The problem is, I know you're going through with this harebrained scheme regardless of anything I say, so I might as well do whatever I can."

Phoebe adjusted her robe and smiled up at him hesitantly. "You've been very understanding about all this." She shook her head. "I'm sorry my sister has put your department in this awkward position."

Alvarez said dryly, "Frankly, Ms. Devereaux, after meeting your sister, nothing about this present situation surprises me. Other than the fact that you two are related. Is Tiffany adopted?"

Phoebe grinned at his sarcasm. "No such luck. But, honestly, she means well. In her own way. I told you about the pregnancy." She shrugged then sighed. "She's just very protective of the baby. Otherwise I know she wouldn't have left." She quickly added, "Of course, Tiffany doesn't really believe that Mr. V. is involved in any crimes, so there's really not all that much risk for me. Or her," she blurted. "I mean, if Tiffany had stayed...well, you understand what I'm trying to say..." Then Phoebe ducked her chin, hating Alvarez to think of her as some sort of sap who did anything Tiffany asked regardless of the danger. Then again, if the shoe fit...

The detective's mouth flattened. "I know what your sister thinks. She told me in quite colorful language. Listen, I wouldn't waste my time if I didn't think the bastard was up to something. That's fifteen years of experience talking. Don't count on your sister's fantasies about Angelo Venzara being innocent to keep you safe. You need to be careful. His man Sonny can be a shark. If he suspects you, get the hell off that boat. Period. I do not want or need your life on my hands."

Phoebe nodded, her throat working against the sudden pressure squeezing her windpipe.

He shook his head, moving on to another topic. "Have you made any progress in replacing your sister this Saturday?"

Phoebe licked her lips. "Um, no. Not yet. I don't have my first show until Tuesday night, so tomorrow I'll hang around the ship and practice as much as I can. Tiffany thinks Mr. V. and Sonny are just waiting to see how I do. But she's confident they'll approach me then."

Alvarez rolled his eyes. "Do you mind if I ask when Tiffany is not confident?"

Phoebe had to laugh, but her amusement quickly faded. She licked her lips again. "If by some chance I'm not asked to work Mr. V.'s private party, would it be possible for me to, say…oh, I don't know, maybe get the information you need another way?"

The detective's dark gaze zeroed in on her. "What exactly are you asking me?"

"Well, I hate to bring this up, but Tiffany mentioned that Tony might be in some trouble with your department as well. So, I just thought that maybe, since I'm already there and everything…"

He muttered something in Spanish under his breath, which Phoebe rather doubted was positive. "I gather you're working yourself up to ask if you can save Tony Venzara's neck by doing his snoop work for us as well?"

Phoebe licked her lips and nodded. "I know that he obviously had a lot more access with Mr. V. and the *Mirage*, but Tony seems to be willing to steer me in the right direction. As a matter of fact, I found out this morning about an island Mr. V. purchased a year ago. The unmarked crates that the *Mirage* has been picking up in Nassau are coming from the island. Tony thinks it's possible that Mr. V. might be growing something and then bringing it into port on the *Mirage*."

"Tony Venzara told you all this?"

"Yes, through Tiffany. He feels horrible about it, but with Tiffany's pregnancy there was no way he could just let her run off by herself. Tony is hoping that once you figure out that Mr. V. is a legitimate businessman, you'll drop the charges against him as well."

"I cannot believe I'm going to go along with this," he grumbled, while he jotted down what she'd said in a little notebook very similar to Trace's.

Phoebe almost bounced up and down in her seat and had to refrain from clapping her hands when she registered his words.

When Alvarez finished writing, he closed the pad and slid it back inside his sports coat. "We knew about the crates, but not where they were originating from. Has Tony ever gotten a look inside one?"

"No. But I'll talk to Tiffany again and see what else Tony might remember."

"For his sake, it better be a lot. All right, I'm gonna get started on finding out what I can about this island. We've never run across it and I thought we knew about every pie Angelo Venzara had sunk his fingers into." Alvarez stood up from his chair, and added, "For the last six moths, Venzara has been liquidating his personal assets like crazy. Turning them into cash. Makes you wonder what he's using all that money for if he's as innocent as your brother-in-law thinks."

He headed for the front door, then stopped and looked back. "By the way. Forget about me not giving you orders. From now on you do everything I say. No arguments. If Tony keeps this crap up, which for his sake I hope he does, then I'm in charge. No going off on your own. Do you understand?"

Phoebe wanted to gush her thanks but settled with, "Yes,

completely." Then she thought about Trace in the next room and knew there was no way that she could be totally compliant with Alvarez's request. Not if Trace was off solving the crime on his own. Though she'd never blow Trace's cover, she'd already come to the conclusion that she couldn't let him write his story until she'd cleared Tony and Tiffany with the police. She slid her hand behind her back, crossed her fingers and said to Alvarez, "I won't make a single move without your permission."

The detective gave her a long look then snorted. "Yeah, right. Now I see where the other sister gets it." Alvarez opened the door, but before he let himself out, said, "You're hiding something, Devereaux. If you're serious about wanting to get your nutty relatives off the hook, you'd better figure out how to tell me. Soon. I don't like surprises." And by the look he shot her, she knew he wasn't lying.

PHOEBE COLLAPSED BACK in her chair the moment the door closed. An adrenaline crash after a long sustained rush. Her emotions were none too steady either. Not with her extra snooping assignments, and Alvarez's suspicions, and Trace's involvement as a reporter, and then just plain old everything about Trace.

His blasted sister, she thought, and cringed. And what on earth was she going to do about Trace and his story? she wondered, groaning softly. At the moment Phoebe didn't have a single clue, but there was no way she could let him interfere with getting the police what they needed so Tiffany and her husband could come home. Their situation was already precarious enough. She closed her eyes, dropping her head forward. If only she could just make time to stop for a few hours and deal with everything later. After she'd bathed and slept.

A noise sounded from the kitchen and Phoebe winced. Any minute Trace would be marching out here demanding the truth, and just the thought made her stomach clench. She could not handle him right now. Not his questions, or the feelings he created. At the very least, maybe she could sneak in a soothing bath before the interrogation began.

Casting a furtive glance over her shoulder, she crept down the hallway to Tiffany's room. She gazed longingly at the bed but forced herself to walk past and into the master bath. Here Phoebe stopped. Her lips curved downward as her gaze circled the room, finally zeroing in on one of her many reflections.

No one should have to face this kind of self-analysis so early in the day, she thought in disgust. Especially with a hangover. What could Tiffany have been thinking when she'd had the room remodeled? Phoebe snorted and thought, well, duh...

Every surface in the room not covered with dark red tile, was one endless mirror. And she meant *everything*. Walls, ceilings, the back of the door, the inside of the huge shower that sported eight heads complete with pulsating sprays at bizarre and interesting angles. Heck, even the shiny gold toilet seat offered a view. The whole effect was a cross of art deco–meets Las Vegas chic–meets the best little whorehouse in Texas. Arousing and revealing and somewhat repulsive at the same time.

Phoebe looked away and removed the dozens of pins digging into her scalp, then set them on the vanity. That finished, she twisted her hair back into a knot, this time without her fashionable quills, then climbed the steps to the sunken Jacuzzi tub. She ducked to turn on the spigot. The sound of the pounding water echoed through the room and Phoebe felt her muscles relax a tiny amount. This was exactly what she needed. A nice long soak in the tub then a quick, painless drowning to chase all her troubles away.

That started, she went back to the sink and brushed her teeth. She also scrubbed her face. Feeling marginally better,

Phoebe slipped off her robe and immediately stopped feeling better. Completely naked, she could see herself from the front, back, side and even from above if she wanted. Not that she wanted, mind you. Heck, even a ballet dancer could have body image issues. Fortunately, the steaming water and sweet relief beckoned.

Dropping to her knees on the top step, she leaned onto her free hand and turned off the tap. Then, almost absently, before she stood, Phoebe glanced up and her mouth fell open. She stared at the reflection ping-ponging into view from behind her. Her lungs froze. Her eyes grew wide. She tried to curse but only managed inarticulate squeaks.

She was having a panic attack, Phoebe realized. Closing her eyes, she told herself to relax. She was lying in a field of grass...the sun was warm against her skin and she saw a butterfly. No, she didn't!

Instead, she saw her naked butt stuck up in the air, and every bit of her female anatomy prominently displayed beneath. She couldn't breathe. This was the same view Trace had gotten this morning.

Her skin felt clammy and she knew her temperature was dropping but she couldn't control her body's reactions no matter how hard she concentrated. Of all the times for her neurotic psyche to go into meltdown mode, why now? So she'd given Trace the crotch shot of a lifetime. That wasn't so bad, was it? The answer, of course, was *yes!*

Phoebe twisted down onto the step and hugged her knees to her chest. Suddenly, all the humiliations of the past twenty-four hours flashed through her head like clips from a movie. Getting drunk at the party. Grabbing a cop's butt. Passing out in front of a roomful of people. And the worst of all, Trace finding her naked...with a vibrator in her ear.

Well, this certainly put any last-minute anxieties about performing as a showgirl into perspective. What was dancing in heels and a thong bikini in comparison to full, canine-position nudity? With that obvious answer in mind, Phoebe dropped her forehead to her knees and cried her humiliated heart out.

TRACE STOOD OUTSIDE the bathroom door, ready to bang it down if he had to. By the time he'd calmed down enough to leave the kitchen without killing her, Phoebe had turned chicken and fled the scene. Well, she owed him some answers and he wanted them now. Her conversation with that cop had all but given him a heart attack.

Forced to sit silently and listen to Phoebe's proposal to Alvarez had been one of the worst moments of Trace's life. If it wouldn't have blown his cover as well as gotten her in trouble, he would have stormed into their meeting and told her to shut the hell up. Anything to stop the words spilling from her mouth as she laid out her dangerous proposition to get Tony Venzara and her good-for-nothing sister off the hook. The minute he finished strangling her, Phoebe was going to explain herself and then he was going to strangle her again.

Trace lifted his hand to the door, but with his first knock it slipped open a crack. She was crying, all sniffles and gulps, and the sound brought him up short.

He hesitated and this time tapped softly. "Phoebe, are you okay?"

Her sobs broke off for a moment, but she didn't answer.

Trace frowned, stymied. He rested his hands on either side of the door frame unsure how to go on. He didn't want to invade her privacy, yet her heartbreaking cries had his own heart pounding. But only an asshole would just storm in without permission. He thought about this for a minute then figured that pretty much freed him up and pushed open the door. He took one look at her and his anger immediately took a back seat.

"Kitten? Honey, what is it? What's wrong?" As he squatted next to her, he caught a reflection of the same movement from the corner of his eye. He turned his head and stiffened, his jaw almost hitting the floor.

It was like standing in a house of mirrors. There wasn't a single damn inch of her he couldn't see if he so chose and, oh, did he so want to choose. Unfortunately, now wasn't the time and Trace cursed under his breath then forced himself to look away.

He kneeled on the bottom step and took her face in his hands. "Phoebe, look at me. What happened?"

"I'm f-fine." She bit her lip and gave him a watery smile and it made his chest tighten. Another tear leaked out, dripping over his fingers. It stung, not on his skin, but inside where her pain had suddenly become his. Still sniffing and wiping, she said, "It's nothing, really," then added, "Honest."

Trace snorted. "Give me a little credit. I may be a man, but even I can see right through that whopper." He let his hands slide down to her shoulders. "Jeez, kitten, you're freezing." In spite of the sheen of perspiration coating her body, she felt like ice. Her torso rose and fell erratically with her labored breathing, and Trace remembered from back in college just how bad one of her panic attacks could get.

His gaze fell on the steam rising from the hot water filling the bath. Trace didn't waste time except to glance at his prized boots and say, "Screw it." Then he scooped Phoebe up, her body still curled like a pill bug, and stepped into the bathtub, clunky biker boots, stripper pants and all.

7

PHOEBE GASPED while Trace ignored the water filling his boots. "Wh-what are you do-doing?" she asked, her breath hitching as she cried, though he suspected that for the moment shock was winning out over panic attack.

"Hush. You're too cold," he said, submerging them both. "I'm getting you warm."

"B-b-but your pants—"

"Are wet." He leaned back then slid down so they both sank deeper into the heat.

She tried to struggle, difficult since she wouldn't let go of her legs, and she managed to choke out, "You're crazy... absolutely crazy."

"That's me. Crazy Trace McGraw. Scourge of naked crying women everywhere."

"You're doing it again," she said, tears obvious in her voice.

"What's that?" He cupped a handful of water and poured it over her trembling shoulders.

"Being nice."

Trace's lips curved. "Sorry."

"You should be." Then she lifted her right hand from its death grip around her calves and rubbed her eyes. But instead of returning her arm back to where it had circled her legs, she rested it on Trace's shoulder. Almost a hug of sorts as she leaned into him. He swore he felt something shift in his chest.

Gradually, over time, she turned fluid in his arms, her

tears drying up, and he heaved a mental sigh of relief. Now, he thought determinedly, to get to the bottom of this.... A faint smile on his lips, Trace began to kiss his way down her neck.

"Phoebe." He singsonged her name, dragging the syllables out against the sensitive flesh just behind her earlobe. He could feel where her mouth was pressed into his shoulder and it curved into a tiny smile. "Are you feeling better?"

She nodded softly. "Yes, actually." Her voice hushed.

Needing to comfort her, and reassure her, and willing to offer just about anything to make certain she didn't go through one of these attacks again, Trace hugged her tight and said, "I know it's been a rough morning, but we'll work it out. All that stuff you agreed to with Alvarez...I'm not thrilled but I'll help. I won't let anything happen to you. I promise. You don't need to be scared or upset. We'll come up with something, okay?"

Phoebe sniffed. "What do you mean?"

"I mean, we'll talk about the details later, but you just scared the hell out of me and I never want to go through that again. I forgot you had panic attacks."

Phoebe nodded, her voice still small. "Mostly when I was younger. I only get them now when I'm really stressed out."

Trace grunted. "Well, I guess if anything was going to trigger one, I'd say you had a pretty good excuse. But I don't want you to worry about the cops or your sister or this thing with Mr. V., okay? Maybe we can talk to Alvarez and work out a deal where I can get him the information he needs." Trace sighed and rubbed the back of his neck. "I'm on the *Mirage* anyway. Once I get my story and find a paper where I can sell the article, I don't mind telling the police whatever I know."

Phoebe popped up like a jack-in-the-box and looked at him, cool air rushing between their skin. Her eyes were red and puffy from crying except now they were also wary.

"No." She wiped the back of her hand under her nose like a child, and Trace almost smiled. "That's very nice of you, but I can't let you do that." And though she still sounded a bit shaky, her stubbornness was certainly coming across loud and clear. "This is my responsibility," she went on, "and I won't—"

"No, it's not." Trace interrupted, ignoring her naked breasts, which she'd apparently forgotten about and were right there in front of him, and said, "I may not have all the details yet, but I know that this is your sister's mess."

Phoebe huffed. "Yes, but now that I'm here I couldn't just dump my problems on someone else—"

"Tiffany did." As much as he tried not to, his eyes started to wander and he figured staring at her breasts was okay as long as he held off touching until they were done with their argument.

She scowled. "That's beside the point. I'm here and I'm staying and I'm seeing this through. Your offer is very thoughtful, but—"

"Oh, yeah? Then what are you going to do the next time you get like this?" Then again, he reconsidered, maybe it was time to move on to the touching part since apparently their argument wouldn't be over anytime soon. "I'm not trying to be mean here, kitten, but how the hell are you going to play spy when you're hypothermic and hyperventilating? If you're this upset just from talking to Alvarez, I can guarantee that you'll freak out when you start sneaking around that damn ship. And if you think—"

Phoebe yelled over top of his tirade, "If you interrupt me one more time, I'm going to hit you and my panic attack had nothing to do with Detective Alvarez." She stopped suddenly. "Well, I mean," she hedged, her face turning red, "that's not what started it, anyway."

Trace looked away from her breasts, though he was still

thinking about them, and met her gaze. "Then what the hell brought that on?"

Phoebe's expression became distinctly uncomfortable and she started to shift awkwardly on his lap and just that small movement almost made his eyes cross. She stammered for a few seconds and then, shocking him near out of his skin, she slid back into his arms and dropped her face into the crook of his neck—which pressed her bare breasts into his bare chest—and wailed, "Oh, Trace, I'm *soooo* embarrassed."

He stared at his stunned reflection in the mirror across from him. "Embarrassed?" He frowned down at her head.

"I don't want to talk about it," she said, her voice muffled against his shoulder.

"Tough. You're talking. Explain."

She said no, and he said yes, until finally Phoebe moaned, "I don't want to," and curled back into a ball, turning her face to her knees and hugging them tight, and Trace realized he was insane because he was pushing her right back into the same situation he'd walked in on and that his stupidity had also lost him all contact with her breasts.

"Shh," he soothed, backtracking in his mind at top speed. "I'm sorry. Don't get upset again, okay? I just want to help." He took a deep breath, his cheeks puffing out as he exhaled. "You know," he spoke softly, skimming his fingers over the delicate ridges of her spine, "I can't make it all better unless you tell me the problem."

She kept her head tucked. "Even you can't go back and erase the last twenty-four hours."

"The last twenty-four hours, huh? Was seeing me again so bad?" Originally he'd only meant the question as a joke, but his heart skipped a beat and he held his breath as the silence dragged out.

Finally, she lifted her gaze to his. "No." She shook her head. "It's not that at all." She sighed then went on reluctantly. "Okay, all this stuff with Tiffany and the police already had me pretty shaky, but it's more what you saw of me that got the ball rolling. Specifically, what you saw this morning."

He cocked his head, and she looked heavenward and said, "When I answered the phone. This morning...and you walked in." Phoebe met his eyes while a blush spread across her skin all the way down her neck and headed toward those darn breasts again that he was so fixated on. Trace couldn't help but grin.

"Now, why would you want to go and deprive me of one of the highlights of my life?"

"Don't laugh at me."

He smiled wider. "I'm not laughing at you, kitten."

"Yes, you are." She looked away. "Though I guess I can't really blame you. You must have thought I looked so stupid."

"I can honestly say that *stupid* is a word that never even entered my mind," he said, his voice dry.

She snorted then rolled her eyes. "Forgive me. You must have thought I was a genius trying to speak into a vibrator."

He did laugh at this. "Honestly, I wasn't capable of thought. At least negative ones." His stomach clenched at just the memory. She'd looked amazing. The stuff wet dreams were made of, and he bit back a groan. "Kitten, if ever there was a woman made for that view," he shuddered, "it's definitely you."

Phoebe opened her mouth then closed it, blushing harder. "Nice line. And here I thought that it was your face the ladies went nutso over."

He grinned. "If you liked that one, I've got a few more." Then he winced. "Though I admit, none as suave."

She said flatly, "It's called extreme amusement. Or pity." She pressed her face back into his shoulder and moaned.

"What can I do to make you believe that the only thing pitiful about this whole situation is how easily you arouse me?

Cripes, woman, the sight of your toes is enough to make my hands shake.'' He tweaked one under the water.

She groaned. ''You're just being nice again.''

The woman was certifiable. And apparently didn't have a clue that she was the most beautiful thing he'd ever seen. Speaking against her cheek, he said, ''Don't you know what you do to me...?''

She must have recognized the intensity in his voice because she popped back up, forgetting she was naked and offering him a clear and unobstructed view of those gorgeous breasts again. He could have wept with relief.

''You're actually serious,'' she said.

He could only nod. He was getting a second chance here and was not about to waste it. Running his finger over her collarbone, he slowly journeyed downward. Her nipples puckered up impudently like ripe berries. She let out a tiny squeak then smacked her hands over her chest, and he almost snarled.

She said, ''I don't understand. I'm not exactly a femme fatale.''

''Oh yes you are...but worse. Much worse,'' he whispered because he couldn't have talked any louder without his voice cracking. ''Let me prove it. Let me show you what I see.'' Gently, he took hold of her wrists. ''I want to touch you... everywhere.'' He stared into her eyes. ''Will you let me?''

PHOEBE LICKED HER LIPS and glanced away. Smacking her hands over her chest had been more a reflex than anything else, but screaming out yes hardly seemed appropriate either, even if it was her gut reaction. Oh, this all seemed so silly now, but it was the position that she'd been in when Trace had found her naked that had mostly triggered her panic attack, not him seeing her naked. But how to explain that he could look or touch just about anything he wanted as long as she didn't have to flip onto her knees and press her face to the floor anytime soon. And then maybe *later* she could try that...when she'd worked her way up to it.

Then Trace lowered her hands and used both of his and she didn't have to worry about sounding inconsistent because she was no longer capable of speech. His palms were gentle and hot on her skin and she arched her back then groaned. Or did he? She couldn't be sure and didn't really care because now his fingers were circling her nipples, doing some sort of magic flicky thing, and her eyes almost rolled back in her head. Her nipples pulled painfully tight, turned dark and red, and she panted with each press and glide.

"Will you?" he asked again. His voice rasped like velvet over her exposed nerves. Steam from the bath had curled the ends of his hair. Pieces stuck to the side of his neck and face. Lord, he was beautiful. And apparently out of his mind.

He was offering to fulfill every desire she'd been struggling with since seeing him again—not to mention the years of late-night fantasies starring the one and only Trace Mc-Graw—and he thought that she might actually say no? Phoebe hardly knew where to start and wondered if he'd find her too forward if she just ripped off his pants and jumped him. She cleared her throat. "Well, uh, sure. Okay. I mean, yes, of course. If you really want to." Oh, nice, Devereaux. Very sophisticated. Begging would have left her with more dignity than that answer.

"Hell yes, I want to," he growled. He cupped her jaw and pulled her close, kissing along the bone. "Damn you're beautiful." He spoke reverently and she almost laughed.

Smiling, she clasped her hands over top of his and closed her eyes. "That's what I was going to say."

"Thanks." He chuckled softly, the sound making her shiver right down between her thighs. He kissed her closed lids. Petal-soft whispers slid over her face then down to her mouth.

Slowly, Phoebe blinked open her eyes. "I need to say something first." She licked her lips then forced herself to meet his gaze. Then as sincerely as she knew how, she apologized. "I'm sorry. For accusing you before about your sister and everything. I was wrong and should have given you a chance to explain back when this happened—" She broke off. "I wish I had. You'll never know how much I really, really wish that I had."

Trace's pupils widened. Gently he leaned forward and gave her the barest of kisses. "I'm sorry, too. I should have made you talk to me, not given up so easily, but I was stupid." He shrugged then sighed. "Really, really stupid," he whispered. She started to protest but he shook his head, and staring at her lips, murmured, "Later," then licked into her mouth, his tongue sliding deep, and Phoebe moaned and turned into him. After far too short a time, he spoke into her mouth and asked, "Do you trust me?"

She nodded absently, thinking, *Yeah, sure, whatever...*, her focus more centered on the fairly massive erection beneath her hip than anything he was saying. He felt heavy and solid, thicker than her wrist, and she had to squeeze her thighs together to keep from squirming against him.

His breath hissed out. "Good." And something about the way he said this grabbed her attention and made her pulse jump.

Trace took her legs then and lifted them until they were on top of his, bent at the knees with her back to his chest, and she moaned and said, "I liked where I was," and he chuckled softly then said, "Trust me. You'll like this, too." Phoebe shivered but not because she was cold. Everywhere she looked she could see them entwined, the picture of her naked legs decadent against the black fabric of his pants.

Then he whispered, "I want to see all of you."

Phoebe swallowed and tried to laugh. "I thought you had. Didn't we already discuss this?"

Trace grinned. "I want another look...." He didn't wait for permission, instead kissed the side of her neck then slowly opened his legs taking hers with him.

Then again, she thought as she squirmed in his hold, her naked core displayed right there before her eyes, maybe she'd been a bit too hasty. "You know what? I'm cold. Maybe we should do this in the bedroom." She wanted to have sex but was starting to rethink the whole decision to let him look at anything he wanted.

He braced his hand low on her stomach, and she got distracted again, this time by his splayed fingers covering her from hipbone to hipbone. "Liar." He made it sound like an endearment. "Watch," he whispered then put his hands on her knees before she could think to close them and positioned them outside his own. Now he had the leverage to open her thighs all the wider, which he did, stretching until his own knees met the walls of the large tub. She rested on top of his pelvis above the water, yet instead of feeling cold, his naked chest radiated heat clear through to her belly, his arousal straining against her bottom.

He spoke softly. "Oh, kitten." His eyes intent on their reflection. "How could you not know how beautiful you are?" He never looked away, as if he was mesmerized, a heady thrill in spite of the roiling sensation in her stomach. She'd never been so exposed—well, other than the whole hands-and-knees episode, but that was different. This time they were both looking and she was pink and wet, throbbing in rhythm with her pounding heartbeat. It was too much. It wasn't enough. And if he didn't do something soon, she was going to kill him.

She decided to take matters into her own hands, literally, and lowered them beneath the water, digging her fingers into his hips and pleading, "Please, you have to...I can't wait." *Oh, Lord, she was begging and didn't even care.*

"Shh." He tried to soothe her, but didn't sound much better himself. His breath whistled out harshly and he lifted his hands to her nipples and she wanted to whimper, "Not there, lower." But then again this felt nice, too, and she hated to appear desperate even though she was.

His gaze dropped down her body. He steadied her hips and said, "I need to touch you there...now."

And this time she wanted to scream, "*Well, it's about damn time.*" But, again, she thought this might sound a bit hostile, so she moaned instead. Yet instead of relief she only became more agitated as she stared, the progress of his other hand still too darn slow for her liking, until finally his fingers mercifully slid through her curls and she jerked then gasped, "Oh, m...y... G...o...d..."

"You're so wet," he groaned. He began to press and slide, fondled her with mind-numbing strokes until he'd spread her essence and she was slick to his touch. Then he slowly, almost gently, began to rub his finger back and forth, back and forth, in an unbearable rhythm until her hips seemed to move on their own, increasing the delicious tension spiraling to her womb from his hand.

Suddenly he broke the intensity and said, "I have to feel you. I can't wait." He circled one arm around her waist then lifted her up his chest. She felt his knuckles nudge against her bottom and heard the sound of Velcro tearing open as he freed his penis. A heavy weight, thick and warm, dropped onto the small of her back.

One corner of his mouth tilted upward. "About time these damn pants came in handy."

Except Phoebe barely heard him. She stared hard enough to melt her eyes, but could only make out the base of his erection in the open flap of his pants. Rats. Knowing her luck, she'd never get a good look.

Trace wasn't finished and he moved himself between her spread thighs then slid her back down until she straddled him, not so he was inside her, but so she was riding the top of his length. Not exactly what she had in mind, but she could deal with this, and she started to slide against him, striving for the friction she needed. He burned against her ultrasensitive skin, hot and thick and hard.

The tendons in his neck were rigid. "Easy, now...easy," he crooned, stilling her untutored attempts at release. "Let me help." Then he slowly tilted her hips in opposition with his and dragged the heart-shaped tip of his penis backward inch by painstaking inch until he reached the smooth skin just past her empty core. She could feel him pulse beneath her like an extra heartbeat and they both shuddered. Their eyes met in the glass and he softly kissed her temple. Then he looked back down and leisurely pushed forward. Her flesh parted for the thick knob as he pressed along her slippery heat to the underside of her clitoris, her nubbin bumping onto his shaft. Phoebe bit the inside of her cheek, holding back a groan. If he felt this good just sliding beneath her, she couldn't imagine how she'd react once he was inside her. She panted. "You feel, you feel..."

"So do you," he moaned, his teeth clenched.

"Don't stop," she pleaded and a muscle flexed in his jaw. In order to keep him in place, she had to arch her back while she moved, her breasts thrust forward, her bottom tilted so that her wet center stayed against him as long as possible. But she didn't care, now beyond any sense of modesty. His strokes grew shorter. His hips pressed firmly and tension coiled in her belly, spiraling tighter like an overwound spring. Her pelvis writhed and she squeezed her eyes shut. Something was happening. She could feel it getting closer, tension banding in her stomach, a sort of panic swelling through her belly. Now. Almost there. Almost there.

"Open your eyes," he whispered. "Look..." He snared her gaze in the mirror then lifted his hands to her nipples and squeezed. Her hips jerked as he flicked and rubbed. Her throat ached from the ballooning pressure, but she couldn't seem to reach the other side, always climbing but never falling over the top.

Then Trace's voice, low and rough, spoke in her ear, "Come on, kitten. Now. With both of us watching. Come for me."

"I can't," she said, sounding breathless and urgent. She licked her lips. "I'm trying, I'm trying..." And then the sweet, sweet man anchored his boots to the floor and his shoulders to the back of the tub and steadily pushed his hips upward and said, "But you are. You're coming right now..." And he was right. Phoebe came hard.

TRACE HADN'T REACHED his own spectacular release yet and his body shook. Any niceties were beyond him as he rode the knife edge of control. The second she recovered he was going to shove down his pants, plunge inside her and pump until he spewed like a geyser. He'd flood her, soak her until she dripped—he would have let his thoughts go on in this pornographic vein except reality smacked him in the chest like a sledgehammer. He had no protection. While all this internal fantasizing about excessive ejaculate might be nice for him, he wasn't sure she'd find it so erotic nine months from now.

He didn't even bother asking Phoebe if she had any condoms. She wouldn't and he could've cried at that moment. Just laid back his head and wept like a baby. Of course, it was too much to hope that she wouldn't move a muscle for the next six hours or so until he cooled down. Already she was writhing her luscious backside against him, making him jerk. Any second his eyes would roll back in his head.

"Hmm," she purred, stretching her arms over her head.

He winced and grabbed her hips. "Careful there, kitten. One false move and I can't promise what'll happen."

"You poor baby." Agile as only a professional dancer can be, she unhooked her legs from around his and swiveled to face him. He clutched the side of the tub, his fingers blanching. She straddled his hips with her thighs and circled her arms around his neck and hugged him tight, her breasts on his naked flesh heaven.

"That was amazing," she gushed. "Thank you, thank you, thank you." She interspersed her words with frantic kisses to his face and mouth.

At least one of them was happy, he thought, pleased even though he still had a hard-on big enough to rival that purple monster under her bed. Then her kisses slowly turned from playful to passionate and she slid her hand down between their bodies and he grabbed her wrist to stop her. If she touched him he'd be gone.

"Let me...I want to touch you." She flicked her tongue across his panting mouth, playing with his lips while trying to pull her hand free.

"Wait," he groaned. "We can't."

Phoebe laughed. "Don't tell me I'm going to have to convince you now."

He chuckled weakly, between gasps from her mindnumbing undulations. "That's not the problem. I don't have any condoms with me."

Her head snapped up and it surprised a bark of laughter from him. "I know you think I'm some sort of lothario who goes around with a six-pack of rubbers always on the ready, but I own about—" he stopped to think "—three condoms, which are collecting dust in my bedside table at home. They've probably expired even if I could get to them." A slight exaggeration, but it had been a damn long time.

Phoebe practically beamed at him. "I don't believe you, but you get oral sex for saying it."

Trace grinned. "Did I also happen to mention that this will be my first time?"

"Did I mention that it'll be my first blow job? I heard that guys like lots of teeth."

He pinched her bottom.

Laughing, she said, "Condoms aren't a problem. There are some in that jar on the shelf over your head."

He lifted his eyebrows.

Phoebe blushed slightly and rolled her eyes. "Tiffany has them stashed in every room of the apartment. I even found some in the knife drawer in the kitchen. How she managed to get pregnant with the number of prophylactics squirreled away in this place is a mystery. The only spot I haven't run across any is out on the balcony."

His heart hammered at the realization that he was being given the green light here. "Not a problem." He leaned toward her and kissed her hard. "Note to self. No sex on the balcony. Got it." Then he stood, unceremoniously dumping her from his lap.

"Hey!" She glared up at him from the floor of the tub, her hair tumbled loose from its knot, her slim arms and outrageously wicked legs sprawled in the most orgasm-inducing way.

"I'm hanging on by a thread here, sweetheart. If I don't get inside you in the next ten seconds I'm going to embarrass myself."

Her lips curved as she sat up. "At least take your boots off."

Trace looked down at his feet, having completely forgotten the ruined leather. Closing his eyes, he took a deep breath and let it out. It was best he calm down anyway. *Slam, bam, thank you, ma'am* had never been his style and he probably shouldn't start the technique with the most important woman in his life.

"Fine," he said, sitting down on the rim of the tub. He worked off the squishy boots and grimaced. "I guess these are ruined." He tossed them to the floor.

Phoebe grinned at him. "Thank you."

"You're welcome," he drawled with a smile, thinking he

might just be able to handle the slower pace. Until he noticed her staring. At his crotch.

"Wow," she swallowed noisily. "You're, uh—" She stopped. "Well, you're big. I suspected, of course, when we did this in college, but mostly I just felt you. And then even a minute ago, I couldn't really get a good look. You know, just a glimpse here and there..." Her eyes had widened and he felt like a villain in a two-penny novel.

He glanced down then cleared his throat. "It's only the angle."

She shook her head, never taking her eyes off the portion of him sticking out of his pants. "No. I don't think so."

In spite of himself, he felt his face slowly heat. "You probably don't have that many to compare it to," he said, though even Trace had been a bit surprised at the size of his good buddy. He was definitely happy to see her. Of that, there could be no doubt.

"That may be true, but I know big when I see it. Unless you're trying to say that thing is average."

He raked his hands through his hair, his wet fingers slicking the strands back wherever they touched. "I'm trying to say I'm not going to harpoon you. It'll work. Believe me. Or don't you remember?" He wiggled his eyebrows at her.

She smirked. "Yes, but will I be able to walk tomorrow without wincing at every step? Now, *that* I do remember."

He nodded, the corners of his mouth turning up. "You can have a nice long soak in the tub afterward."

She swirled her hand through the clear water. "Great, I'll be a giant prune."

"Yes, but you'll be a happy giant prune."

Her hand stilled. "How happy?"

"The kind of happy you were about three minutes ago."

"Good point. What are we waiting for?"

"That's my girl." Smiling like a buffoon, he stood up. He

placed one of the condoms on the shelf then turned back to Phoebe.

Licking her lips, she rose on her knees, her mouth a breath away from his stomach. "You know what?" she asked, her hands on his thighs.

His stomach did a slow flip. "No. What?"

"You're overdressed." She smiled up at him, curling her fingers into the dark, clinging fabric. "May I?"

Trace nodded and thought, *there is a God.* "Be my guest."

Phoebe pulled off his pants in one rip. Laughing, she studied the piece in her hands. The other had slid into the water somewhere behind him. "You're right. This Velcro stuff is handy."

His smile flattened. "A stripper's best friend."

Then she turned her head and he watched as she knelt at face level with his erection. She licked her lips again, and he wasn't sure if it was a sign of anticipation or trepidation, but before he could worry about it she reached out and clasped him.

He gasped. His hands fisted at his sides.

She stared, her lids lowered drowsily. "Your skin is so soft here...but hard," she whispered, taking a firmer hold while moving her hand. Her expression said *gimme. Now.* And if she licked her lips one more time he just might lose it.

"Wait—"

She quirked one of her eyebrows. "You're not going to start this up again, are you?"

He laughed at her annoyance. "No, my greedy little kitten." He reached down and lifted her to her feet, breaking the delicious hold she had on his member. "I'd just like to level the playing field, so to speak."

Warm water swirled around their knees, a contrast to the tiny droplets that dried on their skin. "Chicken," she taunted and lifted a hand to the muscles striating his abdomen. Her thumb bumped over each band down to the hair at his groin and he had to lock his legs to hold his stance. He laughed weakly and dropped his forehead to hers, almost afraid to go on. Afraid he'd wake up and this would all be a dream. The best sex of his life had been with Phoebe and she'd been a virgin. This time just might kill him.

He gripped her waist. "You have no idea how many times I pictured this. Dreamed about your taste...about how good you felt underneath me."

She lifted her head, her gray eyes full of wonder. "Really?"

He flicked a drop of water from his still-wet fingers onto her nose. "Yeah, really. I don't know why you're having such a hard time believing this."

Blushing, she ducked her chin, but her smile was pure sex as she ran her finger up the underside of his erection from base to tip and said, "I don't know, either. How on earth could I ignore proof like this?" Then she stepped into his arms.

Their bodies met, nothing between them, and he sucked in his breath, the reality infinitely better than anything he remembered. His arousal pressed into her stomach and just that little bit made a tear weep from its swollen head. He tightened his fists in her hair, but when he would have lifted her mouth, she began to nuzzle her way down his chest. He stood perfectly still, her enthusiasm almost surreal.

Her lips taunted the brown disc of his nipple to an aching peak as she spoke. "Um, when you pictured this, were we moving?" She nipped him gently.

He grinned. "Oh yeah..."

"How?" she whispered.

"I'll show you," he said, then slowly dropped to his knees. Her pink outer lips were swollen, peeking below a thin strip of curls. She'd shaved or waxed off everything else and she looked so damn delicious he wanted to sink his teeth into her smooth mound. Maybe in a minute. For now he parted her with the pads of his thumbs then gently licked into her.

"Ohmigosh!" Her voice broke and she stiffened her thighs. "Good starting place, by the way," she said, as her hands sunk into his hair.

He chuckled, making his tongue vibrate as he pulled back, and she moaned. "Just wait. It only gets better."

She tightened her grip on his head. "If it gets any better I'll fall."

"I won't let you. Now, watch, kitten. Your sister put up a hell of a lot of mirrors in this place and they're too damn good to go to waste." He nodded to the wall at their side.

She looked at their reflection and gulped. "Remind me to be nicer to Tiffany next time she calls."

Laughing softly, he zeroed back in on his target. He slid his tongue into her heat and once there lapped every inch of her. He spoke against her wet flesh, making sure to keep his lips a constant moving pressure and said, "Put your foot on the tub."

"No—" She groaned. "I'm fine." She gasped. "Like this."

"Wrong answer, kitten." He took hold of her ankle and started to lift it into place.

"No, Trace. Really—" Her voice broke and she arched against his mouth as he circled his tongue around her throbbing core, teasing her inner lips. "Oh, oh, oh," she panted, her head falling back. Smiling, he placed her foot where he wanted and pushed her knee wide. Then he sat back on his heels and stared.

She bit her lip. "You're too close," she complained, squirming her lush heat right there before his eyes. His penis jerked.

He slid his hands beneath her bottom. "Brace yourself, kitten, because I'm about to get a lot closer." And with that, he lifted her to his mouth, making his tongue wide and flat and licked her entire length in one hot sweep.

"Oooooh," Phoebe groaned out the long syllable and he continued to torment them both, lapping and nipping her silky flesh. Trace slid his fingers deep then opened them, licking between. She tasted like nothing he'd ever known, sweet and warm and creamy, and after only minutes, her inner muscles started to squeeze and quiver and he knew she was close. His pulse roared in his ears and his arousal flexed.

"With you. This time I want to be with you. Please," she said, and Trace surged to his feet and grabbed the condom from the shelf. He tore open the foil packet and rolled it down his erection in record time. Then he bent his knees and nudged himself between her inner lips. He pushed, clenching his buttocks. She was so damn tight he had to grit his teeth and force his way in farther.

Her fingers dug into his scalp where she held his head on both sides behind his ears. He stared into her eyes. They'd turned silver, her pupils wide. "Don't stop," she begged.

He dropped his forehead onto hers. A bead of sweat rolled down his temple. He was less than halfway there. Obviously, she hadn't done this very often in the last nine years and the thought alone had him ready to blow. He took a deep breath. "I don't want to hurt you."

She shivered. "You're not." Though he didn't know how her words could be true. Hell, she was so damn tight, it almost hurt *him*. Her inner muscles contracted and he winced.

He spoke softly. "Just a few seconds more," he said, and moved his mouth to her breast. He latched on to her reddened little nipple and suckled and rolled her crest under his tongue until she writhed voluptuously and slid herself farther onto his length. Pressure built at the base of his spine, urging him to move, prodding him to grind deeper, but he held himself back.

"Hold me," she gasped and slid her arms around his neck, pulling her breast from his mouth. He returned her hug, his own arms around her back pressing her closer. Her left foot was still on the tub and he cupped her thigh, lifting her into him. He pressed steadily and with another breathtaking undulation of her hips, he sank deeper into her heat. Slowly, he pulled out, then rocked in, back and forth, back and forth, each time pressing in a little more, until, after what seemed like an eternity, he was almost completely buried in her silky core.

"That's it...that's it. I'm almost done. Just don't move," he was saying.

She gasped out, "That's not the problem," then wriggled and pulled back her hips only to push him in as deep as he could possibly go.

Trace closed his eyes and let his head fall back. His arousal pulsed inside her tight sheath, each beat coursing up his entire length to the crown, until the head of his penis throbbed. The pleasure was indescribable and he gritted his teeth, afraid he'd come if she even breathed too hard. "Don't move," he warned. "Not yet. Not yet." She nodded, the movement jerky, but her internal muscles kept tightening, quivering to accommodate him.

He glanced down at her and sucked in his breath. His hands shook as he slowly dragged them up her sides, over her shoulders till he clasped her neck. He notched his thumbs beneath her chin and tilted her face up to his. Her eyes glistened, damp and shiny.

The sight made his chest burn. "Am I hurting you?" he asked. His mouth hovered above her lips. She slid her mouth back and forth beneath his as she shook her head no. He knew why she cried, and cupped her face then kissed her. He licked soft and deep, pouring everything into the glide and swirl of his tongue and lips that he was too scared to think let alone say out loud. Pressure squeezed behind his ribs because this just felt so good and right.

Eventually, though, Phoebe began to have ideas of her own, apparently impatient with the pace he'd set, and she started to run her hands up his back then over his biceps, charting each muscle until he wanted to grin and ask her if she had them memorized yet. And then he no longer felt like grinning, because she'd gotten tired of that game and had started moving south, down over his backside until she'd charted that area to memory as well. Around her third or fourth pass, their kiss turned from emotional to carnal and Trace could swear that even his feet were sweating under the bathwater.

"Wait," he gasped, her hands back on the move and now between their stomachs until her fingertips wiggled down to where they were joined. She swirled them around and around the base of his penis, searching and feeling where he stretched her flesh taut.

"Can you feel that?" she whispered. "You fill me...all the way."

He cursed, unable to say anything more coherent. He took her hands then and brought them to his shoulders. "Give me a chance here, kitten," he finally managed to say. "You'll give me a heart attack before the good part even gets started."

Frowning, she bit her lip and rolled her hips in tiny circles. "If you don't get started soon, I'm going on to the good part by myself." She looked at him meaningfully.

"Don't worry," he whispered, smiling against her mouth. "I'll catch up at the end." Then he nipped her bottom lip and sucked it between his teeth. Her nails dug into his shoulder and he caught her gaze and held it as he dragged his length from her wet heat.

Her eyes darkened and she moaned, trying to follow him with her hips.

He gave a quiet laugh. "Trust me. I'm definitely coming back," and when only the head of his erection was left inside and she was moaning even harder than before in that deep, breathy way that made his balls clench, he pushed back into her, his pace unhurried and deliberate until their pelvises met and her curls blended with his.

"Ohmigoshohmigosh," she mumbled breathlessly, her eyes glazed. He thought, *yep, that pretty much sums it up*, and painstakingly pulled out of her again. He rocked back and forth, his thrusts measured and steady in spite of her not-so-subtle hints to move it along already. He almost laughed out loud but knew his patience would ultimately be rewarded. Not to mention that if he went any faster he'd be gone with his first plunge.

"More," she begged, a plea that nearly sent him over the edge anyway. "Faster."

He clenched his jaw, then shook his head. "Slower..." And he forced himself to move in even deeper, longer lunges, but this ended up working against him because with each protracted withdrawal Phoebe had discovered that she could watch his shaft, glistening and wet from her arousal, slide between the lips of her sex. And watching her, watching them, as well as watching the show himself, sent Trace over the edge all the harder.

"Yes, yes, just like that," she praised and he wanted to tell his little chatterbox that he'd known what she was after the whole time. Instead, he grinned and did what she wanted, how she wanted, whatever she wanted. Trace didn't care as long as he could feel his erection squeezing back into her tight canal with each drive.

Phoebe pressed hard and moaned, creating a constant strain of tension between where they were joined. He could feel the weight of his testicles swing between his legs. Her nipples stab his chest. Her hot puffs of breath in his ear. Chills broke out across his skin and white lights danced behind his eyelids, and it went on and on, the pleasure stronger than anything he'd ever felt before.

"Trace. You have to tell me," she said, her voice thready. "I'm so close. It won't happen unless you tell me."

Once her words finally penetrated the fog in his brain he frowned, almost losing his momentum. And then it dawned on him what she was after and his lips slowly curved upward. He laughed then whispered low in her ear, "You're coming, kitten. Right...now..." And he was right.

Her inner muscles clamped down on him like a vise, squeezed him with near-painful intensity. His hips jerked forward of their own volition and he plunged deep. He dug his fingers into her hip and thigh. And then he was climaxing with her, until finally, they began to ebb and his heart toyed with the idea of beating again.

He could barely breathe, his limbs trembling, and if he moved, he'd fall. It was that simple, he decided as tiny afterspasms rippled through her sheath, gripping like a fist and sending chills across his skin.

And then something clicked in his mind and he thought, *I'm never letting her go. I can't lose her, lose this. Not again.*

And then he thought, *Aw, hell...*

8

PHOEBE GINGERLY STEPPED over the length of coiled rope next to the curtain. She shifted her ridiculously light load of costumes, the hangers dangling from her fingertips as she made her way to the dressing room. Her high heels moved silently on the rubbery surface purposely designed to muffle the sounds backstage, yet still, all was eerily quiet some forty-five minutes after the showgirls' grueling practice had ended.

A few more strides though, and Phoebe couldn't help but wince, and almost immediately her lips twisted into a smile. Just as she'd predicted, Phoebe ached in places that prior to yesterday hadn't ached in quite some time. She supposed dancing for hours today hadn't helped, but knew exactly where the source of these unfamiliar twinges could be blamed. Phoebe's mouth curved wider. But darn if it hadn't been worth it. And darn if she didn't want to do it again.

"A woman only smiles like that for one reason."

Phoebe jumped at the unexpected voice, her heart pounding beneath her ribs. Turning, she searched the shadows but her pulse only leaped faster as Sonny Martorelli stepped into view. Oddly, two words came to mind whenever she saw him. Big and square. His face, his nose, his body, his hands. Even his hair, which she still didn't quite understand though she was staring right at the brown, boxy locks.

The man didn't have an official title on the *Mirage*, but was Mr. V.'s bodyguard and right-hand man. He was also built like a Mack truck—big and square—and presumably roughed people up on Mr. V.'s orders on a regular basis. Or took them out. Or whatever the heck it was called in Mafia slang.

Sonny leered. "I could tell at practice you looked different...now I know why."

Phoebe hugged the skimpy garments to her chest. Then she told herself to calm the heck down. She couldn't afford to appear anything other than enthusiastic at Sonny's interest.

"Yes, well—" she glanced down at herself then licked her dry lips "—I didn't even recognize myself in this getup," she said, trying to smile. Especially dressed as a sequined bird of paradise, which on the *Mirage* meant a multicolored, spangled bra and thong with huge tail feathers barely covering her from behind. They'd even made her wear this big-feathered hat that kept slipping into her eyes every time she moved her head.

Forcing herself to continue, she patted the bundle in her arms and spoke brightly. "The seamstress was very pleased. Nothing will have to be remade, so I'm all ready for my first show." She almost groaned. Like Sonny gave a rip about her costumes other than how much of her body they revealed.

He grunted. "Good. But it's not the costume. I watched you practice."

Phoebe swallowed. "Watched me?"

He lowered his lids halfway, giving him an almost lazy appearance. "You were dancing different. The way you moved."

Phoebe nodded stupidly and glanced around to see if any of the other girls were still here, but everyone had left. If she hadn't had to stay behind for alterations she'd have been long gone herself.

Still, when she looked back at him, she forced another big smile. "I guess that's because I've learned the numbers and I really enjoy their style and energy. It doesn't take me long, but I always dance better when I'm not worried about stepping on someone's toes," she tried to joke but her effort fell flat.

Sonny stepped closer. He held a blue rubber ball in his right hand. It looked like a racquet ball and he tossed it lightly in the air, catching it in his grip and squeezing it in his fist before casually sending it back up. The sound of it hitting his palm became almost hypnotic, yet oddly added to her agitation. She shifted her feet and glanced toward the dressing room.

"That's not what I meant," he said, against the tapping always now in the background.

Phoebe's gaze followed the bouncing ball, her pulse thudding at near triple its beat. "Oh," she laughed stiltedly. "All right," she said, trying a different tack. "I guess you caught me. I wanted to really knock the audience out at my first show. You know, give them something to remember." Actually, Phoebe was just hoping not to be pelted with rotten vegetables but doubted that would help her case. "So, Barbie and Daisy have been helping me with a few of the moves. I guess nothing gets past you." She silently moaned. She was babbling. Oh Lord, she might as well be wearing a sign around her neck that said Nervous Police Informant.

His smile almost made her take a step backward. "No," he agreed. "Nothing does." The ball drummed on until she wanted to scream. His gaze ran over her again. "You know, I gotta tell you. I envy the guy whoever he is. He's definitely one lucky son of a bitch."

Phoebe's mouth went dry. "I beg your pardon?"

"Now, don't that sound classy?" Sonny laughed, making the little hairs on the back of her neck stand up. "And you can beg me anytime. I bet Tiffany knows how to beg real pretty, too. Did she teach you?" He caught the ball, the sleeve of his shiny, gray coat straining. The suit—with its wide, padded shoulders and tacky material that seemed to reflect every stray beam of light in the room—was so comical he could have come straight from central casting of *Goodfellas*. If the jerk wasn't so terrifying it would've been ridiculous.

Phoebe stammered. "I—I don't know what you're talking about." Though after his multitude of thinly veiled innuendos she had a pretty good idea. It was enough to make her blood run cold and she strained to hear some signs of life from in front of the curtain. Surely there must be someone out there setting up for tomorrow.

"Oh, I think you do, but you like to pretend, don't you?" He stepped closer. "Pretend about lots of things."

"Pretend?" Her voice came out part squeak while her heart leaped into her throat. The conversation had veered off into a new and even more disturbing direction. But how could Sonny already suspect her of being more than she claimed? It didn't make sense.

Sonny nodded. "Yeah. At first you come across all cool and prim, dancing stiff and holding back. But that's just an act, isn't it? Because no priss wears a smile like the one I just saw a minute ago." He shook his head. "Not after your first weekend in town." If he paused here for effect, it worked. "And today at practice, you danced like a woman who's had a man between her legs. And wants it again. Which means you're a lot more like your sister than I thought." Sonny narrowed his eyes, and if Phoebe wasn't mistaken, had begun to watch her with a certain amount of grudging respect. As if her supposed promiscuity suddenly made him view her in a different light.

Heat seared Phoebe's skin from the neck up. If she wasn't already frozen in shock, she was pretty sure her jaw would be resting on the floor. She supposed she should be relieved that he wasn't on to the whole undercover-spying thing, but somehow couldn't work up the right amount of enthusiasm for his rather unsavory deductions, despite that they meant he perceived her as someone capable of pursuing the life of a showgirl. And even though Sonny Martorelli scared the crap out of her and was the absolute last person on earth besides maybe her mother with whom Phoebe wanted to discuss her sex life, a little voice in her head kept warning, *don't blow it, don't blow it.*

She ignored the metallic taste in her mouth and pulled upon every ounce of acting ability she possessed. "Wow." Phoebe raised both her eyebrows, going for the sassy sarcasm Tiffany and the other showgirls had down to an art form. "That's an awful lot to get from a smile. But I don't mind admitting I have a lot in common with my little sister." Not a complete lie if you counted stuff like genetics and the address where she and Tiffany grew up. Phoebe shrugged. "I'm sorry if I acted otherwise. I was pretty nervous last week." She laughed and pushed the hair that kept falling from her bun behind her ears. "I was so worried about making a good impression, I must have done just the opposite."

He narrowed his eyes and rolled the ball between his fingers. After a few moments he finally spoke, but there was a hesitation in his voice. "I think I might have an extra job for you this weekend if you're interested. With Tiffany gone and Remmie hurting her ankle, we're still down a girl. But...there's something about you I can't put my finger on."

He paused again while her heart pounded out of control. Suddenly, her fear took a back seat to the carrot being dangled in front of her. Apparently, sex with Trace had been the answer to more than one of her problems. And as slimy and disgusting as Phoebe found Sonny, she seemed to have successfully stumbled across a way of getting hired for the party. She couldn't let this opportunity pass.

"Sonny—" she cleared her throat "—the *Mirage* is a chance for me to get my career going in a new direction. Anything you can throw my way would be great. In spite of the impression I gave you last week, I'm looking forward to performing for an audience that can appreciate all I have to offer." She stopped there and smiled provocatively. At least she hoped that's how her expression appeared. Nauseated definitely wasn't the look she was going for but far closer to the truth.

He nodded slowly. "Tomorrow night's your first show, right?" He began to absently toss the ball again. "We'll see exactly what it is you've got to offer and talk then." He shook his head then cocked his eyebrow. "Though, if I were you, I'd call your new boyfriend and tell him he's in for a busy night. He did more for your dancing in one weekend than you could have gotten from a month of practices." The creep chuckled lewdly. Before he left, he said, "And remember, Devereaux. I'll be watching you."

Phoebe stared after him, the sound of the tapping ball fading as he moved out of sight. Then she heard Trace speak from right next to her, and all but leaped into the air.

"If the bastard ever tries to do more than watch, I'll kill him."

Setting her stupid feather headdress back straight, she frowned at Trace. "If he ever tries, I'll let you. Where did you come from?" This was the first time she'd seen him since yesterday when he'd left Tiff's apartment, and just looking at him made her body tingle. A mental image of her writhing in Trace's arms flashed in her mind and she didn't know whether to grin like the village idiot or duck her head in shame.

"I'm going to start as a bartender on the nights I'm not dancing. I told management that I wanted to pick up some extra cash, but it gives me an excuse to be around. I'm supposed to help stock the bar today. I figured while I'm down there with all the crates, I'd try to check out the hold again," he said, still looking in the direction Sonny had left. Then he glanced down at her and did a sort of double take. He let out a soft whistle. "That's quite a tail you got there, kitten. Or should I say Polly, and ask if you'd like a cracker?" Grinning, he slid his hand up the back of her thigh and rustled the feathers draping her mostly bare bottom. Then he palmed one of her naked cheeks possessively and she shivered.

"Careful," she said, as a feather floated by in the air. "I think I'm molting."

He laughed and tugged her against him. With her arms full of costumes, Phoebe had no defense when he pulled her pelvis into his. Not that she wanted one. He stared down at her and she licked her suddenly dry lips.

"Here, let me," he said, and gently ran his tongue over her top lip, bathing the peaks along the upper line then slowly lowering to her bottom lip, giving it the same moist attention. His breath was warm and sweet and she wanted more. Unable to bear it, she squirmed one of her hands free from between their bodies and took the back of his neck, pressing him closer and deepening their kiss. He laughed softly but seemed happy to comply. He smelled wonderful and clean and like himself and she could've climbed right up him. He released her lips and she groaned.

Trace smiled and nuzzled his nose to hers. "Hi," he said softly.

And with just that one word, a pool of warmth flooded her chest and Phoebe thought, *I could love this man for the rest of my life.* Then she realized what she'd said to herself and thought, *no, I can't. I mean, I could have sex with this man every day for the rest of my life. No, wait, that can't be right either.* And then she thought, *if I don't say something soon, I may be standing here for the rest of my life.*

"Hi." She smiled back.

"Are you okay? I mean after yesterday. I wasn't too rough or anything?" he asked, his voice quiet and low.

Blushing, she pressed her face into his neck and shook her head. Trace was so sweet and protective, it made her go all weak in the knees. Heck, she was one step away from lifting her hand to her forehead and sighing like a southern belle and didn't even care. Oh, brother, if she wasn't careful, she'd start spouting off romantic nonsense about love and Trace, and being in love with Trace. Phoebe stilled and her eyes widened. *Oh, nooooo...*

Jerking herself back from her crazy, insane thoughts, she said, "No. I'm great." And he responded by giving her a hug.

They stood there quietly, content for the moment, and she relaxed into his hold and rested her head on his shoulder. After her conversation with Sonny, she needed the comfort of being held in Trace's arms. Of course, his hand on her butt was pretty nice, too.

"Practice was long," she finally said, "but my dancing is getting better." She wasn't about to tell Trace just how much better, at least according to Sonny, assuming he hadn't already heard.

"I guess that means you can still walk."

Phoebe laughed then poked him in the stomach. "Not easily, but I've managed. Though, I am a bit, er, tender."

"Ouch." He rubbed his stomach, feigning injury. Then he dropped his voice suggestively and said, "I guess I'll just have to kiss it and make it better." He took hold of her hips and her eyes widened.

"Not here!"

"Nope," he agreed. "The dressing room should be fine though." He wiggled his eyebrows.

She wiggled out of his arms. "No way." She lowered her voice. "Besides, we have more important things to do, like check out that cargo. Did they get another shipment or something? I didn't hear about one coming in." Her headdress slipped again, drooping down over one eye. She shoved it back in place, blowing a feather from her face.

Trace rolled his eyes. "Not that I know of. Which is why I'm checking." Then he scowled. "And *we're* not doing anything." After a quick glance around, he took her arm and steered her toward the dressing room. He led her inside and locked the door behind them.

Trace turned to her, his voice low. "This is no time to be stubborn, Phoebe. I told you that I'd tell the police everything I know. There's no reason for you to still put yourself in danger."

"And I told you thanks but no thanks. I have to do this." Phoebe walked to her locker then hung her costumes inside.

"Why? This is crazy. You're pinning all your hopes on that darn meeting Saturday night. And you still haven't even managed to finagle your way into it yet."

"That isn't true. I'm starting with Mr. V.'s island." She took off her stupid hat then unhooked her tail plumage before plopping down into her chair. "I know you heard me telling Alvarez about the place. Tiffany thinks it's called Isola Pomodoro or something else Italian. And Sonny already implied that he had some extra work for me this weekend if I danced well during the show tomorrow night." Her torturous heels were the next to be immediately removed.

Trace snorted. "I bet he did."

Phoebe flashed a look of disgust then slipped on the robe hanging from the back of her chair and sat back down. "Anyway, I also talked to Tony this morning. He told me that Mr. V.'s cousin, Vinny, has a son, Rocky, who works here, too, and that Tony called him and said—"

Trace held up his hand. "Wait a minute. Who the hell said what to whom?"

Phoebe rolled her eyes. "Mr. V. has a cousin, Vinny. Vinny has a son, Rocky. Rocky works on the *Mirage*, too. Tony called Rocky. Are you still with me?" Trace looked as if he'd sucked on a lemon. His lips were twisted, and he had a sort of frowny, scowly expression taking over his face and she couldn't help but laugh.

"Yes, I'm with you. Though the Venzara men have worse

names than the showgirls. But go on." He motioned with his hand for her to continue.

"Tony called Rocky. They're around the same age and I guess they're friends—"

Trace looked at the ceiling and growled her name in warning.

"Just bear with me. Rocky is Mr. V.'s accountant."

"An accountant named Rocky. Why doesn't this surprise me?" Trace muttered, though he did appear to perk up some at this interesting tidbit.

"When Tony spoke with him, Rocky complained about how uptight Mr. V. has been lately. And I guess when Mr. V. gets tense he cooks, and wants everyone around him to eat, which means poor Rocky has put on ten pounds in the last two weeks."

Trace started tapping his foot, but Phoebe ignored him. "Rocky said that Mr. V. is really being crazy about this Saturday night. Wants everything to be perfect, including the menu. He's made eighteen batches of tomato sauce since last week, which, if you've ever met Mr. V., is a big deal. The man takes food seriously. I talked to him once and half the time we discussed seasonings."

Trace glanced at his watch and said, "This is fascinating. And I mean that. Really. Unfortunately, I have a bar to stock, otherwise I could listen to this all day."

Phoebe shrugged. "Fine. If you don't want to hear about the launch that's meeting the *Mirage* tomorrow night out at sea, then what do I care."

Trace rubbed the back of his neck. "No, the launch I want to hear about. It was the Chef Boyardee chronicles that were starting to drag."

She merely sniffed then lifted her chin before continuing. "You heard Alvarez say that Mr. V. is liquidating his assets. Apparently, Mr. V. has put a lot of money into his island, and if this meeting goes well, hopes to throw in a lot more. Everything is riding on the outcome of Saturday night. Mr. V. has gone so nutso over all this that he refuses to wait until Thursday for the next shipment when the *Mirage* stops in Nassau—the same day that Renaldo and Delefluente are arriving in Miami. Though Rocky has no idea what the shipment actually is. In fact, it turns out Renaldo and Delefluente are both apparently bringing something on board, too, each with his own men to guard his separate stuff. Rocky also said that Mr. V. keeps ranting about his samples and how they have to be ready for Saturday night and that Renaldo and Delefluente will only accept the best. So, a boat from Isola Pomodoro will meet the *Mirage* at sea tomorrow night and deliver Mr. V.'s shipment one hour before the ship heads back to port."

Trace stared unseeingly, his eyes narrowed on some spot behind her. Then he said, "I guess I won't waste my time going down there today." He rubbed his finger across his bottom lip. "I'll have to get the other bartender, Brett, to cover for me, but I can work that out. This is great." He gave her a huge smile. Then he hesitated and asked, "Have you told Alvarez yet?"

"That is the whole point of all this," she answered dryly. "Me passing along information to the cops. Of course I told Alvarez, and he wants me to find out what's in those crates. Fortunately, the launch should be meeting the ship right before my last set, so I can be down there when they're unloading. If I don't have enough time, I can see where they're keeping the shipment then go back later."

Trace shoved both hands in his hair, and he looked as if he was ready to yank it out at the roots. "I can't believe Alvarez is actually using you for this crap."

Rubbing her blistered feet, she said, "Yep," and smiled smugly. "I told you it would work."

"Great," Trace muttered and spun away. He started pacing back and forth then finally said, "Listen, not only is this way too risky, you have no experience. What if you mess everything up? If Sonny or Mr. V. finds out about you, your life could be in danger. Besides, I have to consider my story. If I don't get it, I'm screwed. Let me talk to Alvarez. He'll probably agree with me."

"I've got an idea. How about I take care of everything and after the police make their arrest, I'll give you the inside scoop?"

His scowl darkened, and when he spoke it sounded as though his teeth were clenched. "First, because you could get killed if Sonny figures out what you're doing—"

Phoebe interrupted. "So could you. What's the difference?"

She noticed a muscle had started ticking in Trace's jaw. "There just is," he said. Then he pointed his finger at her and said, "I do not want to find your body floating in the water down by the docks. It's a nice body. I'm partial to it. I have plans for that body."

Phoebe didn't bother pointing out his inconsistencies, instead choosing to be flattered. Of course, his words had so excited her, she didn't have any breath to argue with him anyway.

"And second," he went on, "because I need my story before the police make their arrest. Once the newshounds get wind of this, a hundred other reporters will be on the trail. All the good papers will use their own staff and I won't have jumped the gun on any of them."

Phoebe shook her head. "Why don't you just sell your story to the one you're working for now?"

A flush of red crept up Trace's neck. Too casually, he sauntered over to the makeup mirror and started fiddling with the little jars of cosmetics. "Working at the same place gets stale. I thought I'd shop my piece around and see what sort of interest I could drum up."

She pursed her lips, studying him as he fidgeted and

blushed. Finally she asked, "What's the name of this paper where you work?"

He wouldn't look at her and mumbled some indecipherable answer.

Cocking her head so her ear turned toward him, she said, "I'm sorry, I didn't quite catch that." He said a bit louder, "The—" and then everything else was slurred again.

Ooh, the darn man could be annoying when he wanted. "Will you please speak normally? I can't understand a word you're saying."

"The *Daily Intruder*," he all but shouted this time.

Phoebe widened her eyes. "Oh, well then." Her lips started twitching. "I can see your dilemma."

Trace turned to glower at her and she tried not to snicker. "Though you never know," she said. "You might come across something they'd be willing to print. Maybe we'll find out that Mr. V. is secretly dating J.Lo. She's from Miami, right? Or maybe," she sputtered between guffaws, "Mr. V. is really from outer space and he's cloning pod people on his island as we speak." Phoebe had to stop and she hugged her sides, bending over in laughter.

Trace's eyebrows lowered ominously. "Ha-ha-ha. Very funny. I'm glad my life amuses you." He rubbed the back of his neck. "Perhaps now you can see why this piece is so important to me. After I'm done, I'll tell Alvarez everything. But I can't let him arrest Mr. V. before I'm ready. Every reporter in the next three counties will jump on this one. The *Herald* or whichever paper I go with will have no incentive to pick me up unless my article breaks the story."

Wiping her eyes, Phoebe's chortles died down. "I understand that, but what if your story messes up the police's arrest?" This thought sobered her, and she asked, "What if Mr. V. has enough time after your big exposé for him to get away? Or destroy evidence or something? My sister and her husband are waiting to get back into the country. They could feasibly go to jail if I don't come through on this."

Trace shook his head. "Your sister won't. I heard Alvarez say her charges were minor." Then he shrugged. "The husband might."

Phoebe could feel her face growing hot and said, "Tiffany is pregnant. Her child needs its father. He cannot go to jail."

Trace sent her an angry look right back. "Yeah, well, I need my career. And I haven't committed any crimes or shifted my responsibilities onto someone else. They have. I'm getting my story."

"No, you just got fired from the *Herald* for some mysterious reason you don't seem anxious to explain and now write for a trashy tabloid. That's much more noble." Trace's expression turned thunderous but she was on a roll. "I'm keeping my sister and her husband out of jail. Period. You can get your story after the police get their evidence." She held up her hand when he would have cut her off. "I can sympathize, but there's no way I'm backing down. Especially now that Sonny thinks my dancing is great and there's a good chance I'll be included Saturday night."

Trace propped his hands on his hips and glowered down at her. "For the record, I was completely innocent when I lost my job. And when did this magical transformation supposedly take place? Two nights ago you were the worst dancer Candy and Barbie had ever seen."

Heat stole across her face, but she sniffed and said, "Sonny just said he could tell at practice that I was dancing differently."

Trace smirked. "Don't tell me. He saw you in your costume and decided you were friggin' Ginger Rogers."

Her mouth pulled flat. "No. He saw the way I performed my routines and was impressed with my moves. His words not mine." She was not about to quote the whole bit about "a man between your legs."

Trace practically growled. "And just how exactly were you moving?"

Phoebe shrugged, then went to her bag and pulled out her jeans. "As if I'd had a good time this weekend or something like that." She waved her hand. "I don't know—you'll have to ask him. He scares the heck out of me, so I try not to drag out our conversations." After slipping the bottom of her costume off beneath her robe, she stepped into her pants.

His eyebrows lowered ominously. "A good time?"

A sigh welled in her chest. Obviously, he was a reporter for a good reason. The man quite simply never gave up. She decided to come clean now before he nagged her to death. She didn't have to like it though, and said crossly, "Sex. Sonny could tell that I'd had sex. All weekend long. I didn't bother to correct him on that assumption. The marathoner you pulled on Sunday probably made up for Saturday's absence. As a matter of fact, he suggested that I call you and see if you were interested in another tussle tonight. He said you did more for me than all the practicing in the world could ever hope to achieve." After turning her back to Trace, she threw off her robe, unclipped her sequined bra and jerked her shirt on over her head.

When she turned around he was wearing a ridiculously smug expression on his face. Then their eyes met and his gaze turned hot. Flaming hot. Yikes. She recognized that look and could swear she grew moist between her legs in some sort of Pavlovian response. She was mad at him about something, but for the life of her couldn't remember what it was.

Still giving her the look, he added a half grin to complete the devastating effect. "Hmm. Then it looks like I've got myself a problem."

"You actually have quite a few, the worst of them being stubbornness, but to which one in particular are you referring?"

"Oh, just that I hate playing right into Sonny's hands."

"What are you talking about?"

He rubbed his jaw. "And yours, too, now that I think about it."

Phoebe sighed. "Would you at least try to make sense?"

"Didn't you say that having sex with me was better for your dancing than all the practicing in the world?"

She rolled her eyes. "Sonny's words, not mine."

"And you're still planning on dancing tomorrow night, right? I believe those were your words."

"Yes, and your point?"

"Just that I had hoped you'd quit on your own or at least get fired, but," he sighed, "I guess that's not going to happen. A major pain in the ass, since now I not only have to keep your butt out of trouble, but I have to figure out a way to get my story before you help the police make their arrest."

Phoebe narrowed her eyes. "You're mostly right. Except for the part about me and my butt. However, if you don't mind me asking, what great insight finally brought you to this realization?"

Trace had moved closer. He reached out and slid the tip of his finger into the front pocket of her jeans then yanked her forward until she stumbled into his chest. "Because if Sonny's correct, then I guess pretty soon here you're going to be the best damn showgirl the *Mirage* has ever seen. Hell, you'll probably end up the star of the show."

His mouth hovered above her own and she licked her lips. "I will...?"

He lowered his voice. "Uh-huh, because you and I are definitely having sex again."

He was staring at her mouth and she could barely breathe. Her lashes fluttered and she gulped, "We are...?" Jeesh. Wasn't she the witty conversationalist? Unfortunately, since he'd said the S word, these pitiful responses were the best she could do.

She could feel his erection straining against the fly of his jeans, since he'd notched himself right into the V at the top of her thighs, and she thought, *oh, what the heck, why start fighting this now?* then widened her legs farther apart. And Trace, the clever man, knew exactly what to do.

He pushed his hips forward then pressed from side to side and she moaned. Loudly. Oh, jeez…she *was* a moaner.

He sounded hoarse and said, "Oh, yeah. A lot of sex. And soon." He paused and with a frown added, "And then I'll get my story."

She wasn't sure if he was talking to himself or to her, since he'd yet to look away from her mouth, but she nodded dumbly and said, "And I'll help the police."

He nodded back, distracted, his nostrils flaring while he did the amazing circle-push thing with his pelvis again that made her toes curl. Then he said, "First sex then story. In that order. I mean—first I get my story and then I get sex. No, wait—" And then he broke off and muttered, "Aw, hell…"

9

"THERE," Barbie said, patting the final sequin onto the side of Phoebe's breast. "Just sit here for a couple of minutes until the glue dries. Then you'll be good to go."

Phoebe quirked her mouth. "How the heck am I supposed to scratch underneath these things? I'm itchy already." She squirmed in her seat.

"Like this," and Barbie lifted her hands to her own breasts and grasped herself as if squeezing the Charmin. "Then once you peel them off after the routine, you can give yourself a good long scratch."

Phoebe looked down at her chest, naked except for the sequins glued over top. Her bottom half was modest, in comparison, with the low-slung, sequined hip huggers. The two-and-a-half-inch heeled go-go boots completed her new look.

"Hey—" Daisy and her jiggling double D's stopped next to Phoebe "—you nervous, kid?"

She was, but not for the reasons her new friend probably suspected. Still, Phoebe smiled and said, "A little, I guess. But I'm kind of excited, too."

Barbie laughed. "Good. Because you're going to be great, thanks to our master coaching," the showgirl teased, referring to their lengthy practice the day before. "But now I've gotta go fix my hair before we head backstage." She headed to where her own things were set up a few seats farther down the lighted mirror.

Daisy nodded. "I don't know what the heck happened between your first practice and the one we had yesterday, but you're dancing like a different woman." Daisy stopped for a meaningful pause, then said with a wink before she turned to leave, "Though I have my suspicions...."

Phoebe blushed and glanced at her reflection. All right, she thought, staring at the satisfied face beaming back from the mirror. So it might be a bit obvious she'd been ridden hard and put up happy. At least her satisfied glow should convince Sonny that she was the right Devereaux sister for the job.

The real test came later tonight when the secret launch arrived. Trace was right. Phoebe didn't have any experience with this sort of thing and there were moments when she feared her heart was going to pound right out of her chest. But she needed to get control of her nerves if she was going to find Alvarez his information before Trace printed his story. Unfortunately, she and Trace still hadn't resolved a thing other than to agree that neither one of them was going to step aside in their race to catch Angelo Venzara. Or give up having wild monkey sex.

Smiling to herself, Phoebe supposed she should be relieved that at least these ground rules had been established. Now if only she could get her heart to stop going mushy every time Trace came within ten feet of her, she'd be doing fine. And the L word had started creeping into her thoughts with startling regularity, a recent problem that had become all but unmanageable.

Of course, Trace didn't make it easy to harness her emotions on any of these fronts. He was so darn likable. No matter how she danced, or how much she frustrated him, or how stubborn she acted, he seemed genuinely to like her. She could probably fail at everything and he wouldn't care. So, how the heck was she supposed to fight all this and wild monkey sex, too? It plain wasn't fair.

Maybe she should just start acting like herself instead of the new and improved Phoebe she'd been pretending to be since she'd arrived in Miami. If worse came to worst, and she didn't get control of her runaway feelings, that would scare him off in a heartbeat. That or bore him to death. Either was an option. But a necessary one if she wasn't strong enough to end their fun and games before she fell in love.

Her thoughts were broken as one of the backstage technicians came by and yelled out first call. She bit back a sigh, no closer to solving the dilemma of how not to fall crazy in love with Trace than before. "All right. I'm off." Phoebe gave a quick wave to Barbie and the other girls still in the dressing room, and started for the door. But as she walked into the hallway, she quickly became overwhelmed by her itchy sequins. "Oh, I can't stand this," she said, not even caring if the glue was dry enough when she grabbed her chest and squeezed.

"You need some help there, kitten?" Trace grinned as he rounded the corner, looking positively yummy as always.

When he reached her, he took hold of her wrists then lowered her hands. "Holy hell," he scowled. "Where's the rest of it?"

Phoebe raised an eyebrow. "It's a heck of a lot more than you wore at Candy's"

Trace frowned. "Stop using logic. It won't get you anywhere with me."

Phoebe laughed and Traced sighed. "This is going to be the longest night of my life," he grumbled.

"Poor baby. At least you won't have to watch some floozy pulling money from her bra then slipping it into my costume."

"Darn. That kind of sounds good."

Phoebe hit him in the chest and Trace laughed and then kissed her until she felt dizzy. Lord, what this man could do with his mouth. Then his hands caressed her naked back and she feared her knees were going to buckle.

A few delicious seconds later, he pulled away and stared

down at her breasts. "Now, where were we? I seem to recall catching you in a rather private moment when I walked up."

Phoebe wrinkled her nose. "I was itchy. These darn sequins are glued on and I have to squeeze myself if I want any relief."

"I'm dreaming this, right?"

"Gets you all hot and bothered, huh?"

"I don't know what I want to do more, watch or help."

"Oh, by all means, help me. Please...." She sighed as his warm hands enveloped her then gently contracted.

"You two really have a thing for hallways, don't you?" Barbie stood inside the doorway of the dressing room, the rest of the dancers crowded around behind her.

Phoebe pressed her face into Trace's shirt and laughed while he shrugged his shoulders. "What can I say? She's an exhibitionist. Loves getting caught. She doesn't even care that I'm shy."

Phoebe tickled his sides and he jumped back. "Ooh, ticklish, are you? This is good to know."

He snorted. "Just what you needed. More weapons in your arsenal. I've gotta go, anyway. I'm tending bar tonight and my break's over."

"You, too, Madame Butterfly. It won't look good if you miss your first number." Barbie smacked Phoebe on the butt playfully as she walked by.

As the other dancers headed toward the stage, Phoebe grabbed Trace before he could leave. She lowered her voice and asked, "What are you going to be doing while I'm on-stage?"

"Mixing drinks. Why?"

"At the bar that's set up in the showroom?"

Trace crossed his arms. "Yes...why?"

Phoebe looked around to make sure no one could overhear them. "I'm just making sure I know where you'll be. I don't trust you not to go digging around while my back is turned."

Trace smirked. "There's nothing you can do to stop me."

Since killing him wasn't an option, Phoebe shrugged and pretended an indifference she was far from feeling. "Fine. But I guess that goes both ways, doesn't it?" she said, and Trace scowled. Then she realized there was another minor snag in her plan and asked, "Do you know where the hold is? I assume that I just keep going down the service stairs until I reach the bottom of the ship, but—"

He let out a curse. "Are you *trying* to get killed?"

Phoebe pointed her finger at him and said, "Listen, O Great Master of the Snooping World, you wouldn't even know about this special shipment if it wasn't for me. I could call Tony and ask for the layout of the ship, but since you're here, I figured I'd save myself the hassle."

Trace grabbed her finger and jerked her into his arms, and most of her anger was replaced by pure arousal. "When dinner clears," he said, "housekeeping drops off the linen, and the laundry area is usually empty until after we dock. I'll be at the service entrance at ten o'clock. If you're not there by 10:01, I'm going down without you and you can find your own damn way to the hold."

"I'll be there," she said, trying to sound annoyed but having a hard time because his chest was so warm and hard, and the stupid man was really just worried about her.

"Oh, one last thing," she said, because she had another small piece of revenge to deliver. Trace eyed her warily as she leaned up and put her arms around his neck. Automatically he lowered his hands to her hips.

Giving him a brief, wicked smile, Phoebe licked his ear then blew on it and said, "I just want you to know...while I'm out there performing, I'll be thinking of you...." She could feel Trace's muscles go stiff beneath her hands and, laughing softly, she delivered the rest of her payback. "I may be dancing for the men in the audience...but I'll be thinking of you the whole time." And with that, she shot him a cocky wink and walked backstage.

TRACE CROUCHED silently behind the wall of crates while some twenty or so feet away Sonny Martorelli waited with three of his men. The ship rocked with another wave and Trace grabbed on to the wooden box at his side as a series of curses reached his ears, and he found himself in complete agreement with Sonny's men. Trying to stay on your feet and off your butt was almost impossible with the swells tossing about the *Mirage*.

The suddenly rough sea conditions also meant that the launch wasn't coming tonight. It couldn't be. In the last half hour, the water had turned unusually turbulent, with caps breaking at twelve to fifteen feet, some surging higher. The onset of the sudden weather would knock anything smaller than the *Mirage* around like a toy boat in a bathtub. Why the hell didn't Sonny and his men just go back upstairs so Trace could get out of here and find Phoebe? Probably because that would make his life too easy—a concept God seemed personally opposed to.

Instead of leaving like a good Mafia henchman, Sonny stood smoking a cigarette by the small upper hatch that was partially opened. The acrid scent of tobacco filled the air as the minutes all but crawled by. The men had only bothered with the one light next to Sonny, leaving everything else in the cavernous room dark. And the only noise besides the occasional comment from one of the goons, and the roar of the sea, was the tapping. Never-ending. On and on as Sonny tossed a hand-size ball into the air until Trace thought he'd go nuts.

For what felt like hours, though realistically was probably more like twenty minutes, Trace had been stuck behind this crate with nothing to do besides count the taps. And sweat.

And try to stay upright. And wonder where the hell Phoebe was. She'd never shown up at the laundry service, though Trace had waited until well after 10:01. A nervous wreck, he'd eventually had to leave or risk missing the shipment altogether. Of course, by then, the sea conditions had gotten so turbulent it hadn't mattered anyway.

Damn it, he should never have let the crazy woman out of his sight. Well, from now on he wouldn't unless he'd tied her up and locked her in a safe place first.

"I think Mr. V.'s lost it this time." Trace recognized the voice of one of Sonny's goons. "I mean, come on. Why do we have to be stuck down here when we could be up there watching that new girl onstage?"

"Hey," Sonny answered, "watch your mouth, Joey. Nobody questions Mr. V.'s orders. He wants the shipment tonight. That's all you need to know."

A different goon chimed in and said, "Besides, if we go back upstairs, Mr. V. will probably just make us eat more of his spaghetti. Every time I see him, he makes me eat some more of his spaghetti. My stomach doesn't feel so good. And these friggin' waves are only makin' it worse."

Not to mention the overwhelming smell of tomato sauce, Trace thought to himself. Mr. V. may be a great cook, but the entire ship was starting to reek of garlic. Not entirely unpleasant, but it was like sailing the high seas in an Olive Garden.

"Hey, Bobby, nobody said that you had to stuff your face until you puked. If you weren't such a friggin' pig, Mr. V. wouldn't give you all the leftovers." The third man laughed and Trace could hear scuffling.

"Would you two putzes knock it off," Sonny commanded.

"I don't hear no boat, Sonny. You think they aren't coming? It's really bad out there."

Sonny cursed. "Until Mr. V. tells me different, they're coming."

Someone sighed. It must have been the bastard they'd called Joey because then he said, "Yeah, but even if the shipment does make it, they won't be here before the last set. And I wanna see Tiffany's sister in that costume the dancers wear for the final number. Damn is she *hot*." He dragged the word out. "That woman has got a pair of tits to die for and that booty. Man, oh, man—"

"What about her legs?" one of the guys broke in. "Those bitches must be ten feet long."

More laughter erupted, then another said, "Give it up, Joey. What she needs is a real man. Lucky for her I've got eight inches just waiting to make her day." More guffaws followed.

While Trace decided which one to mutilate first, he heard a tiny squeak from off to his right. Eyes narrowed, he cursed silently. Apparently he wasn't the only one offended. Just able to make out a flesh-colored shadow in the distance, he crept over to where the pain-in-the-butt showgirl was hiding. Not easy with the floor rolling and pitching, but he finally made it to her side. Phoebe didn't hear him, but he wasn't surprised since she wasn't supposed to. And then he saw what she was wearing, or rather wasn't wearing, and he was surprised. In fact, he almost swallowed his tongue.

Clamping a hand over her mouth, he breathed directly in her ear, "Where are your effing clothes?"

If Trace hadn't been holding her, she'd have probably jumped a foot. Instead, she glared at him from the corner of her eye. He did a quick scan of their surroundings, or what he could see of them in this light, then motioned with his head to the open door in the corner. It was probably a storage closet, though he couldn't be sure since it was pitch-black inside like almost everything else down here.

He pointed for her to go in first. Holding his finger to his lips, he inched the metal door closed. If the launch actually did show up, Trace had no doubt the men would make

enough noise for them to hear its arrival. Except now it really
was pitch-black and he couldn't tell where she was. The ship
rocked through another swell and Phoebe fell into his back.

Turning, he took her by the arms and dragged her to him.
"Where the hell were you?" he whispered almost noise-
lessly. "I waited close to half an hour." Then he remembered
her costume and his heart pounded hard enough to break
through his ribs. If one of those guys saw her dressed like
this there would be a mass stampede for her body.

Damn. She was wearing some sort of netting. That's the
most he'd been able to discern when he'd found her. A sleek,
flesh-colored suit of stretchy mesh. Without a single friggin'
thing on underneath, damn it.

She turned her head, her voice only slightly louder than
his. "I have plenty of time, if the show's still even on. We
can't possibly dance with the ship swaying like this. Besides,
I don't perform until the final few minutes. That's why I'm in
my costume, so I can head right backstage."

Trace gritted his teeth. "Oh, yeah. That's a great reason to
come down here naked."

Phoebe made an angry little huff then nipped his ear,
which shocked the hell out of him because he wasn't expecting it. The sensation made his entire body stiffen, including
his penis, and he said to himself, *screw it*, and slammed his
mouth down on hers. And for the moment when their lips
met, he actually felt human and okay. All because he was
kissing this nut. And the thought popped into his head, *I
cannot lose her*, which made him hold Phoebe even tighter.

But after only moments, she began to wriggle against him
enticingly and he ran his hands down her length, skimming
all his favorite hills and curves in spite of how stupid and in-
appropriate their blatant groping was at a time like this. And
of course, she *would* press her pelvis against his, moving the
way he'd taught her. And being the obliging fellow that he
was, he pressed back, then swallowed her moan. Damn, he

loved that sound, just not now. Not when the breathy noises sent darts of pure lust shooting from his brain to his groin and had him ready to strip off her ridiculous covering in one rip.

Phoebe broke their kiss, though she kept her hips grinding against him. Then she whispered, "Is this your plan?"

"What plan?" He breathed the question against the top of her jaw then licked the scented skin. Cripes, he could barely think. He locked his knees, fisted his hands, wondering when this would end. This overwhelming desire to mate with every inch of her body. And it was only getting worse the more he touched her. The times that they'd had sex had not even come close to taking the edge off. The minute he'd pull out of her wet heat the craving to drive himself right back into her would crank through his gut.

"Making love?"

But before he could figure out what the hell she meant, the floor tilted and Trace stumbled. The back of his legs met a low shelf or ledge of some kind and he leaned onto it, resting his weight and bringing his groin into perfect alignment with hers. Then she lifted her thigh to his hip. Not about to ignore the invitation no matter how stupid it was to lose his grip on reality with Sonny's men out there, Trace slipped his hand beneath her knee then wrapped her slim leg around his waist and pressed hard against the heat searing his fly.

"The tapping," she mumbled, her lips caressing the side of his face while he slid his hands to her sweet bottom. "It's getting louder. Sonny's coming. Is he supposed to catch us doing it...?"

Trace frowned, and shook his head to clear it. For the first time he heard that the strangely ominous sound seemed to be growing louder. He stilled, quickly weighing their options and, predictably, Phoebe made the task even harder for him by grinding harder against him. Using sex as a cover was the oldest, most overused cliché in existence, but was also so corny that it just might work for that very reason. After all, how many people would be stupid enough to play *hide the salami* with a passel of trained Mafia killers less than ten feet away? Trace scowled, hardly believing that he was one of those people stupid enough.

He growled out, "That wouldn't be a bad idea if I could figure out how the hell to get inside this damn thing." The whole time he spoke he ran his hands up and down her ridiculously arousing body, searching for a zipper, or a snap, or a button, or any spot of entry he could find on the gossamer-thin fabric.

Then Trace noticed the tapping again, only closer. And one of Sonny's guys was talking about the shipment and the weather and this sounded pretty close, too. For a moment, Trace stopped, then with growing urgency began tugging at her costume. "Take it off," he whispered.

"Not enough time," Phoebe answered, dropping to her knees. She had his pants unbuckled before he could blink. The next thing he knew, his penis was out and her mouth was sliding over the head.

Trace's heart pounded, and he cursed under his breath as her tongue flicked out, licking the tear of fluid seeping from the slit. He gripped the shelf hard enough to make his fingers go numb while he spread his other hand through her hair and clasped the back of her head.

Then the tapping stopped, and Trace froze. He twisted the silky strands in warning, but of course Phoebe ignored him and merely grasped his shaft and sucked him deeper. He bit the inside of his cheek, hoping to draw blood—which was stupid, really, considering his entire blood supply had surged to south of his belt buckle. But he had to do something, anything, to bring himself back to sanity. Because the feel of himself gliding over the roof of her mouth, everything tight and wet as she worked him between her plump lips, was driving him right over the brink.

He gasped for breath, his respirations no more than labored pants that burst from his lungs, when everything became eerily silent on the other side of the door and he could no longer hear Sonny or any of his men. Trace's body tensed. Yet, still, Phoebe didn't stop and pressure hammered through his lower back, his arousal perversely heightened by the increasing danger. He scowled into the darkness, his lips pulled back from his teeth. His length swelled and he winced, his skin stretched taut enough to burn. Then again, all that burning might be from the heat generated by Phoebe's agile tongue, which she was now wriggling under the thick ridge circling the head of his erection.

Then he heard Sonny say, "Hey, Joey, I thought you left this door open for the shipment?" and Trace's pulse skittered wildly.

Meanwhile, back in his pants, Phoebe slipped her free hand beneath his testicles and cupped their weight. Trace's thighs grew rigid and she began to move the hand on his shaft, twisting her palm up and down, in rhythm with the pulls of her mouth, and he could feel the jolt all the way up his spine.

Joey answered Sonny, saying, "I did exactly what you told me. The way this bucket is rocking, it probably just got knocked closed. Don't sweat it."

"I didn't hear it close," Sonny said, clearly doubtful, but the ship swayed again and a muffled thump and grunt followed. "Hey," Sonny barked and Trace figured the man had been knocked into the wall.

Relentlessly determined, Phoebe's weight pressed into Trace's thighs and her lips slid farther down his erection as the floor tilted back. He almost gasped aloud. His head fell back, and his neck arched. He had to work his throat just to breathe and his balls tightened unbearably. Apparently her goal was to make him come the moment Sonny and his idiots swung into the room, but he didn't want that. The coming part, yes, the loss of control when he needed it most, no. He clenched his jaw until the bone ached painfully.

Trace grabbed her shoulders to jerk her away, unable to take a second more, when he heard the door handle jiggle and all he could think was, oh crap, oh crap, oh crap, they were going to get caught then killed. And right now, right now, right now, he was going to come. His hips moved independently of his brain, pushing him in and out between her slick lips, when suddenly the lock clicked ominously and he heard Sonny say, "Tomorrow night one of you idiots stays by the door. Looks like we'll be waiting till then for the shipment."

Then, unbelievably, the taps started to fade. And right when Trace began to think that they might actually live to have sex another day, Phoebe took him in all the way to the back of her throat and the spasms started. Holy hell, he thought as liquid heat seared the inside of his erection. His vocal cords strained to hold back the groan building in his chest, while Phoebe swallowed each drop of his release, milking him until he felt empty. Rung dry. Content.

Countless moments of silence passed. Then Phoebe suddenly giggled and Trace shook his head, jerked back to reality. "What the hell is so funny? We almost got killed." He turned his ear toward the door, though fairly sure Sonny and his men had left.

Phoebe snapped the front of his briefs into place. "Guess we didn't need to do that after all," she snickered. "You got a freebie for nothing. They never even opened the door."

Buckling his belt, Trace said dryly, "No. They just locked it. And thank you. I'm sorry you were put through that kind of torture when clearly such a sacrifice was unnecessary."

Still unable to see her in the pitch dark, he felt Phoebe's arms suddenly around his neck. "Don't pout," she said, nipping his bottom lip, and he could taste himself on her tongue and shivered at the proof of how he'd filled her mouth. "I was only teasing," she continued. "Besides, I owed you one anyway."

After that spine-wringing climax, Trace wanted nothing more than to fall on the ground and never move again, but he made his way to the door. "Really? Since when did you start keeping score?" When he got there, he skimmed his hands along the wall. "Because I hate to break the news to you, but if you're trying to even things out between us, you're going to have a hard time keeping up. You, kitten, are the queen of multiple orgasms." And just the thought of how wildly she responded to him every damn time he touched her caused a twinge of life behind his zipper. Something he would have said was physically impossible for at least another hour or so but had become habitual around this woman.

"Nope. Oral sex," she corrected. "I want to be fair about this and I'm ahead. First it was me, then both of us at the same time—" a memory Trace would take with him to the grave "—then me, and me again, and now you."

"So you're saying I've got two more blow jobs coming my way?" He laughed then said, "Excellent. I'll let you know when I'm ready to collect." He found the light switch and flipped it on.

He winced, blinking until his eyes adjusted. And got his first real look at Phoebe's costume and frowned hard enough to make his eyebrows hurt. Yep, he'd been right. She had on netting. Without a stitch underneath. Completely see-through except where the material grew cloudy over her nipples and at the apex of her thighs. He assumed her butt had the same murky coverage. In the garment's own way it was more seductive than total nudity. The important parts in shadow, yet with enough hints to make him swallow hard.

Trace scowled and said, "Hell, why bother?" but when Phoebe rolled her eyes, he held up his hand. "Never mind. Wear the damn thing to the grocery store for all I care. You're gonna argue with me whatever I say anyway." He rubbed the back of his neck.

"Not true," Phoebe said, arguing on purpose then laughing.

He shook his head then looked around their closet. Except they weren't in a closet, they were in a small room. Maybe ten by ten with tube lights that ran across the ceiling. Trace narrowed his eyes. "Huh," he mused. They weren't fluorescent but high wattage. A long wooden table sat directly underneath and he took a step closer. The surface had about a six-inch rim all the way around it, making the top a wide, shallow trough. Black plastic lined the inside. As he ran over the possibilities of what this could mean, he happened to glance at Phoebe and quickly became distracted by the three crates in the corner where she stared. Two of them were rather large, the third barely medium in size, and Trace froze.

"Do you think they're important?" Phoebe asked, her voice soft.

Trace blew out a breath. "Well...the *Mirage* has been picking up unmarked cargo and Sonny wanted this room locked for a reason." He gestured with his head toward the wood-slatted boxes. "I'd say there's a pretty good chance that all our answers are waiting in there."

But when he would have gone over to them, he hesitated, a realization striking him. This could really be it. Once they discovered the contents of those crates, all bets were off between him and Phoebe. Their truce would end and if he rushed out and sold his story tomorrow—they'd be over. His chest grew tight. The idea shouldn't be so painful, but it was. The thought of ending this, this *thing* he had going with Phoebe was unbearable. He'd miss her even more than he had nine years ago. Her smile and her laugh. Her feisty comebacks. The way she let herself go in his arms. The woman she'd become, so appealing to him on every front, he didn't know how to fight the feelings she created inside him. And then the truth hit him. It was too late. He'd already lost the fight.

"Well, aren't you going to do something? You know, go open them up?" she asked.

Trace glanced at her, startled. "Oh, yeah." He shook his head. Phoebe was licking her lips again, and he knew she was nervous. It made him want to pull her into his arms and tell her everything would be okay, but he'd be lying, and he wondered if she had as mixed emotions about opening those crates as he did.

"They're probably still nailed shut," he said with a sigh. He walked over and checked just to be sure. "You stay here. I'm going to find something to open them with."

Phoebe's gaze darted to the door. "Are you sure Sonny or the others won't come back?"

"Yeah. They're gone." He glanced at his watch. "We should be okay. I doubt Sonny will notice I'm not at the bar. And you've got another fifteen minutes or so if the show's still on. I'm going to turn off the light, though, when I leave."

"Wonderful," she said dryly, rubbing her arms as if suddenly cold.

Trace had to touch her. He pulled her into a hug and softly kissed her forehead. "I'll be right back. Don't move from here, okay?"

Phoebe nodded. He gave her another quick kiss, reluctant to let her go, before he walked to the door. Fortunately, the lock didn't require a key from both sides as he'd feared and Trace slid the dead bolt open. Pulling a lighter, which he'd taken from the bar, out of his pocket, he managed to find his way to the engine room and came across a thick screwdriver in with some other tools. He returned within minutes and flipped the lights back on.

"This was the best I could do." He held up the screwdriver before setting to work on one of the larger crates.

Phoebe tried to see over his shoulder. "What's in there? What is it?" The wood gave a high-pitched groan as Trace raised the lid, and they both stared inside.

"Dirt? He's smuggling dirt?" Her mouth turned downward.

"Maybe Venzara's hiding drugs in here to throw off the scent." But after repeatedly jabbing the screwdriver into the pile of earth, he shook his head.

Phoebe's eyebrows pulled down in worry. "What about the others?"

Trace nodded then tugged and jerked the next one open.

"Dirt again," she said despondently. "This doesn't help us at all. Why would Mr. V. be sneaking dirt into the country?"

"I haven't the foggiest," Trace muttered. He dusted the rich soil from his hands and moved to the smaller crate. When he opened this one they both raised their eyebrows. "They look like mason jars."

"Two crates full of dirt, and one more filled with glass jars. Not even enough to get you on America's Most Wanted." Phoebe sighed and shook her head. "Maybe Tiffany is right and Mr. V. isn't doing anything illegal."

Trace pulled out a mason jar and held it up to the light. "It could be that they'll use the jars for sealing the drugs in. So dogs won't be able to pick up the scent." Nothing out of the ordinary there, he thought, then set the glass back inside. He looked through them all but found nothing. Shrugging, he glanced at his watch then retrieved the nails and began to knock them back in place one by one with the handle of the screwdriver.

"But wouldn't they hold a liquid or something similar? It would take an awful lot of cocaine to fill all of them." Phoebe pointed out.

"True. But Mr. V. doesn't have to fill them the whole way. Though he could be making a liquid drug. Like that date rape stuff."

Phoebe's shoulders slumped. "Mr. V. could be running moonshine from his own still for all we know."

Trace finished with the last crate then leaned against it. He pointed the screwdriver at the light bulbs overhead. "Those are growing lights."

"You mean sunlamps?"

"Sort of. They put out a really high wattage. Dopeheads use them to grow pot. Except it gives them huge electric bills. It's often how they get caught. The cops screen utility bills for high usage. Though the *Mirage* wouldn't have to worry about something like that since it has its own generators."

Phoebe stared at the crude plywood table underneath. "Maybe this is like a tanning room or something," she said hopefully.

Trace snorted. "Oh, yeah. Just what a cruise ship in south Florida needs. A tanning room. I can picture Mr. V. now, slathering on the cocoa butter then coming all the way down to the hold to catch some rays. On a black plastic-lined tanning bed, no less."

Phoebe made a face.

"Mr. V.'s definitely growing something. Or rather will be. But why on the ship?" Trace asked, thinking out loud. "It doesn't make sense. Usually drug smugglers only bother with the finished product."

"And haven't you noticed something else?" Phoebe turned to the thermostat on the wall. She walked over and looked at the setting.

"The rest of the hold is hot as hell." Trace spoke slowly. "This room is climate controlled." The room was warm but nowhere near the hundred-plus temperatures it had the potential to reach during the peak hours of the day, especially if those mega-lights were on.

Phoebe sent him a cocky grin. "That explains why you looked so cool and comfortable after I'd finished with you. You barely even worked up a sweat."

Trace quirked his eyebrow, though just thinking about what Phoebe had done to him made heat slam through his gut as if he'd swallowed one of those high-wattage bulbs. And then Trace realized that their truce would last a bit longer since they still had no idea what the hell was going on with Mr. V. He was so damn relieved that he could have pumped his fist in the air and shouted out *Y-E-S*. He settled with saying, "Believe me. I was sweating plenty. But because we were going to die." Hiding a smile, he shrugged. "I guess what you were doing wasn't too bad, either. Though I was pretty distracted."

She lifted her chin. "Then I guess I won't waste my time doing it again."

"Uh-uh. Not a chance. I've already got two on credit waiting for me." And Phoebe gave him a knowing look, and he grinned back.

Trace forced his mind to return to the topic at hand. "Well, I think it's pretty obvious Mr. V. is going to be transporting some kind of plants in here." He waved his hand, indicating the room. "Probably marijuana, but you never know. Could be coca. Maybe poppies. Though the table isn't really deep enough for full-grown stalks of any kind."

Phoebe licked her lips, staring at the table. "My mother is really into gardening." She fingered the plastic. "She uses a setup similar to this one for her seedlings."

"Seedlings," he said quietly. "Maybe." Then he nodded at her. "We better leave now, though, before anyone notices we're gone."

"I know that we can unlock the door from the inside, but what is Sonny going to do when he finds the dead bolt open?"

Trace walked around the room to make sure he hadn't missed anything and answered, "I'll sneak back later and re-lock it."

She frowned, clearly not liking the idea of him down here without her. "How?" she asked.

"I've got a few tricks." He shrugged. "I know how to pick open a lock. I should be able to close one, too."

Phoebe didn't seem to like this answer any better, but sighed and said, "Well, at least Sonny asked me to dance on Saturday. This room will be guarded tomorrow night. We may get to see the shipment coming on board, but we won't be able to open any of the crates. Let's hope whatever I over-hear during the cruise will be enough." She looked at Trace and must have clearly caught his scowl because she waved her hand, dismissive. "I forgot to tell you before. Sonny met me backstage after my first set and offered me the extra hours."

Trace pursed his lips, his teeth working the inside of his cheek. If his plan for tomorrow night worked, he'd have most of his answers after the shipment came and have his story in the bag. And Phoebe's private dancing would no longer be an issue.

Phoebe eyed him. "You're taking my news a lot better than I thought you would."

He shrugged. "A lot can happen between now and Saturday."

Phoebe stood straighter. "What are you planning to do?"

"Why, take one of the seedlings, of course."

"Not by yourself you're not," Phoebe said, her expression dark. "I'm the one who told you about this shipment. If any-one gets one of these seedlings or whatever Mr. V. has in those crates, it's me."

But Trace didn't offer her any promises. They both knew that Sonny's guards would make the situation that much more arduous, not to mention dangerous. Instead, he switched off the light then took her hand and led her out of the hold.

IN THE END Phoebe got her way.

Later that night, when Trace was in Phoebe's bed, inside Phoebe, the most shocking thing happened. Unbelievable really, when he considered how screwed up things usually turned out for him.

It began when he was staring down into her eyes. They were going slow this time. Their fingers entwined, hands clasped together, each plunge and retreat too perfect to rush. The sensations more than just physical. The reality of her narrow heat around his erection was excruciating as he pushed his hips forward.

Phoebe gasped but didn't look away, never breaking the contact between them, and a strange tightness swelled behind his ribs. Then, at the apex of his next downstroke, she plain and simply blew him away. Well, that's what started it anyway. Her climax slammed through her and she arched her back, crying, "Oh, no. No, not yet...."

"Shh, you're perfect." He whispered, "Come for me," while he pressed deep then held still, knowing this would make her come harder. Which it did. And when he kissed her nipple and flicked it with his tongue, just as he suspected, she clamped down on him even tighter instead of easing off. He squeezed his eyes shut, his own muscles clenched against her contractions, the need to pump and thrust himself inside her a consuming pressure, but he wasn't ready to give in to the craving yet.

Trace's chest ached, and he knew why but couldn't face the reality of all he felt. Loving her when he knew better than to lose his heart. Instead, he focused completely on each ripple and tremor of her body, wishing he could bind her to him physically until she'd never want to leave his side. And after she stilled, he rubbed his pelvic bone against the tiny button where her pleasure centered, pressed in slow pulses that made her buck, and she cried out, "I love you," right before her final orgasm slammed through her.

Trace froze at her words, his heart skipping some essential beats, he was sure, but he couldn't do anything more productive than stare into her stunned face. She whimpered, whether in shock or horror he wasn't confident, but it didn't matter because the words triggered his own release and he threw back his head, a long "aaahhhhh" straining from his throat. And then he thought, *this time might actually kill me*, because he'd never wanted to hear the words so badly, and having her cry them out, even under duress, made his pulse pound fast enough that he was afraid he'd pass out. But they kept moving and straining together as he came in hot throbbing gushes while chills raced over his flesh. His scalp tingled and his arms shook and with one final gasp, he fell to his elbows.

He buried his face in her hair, unable to stop smiling or drinking in her unbelievable scent...or stop smiling. He managed a quick laugh and tried to raise his head so he could talk to her, look into her eyes. But he couldn't move. His neck was limp, the muscles in his shoulders and at the top of his back trembled. And in that moment of absolute emotional and physical perfection, he knew nothing mattered more than Phoebe. Not his story. Not even his career. Without her, Trace didn't care where the hell he worked or what the hell he did. He'd write obituaries if that's what it took for him to be with her. Anything to feel like this every night and every day. It was too good.

"Did you mean it?" he asked, unable to catch his breath.

Phoebe didn't answer for what seemed like an eternity. Then finally, a wealth of reluctance obvious in her voice, she said, "Yes."

Except Trace could live with her lack of enthusiasm because he knew she wouldn't lie. He smiled even bigger then gasped out, "Excellent." Then he realized what he had to do, and the decision felt good and right. "Tomorrow night after I dance..." He paused briefly, realizing that at this moment even the thought of dancing couldn't depress him, and he went on, "You and me, we'll meet outside the dressing room." He took a quick breath. "After my last set, we'll go down to the hold together. I'll get it for you." Trace shook his head and explained, "The plant. Whatever Sonny brings on-board. We'll find it. You and me. We'll get the evidence to Alvarez. That's more important than my story."

Phoebe stilled, not even breathing. "What did you say?"

He mumbled with a grin, "You heard me."

"Are you serious?" He nodded into her neck and Phoebe hugged him hard enough to squeeze the air out of his lungs. She tried to push on his shoulders to make him lift up but he merely shifted his weight off her.

Trace knew he was doing the right thing for the woman he loved, and languor and contentment spread through. Then it dawned on him that he hadn't told her the words—that he loved her, too. But he couldn't keep his eyes open. They were too heavy. And right before he nodded off he thought, *I'll tell her tomorrow. There's plenty of time. All the time in the world...because I'm never letting her go.* Then, wearing what was probably the goofiest, most satisfied smile known to man, he fell asleep.

10

TRACE KNELT behind the huge crate, Phoebe crouched next to him. Her hand squeezed his in a killer grip. She was scared and with damn good reason. Sonny was more alert last night, checking out every little noise as if they feared a squadron of DEA agents were hiding down here in the hold.

The lady was also more than just a little jealous after watching him dance again, Trace thought with a grin. Though he supposed he shouldn't enjoy the idea so much. He knew she was feeling insecure after her heated declaration last night in bed. But he'd needed to leave her apartment this morning before she'd woken up and they hadn't had a chance yet to talk everything through. A man with a mission, Trace had had quite the busy day.

First, he'd stopped by the *Intruder* and quit. He couldn't look Phoebe in the eye as long as he still worked for that rag and he planned on looking into her eyes a whole hell of a lot. For the rest of his life, as a matter of fact, and he would find a job somewhere else. After that, he'd gone shopping. Smiling to himself, Trace brought Phoebe's left hand to his lips then kissed the smooth skin on her third finger. She shot him a funny look, which he returned with a wink. She'd understand soon enough.

But before he could grow even more smug with excitement, the voice Trace now easily recognized as Joey's interrupted his thoughts. "Where do you want this one, Sonny?"

Trace looked around the side of the crate, Phoebe peeking over his shoulder.

"Stick that in Renaldo's room." Sonny pointed to a room identical to the one Phoebe and Trace had hidden in last night. There were three of these special rooms in all, the doors wide open and spilling light into the hold. Then Sonny looked at the other man. "Bobby, you take yours to Delefluente's. And both of you dump that dirt out on those tables Mr. V. put in there."

"We're friggin' gardeners," Joey grumbled.

Sonny made a rude sound. "Breathing gardeners. Remember, it don't have to be that way." Before long, both men were back, and Sonny pointed to the next crate—this one had wider slats with large spaces between. He told Bobby, "That one goes into Mr. V.'s room, so be careful. He'll be down later to set up those damn plants." Water dripped from the bottom of the crate as Bobby lifted its weight.

Trace glanced at Phoebe. She nodded back. At least the plant issue had been confirmed, though, so far, any chances of seeing them firsthand didn't look good. Until he noticed Phoebe's eyes widen and she pointed behind him. Trace turned just as a small dark object fluttered to the floor as Bobby carted off his load. Then again, Trace thought with a smile, things might be looking up after all. Damn, Phoebe was turning out to be a lot better at this than he'd given her credit for.

Sonny pointed to another box and said to Joey, "Mr. V. said to take this last one up to him now. He wants to make more sauce. He's in the kitchen, waiting." Sonny had raised his voice so both men could hear, but then he suddenly paused. Eyes narrowed, he took another look around. "I gotta funny feeling," he said gruffly, then trailed off. He grunted, shaking his head. "Bobby, you stay down here and start setting up. Mr. V. said to get these onto the table, pronto. If even one of his babies dies, it's on your hands. So, I don't want any of these rooms left alone between now and Saturday night. *Capisce?*"

Bobby poked his head out of Mr. V.'s storage room. "Yeah, yeah, I got it. We stand around playing guard dog until after the meeting this weekend."

"More like baby-sitters," Joey complained.

Sonny grunted. "You two idiots have it easy. When Renaldo and Delefluente get here tomorrow, they'll have their own people. Quit complaining. Between all of you idiots, you should get the job done."

"At least Mr. V. can't make me eat nothin' if I'm stuck down here makin' mud pies," Bobby muttered.

"What? You're hungry again?" Joey snickered. "Hey, when I go upstairs, I'll tell Mr. V. you didn't get no dinner. He'll love to hear how you asked special like for more of his spaghetti. With extra sauce."

"Don't you say nothin'," Bobby shouted, but Sonny and Joey were already walking away, the second man's obnoxious laughter floating back. Bobby cursed then went back into Mr. V.'s room. After a minute, Trace heard the sound of dirt hitting the plywood table.

"Stay here," Trace whispered to Phoebe. He silently crept toward the small, dark spot on the ground. He lifted it and ran his finger over the dewy surface. Recognizing the soft texture of a damp leaf, he smiled then slipped it into his pocket. This little baby would be enough for the police lab to identify what Mr. V. was smuggling.

Back at Phoebe's side, Trace held his finger to his lips to stop her from voicing any questions right now. He took her hand in his. But the second they were in the hallway that ran backstage, Phoebe opened her mouth.

"What is it, what did you find?"

Trace frowned. "Lower your voice. It's a leaf." They were too close to succeeding to let their guards down now.

Her eyes glowed. "That's what I thought. Great. Let me have it. I'll take it straight to Alvarez when we get home.

There should be people in the department who'll be able to figure out what plant it comes from, right?"

Trace nodded absently, scanning the hallway. "It's not safe to talk here." He dropped his eyebrows. "Crap. Someone's coming."

Phoebe's gaze shot down the corridor. "Quick, give me the leaf," she whispered.

Trace shook his head as one of the male dancers rounded the corner. "I'll meet you at your apartment." Then he kissed her hard and ducked into the men's dressing room. Smiling, he knew she was frustrated. But he'd bring her the evidence tonight, although she'd have a small wait before handing Alvarez her precious leaf. Because Trace had plans that would keep her busy until morning....

PHOEBE PACED back and forth across Tiffany's living room. Annoyed with herself, she stopped and took a deep breath then let it out slowly. She had no reason to be nervous just because Trace was a little late. Everything was going as planned. Once she gave Alvarez the leaf they'd know exactly what they were dealing with, and after that, it was simply a matter of being patient until Saturday night.

She plopped down onto the couch with a sigh. Too bad her personal life wasn't shaping up as easily. She could almost hear herself now, telling Trace she loved him as she came her brains out. Phoebe groaned, her face hot while she stretched out on the sofa. Unfortunately, her embarrassing declaration to Trace changed nothing other than making it all the harder when they finally went their separate ways. Because as much as she may wish otherwise, she could never have a future with Trace.

Even though she'd been wrong these past nine years in thinking that Trace had thrown her over for another woman, if she were honest with herself there was a part of her that feared it would eventually happen. Men may fall in love, but it didn't last. Especially men who looked like Trace. There was always a willing woman somewhere and usually more than one. A lot more. She was talking into the double digits here. Heck, her own father—the most handsome man she'd ever known besides Trace—had taught her that lesson and she hadn't forgotten. From childhood she'd known that in a competition, the other woman won every time.

Phoebe rubbed her forehead. Of course, she was probably getting herself all worked up over nothing. Trace hadn't exactly been dropping the hints that he was after more than great sex. She stopped and frowned, the thought depressing her far more than it should, and to distract herself she went back to worrying over what was keeping him. She bit her lip and glanced at the clock. He'd had plenty of time to get here by now. Then she heard a knock on the front door and almost wilted with relief.

"I was so worried," she said, swinging open the door, but it was Alvarez who scowled down at her.

"Good. I am, too. Where's the reporter?"

Phoebe's mouth dropped open. "Reporter?"

Alvarez brushed past her and walked into the living room. He took over the path she'd earlier been wearing into the carpet. "Don't play games with me. I'm not even close to being in the mood. Just tell me, do I have a friggin' case left or did you blab everything?"

Slowly, she closed the door, her mind scrambling for a rational response. "I'm not sure I know who you're talking about—"

Alvarez interrupted, shooting her a dark look. "Yes, you do. I'm talking about the guy who's spent the last three nights here." The detective made a rude sound in his throat. "Everything was going good, so I figured it was none of my business who the hell you shacked up with. I've seen the way your sister operates and wasn't all that surprised to find out you were the same." He shook his head, clearly disgusted with himself. "I didn't get a good look at the bastard until I saw him leaving here this morning when I came by. I recognized him, but it didn't hit me till tonight from where. He interviewed me for an article a couple of years back. A murder case. He used to be with the *Herald*, but I had him checked out. Now he's with the *Intruder*, though I doubt he's writing his story on Venzara for that piece of trash."

Phoebe's heart seemed to stop then began pounding out of control, but he didn't give her a chance to interrupt.

"Knowing my luck, lover boy is probably turning in his story right now."

Frantically, she shook her head. "No, no. I promise. Trace is coming over here right now. He's on his way." Phoebe knew she could either come clean now or make everything worse by trying to pass off a string of lies. "Listen, I can explain everything," she pleaded. "It's not as bad as it looks."

Alvarez scowled and opened his mouth, but Phoebe rushed on. "Do you remember me telling you about Candy's bachelorette party?"

The detective's eyes narrowed, though he nodded, and she took his silence as permission to continue.

Phoebe swallowed. "Okay, good. That's good. I ran into Trace at the party. He was there as—" she hesitated, her face going hot "—well, as the stripper, of all things," she said, then forced herself to laugh. "I used to know him in college when I lived here in Miami. We were friends, I guess you'd say." Alvarez rolled his eyes, but she hurried forward with her explanation. "I'm not r-really used to drinking," she stammered, "and he drove me home. The next morning, he heard me talking to Tiffany on the phone and knew I was lying about my reasons for dancing on the *Mirage*. You were on your way over and I tried to get rid of him, but we started to argue and Trace was worried about me. He told me the truth then, but I didn't know what to do."

Alvarez's skin looked flushed. "So that's what you were

hiding when we talked. I knew something was up, but you distracted me with that crap about Tony Venzara and the island, so I let it pass."

Phoebe squeezed her hands together, her fingertips going white. "I felt so guilty, but Trace is a friend. Protecting him was my only choice," she said beseechingly. "Besides, even if I had blown his cover, he could have turned right around and done the same to mine. Don't you see? At that point, he'd have had nothing to lose. One word about me dropped to the wrong person on the *Mirage* and it would have all been over. But none of that matters anymore," she said hurriedly, jumping to the important part. "Trace is helping me. Really. He's given up on the story until your investigation is finished, so we're fine."

The detective gaped. "Tell me you don't actually believe that."

Phoebe couldn't afford to hesitate with her answer, though with each minute that ticked by without Trace showing up, her own doubts grew by leaps and bounds. "Yes. I do. Trace has been a huge help right from the start. He even found a leaf off one of the plants Mr. V. brought on board tonight." A slight exaggeration but close enough. "Trace is bringing it over now. Oh, and you should know, there are three climate-controlled rooms down in the *Mirage*'s hold. One for Mr. V. The other two for Renaldo and Delefluente. I was going to tell you when I brought you the leaf."

Alvarez snorted, though he seemed slightly less upset. "Let's hope it still matters. If your boyfriend is off turning in his article and it shows up in tomorrow's paper, Venzara will stop using the *Mirage* and switch to another method for his smuggling. And I'll be back to square one. I can't do a damn thing about what he does on that island. It's out of the country."

Phoebe twisted her hands together. The only thing she could think to say was, "Trace will be here. I know it."

He cursed, glaring at the clock on the mantel. "Then I'm sure you won't mind if I just wait here for him to show up."

AN HOUR LATER, Alvarez got to his feet. "He's not coming."

"Wait, Trace'll be—"

"He's not coming. Whatever he found down in that hold is long gone. From now until the end of this investigation, you stay away from him. After that, I don't care what the hell you do," the detective said, not stopping on his way to the foyer.

Phoebe made a noise. "So that's it?"

"I can't exactly arrest the man for tampering with evidence, since you all but gift wrapped whatever fell off that plant for him." Alvarez stopped at the door and looked back at her. "But while we've been sitting here I've had time to think. I'm pretty sure McGraw is going to wait until he knows exactly what Venzara is doing with those seedlings before he tries to sell his story. If I'm right, I may still have a case. But not for long. Lover boy already has the advantage by having whatever you two found tonight."

Phoebe shook her head, refusing to jump to conclusions, as she had nine years ago. "I know how this looks, but Trace wouldn't do this to me. Something must have happened. He'll be here. Besides, I told you that he promised to wait on his story until after you've wrapped up your case."

"Oh, he'll show up all right. Without the evidence. He'll have conveniently lost it or something along those lines. And there's no way in hell that reporter is backing off on this. The guy's selling you a line, Devereaux, so you'll keep him in the loop. So far it's working, too. He's got the evidence and we've got jack. I know the bastard's type. He's lying." Alvarez held up his hand when she would have jumped in to argue. "Just answer this. Do you know why he lost his job at the *Herald*?"

Phoebe's stomach dropped. She could pretend that there hadn't been time for Trace to explain, but the truth was, she hadn't asked. And though she hadn't wanted to know why he'd lost his job, his silence on the subject didn't exactly sit well with her, either. "No," she answered briefly.

Alvarez chuckled though he didn't sound amused. "He slept with his editor's daughter—during the paper's Christmas party. Got drunk and screwed her in the supply closet. On top of the copy machine, I heard, but that part could just be gossip. In either case, the woman's daddy made sure McGraw had a damn hard time finding another job. Ask him about it when he shows up."

Phoebe stared at Alvarez wide eyed, unsure at the moment of exactly how she felt. She hadn't given Trace the benefit of the doubt nine years ago, and part of her really believed that Trace had been telling the truth when he decided to wait on his article. She trusted him in matters that didn't include her heart. Nope, the detective's little revelation didn't make her mad, as much as resigned. Because she'd just been given a perfect example of why she could never feel secure with a man like Trace in a committed relationship. She opened her mouth then closed it, feeling everything inside her collapse with a rush, like a wilted balloon. After all, what could she possibly say to that?

"Finally," Trace grumbled as the lock clicked open. Sliding the pair of thin metal sticks back inside his coat, he didn't waste time once he got inside the apartment. No matter how hard he'd banged, Phoebe hadn't answered the door and he had a sinking feeling it wasn't just because she was fast asleep.

Stepping into her room, Trace winced at the empty bed then rubbed the bridge of his nose. Everything that could possibly have gone wrong in the last few hours had and did. He'd wanted tonight to be perfect and, so far, it had been anything but. Though, he supposed, the evening had started out well enough.

Not long after his and Phoebe's success down in the hold, the *Mirage* had docked and—his brain full of romantic images of all he had planned—Trace had gone home to shower and change. Thirty minutes later, with two dozen pale pink roses in hand and a diamond ring in the front pocket of his leather jacket, he'd headed straight for Phoebe's place. But that's where things had gotten tricky. Believing there was plenty of time, he'd decided to pick up some wine. What he hadn't planned to do was run over a broken beer bottle in the liquor-store parking lot. Unfortunately, he hadn't realized that he'd gotten a flat until a mile later when the thwumping noise from the front end of the car had grown loud enough to sound like a helicopter was landing on the roof.

Next had come the fun and antics of trying to jerk the deflated tire free. The darn lug nuts wouldn't budge an inch even though Trace had tugged hard enough to pop every blood vessel in his brain. Realizing that he was now going to be inexcusably late, he'd pulled out his cell phone to call Phoebe then promptly dropped it when a group of young women had driven by whooping and yelling out, "Sea Stud." The phone had skittered into traffic where it had been immediately demolished by a passing tow truck, the oblivious driver unfazed by the irony.

A mere two hours later and Trace was back on the road when he'd remembered the leaf. The leaf he'd accidentally left in his other pair of pants when he'd changed. But at that point, there was no way in hell he was going back to get it. As far as Trace was concerned, Alvarez could wait for his freaking evidence. After that, everything had been relatively easy. A quick break and enter, and here he was, standing outside Phoebe's bathroom door with her on the other side crying her heart out—if the sobs just barely audible over the pounding water from the shower were anything to go by.

Trace dropped the bouquet onto the dresser and set down the wine. He called out her name, not wanting to scare her as he walked inside. But once there, he hesitated, staring at her blurry image through the steamy glass, his pulse racing.

"Phoebe?" He cursed under his breath. Yep, she was crying, all right. Hard. And it was all his fault. Unable to take a second more, Trace shrugged off his jacket then opened the glass door. She looked tiny standing in the corner. Of course, the shower was ridiculously huge and clearly designed for more than one person. More around five. Maybe six. Seven if a few of them were small.

Phoebe's eyes were red and swollen and Trace said, "Oh, kitten."

Her voice broke. "Wha-what are you doing here?" Tears dripped down her cheeks and mixed with the water pelting her body from all sides. And those damn mirrors Tiffany was so fond of even covered the walls in here, though they were now fogged from the steam.

Holy hell, he'd get good and soaked this time, but he couldn't let her cry over him a second more. Trying to smile, he teased her as he stepped inside, "Here as in, *here with you in the shower,* or here as in, *here inside your apartment?*"

She answered, her voice oddly flat and quiet, "Both. I didn't think you'd bother."

Trace frowned, making a tsking sound as he moved toward her, but she shrank from his touch and his stomach clenched. He hadn't fought for her nine years ago, but this time he'd make her listen. He crowded her to the wall, pressed himself against her from chest to hips. "I know it looks bad, but you have to let me explain."

She wouldn't meet his eyes. "Please don't. It was silly for me to expect you to wait on your story. I'm not mad. I should never have asked." She sounded tired, defeated, and that scared him even more.

"Don't do this. I know you, Phoebe. You wouldn't be so upset if you didn't care. I wanted everything to be perfect tonight, but instead everything went wrong. I didn't lie when I said I would help you. I'm not going to try to sell my article until you've done everything you have to for the police. I was just late, but I'm here now. Look at me." He could feel his heart pounding in his throat. "I got a flat tire and it took forever to change and then you wouldn't answer the door. I wasted another twenty minutes picking the damn lock. But I'll make it up to you. I promise."

Her expression blank, she asked, "Why didn't you call?"

Trace winced. "Well, uh, my cell phone got run over by a truck."

Phoebe briefly jerked her gaze to his, clearly not expecting that answer. "Oh. Did you bring the leaf?"

Cursing, he rubbed the back of his neck. "No, I left it in my other pants. I wanted to wear something nicer than jeans though I shouldn't have bothered." He gestured to the streak of grease smeared down the front of his now see-through white shirt. "I know this all sounds like I'm making it up as I go, but I swear—"

She shook her head then smiled sadly. "I told you before. I'm not mad." Phoebe laughed softly. "Part of me even thinks you're telling the truth. But it doesn't really matter."

"The hell it doesn't." His voice rose. "How can you say that? If you love me it matters." She didn't respond and every muscle in his body tensed. "You meant it, didn't you? When you said that you loved me." This time he took her shoulders. "Phoebe?"

"Yes. Of course I meant it." Her voice broke. "I love you, but it doesn't change a thing. It's not enough. We can't just turn away from—"

"Not enough?" he interrupted, hugging her close, his body trembling. "You're crazy. It's more than enough. It's perfect." She tried to push away and then it dawned on him. "You silly thing. You want the words, don't you? You're not sure how I feel and want to hear them back." He laughed and hugged her tighter. "I love you, kitten." Trace kissed her hard, then smiling, said, "I've never said the words before to a woman who's not my mother. Well, maybe my sisters, but only on big holidays or their birthdays. But no one else. I haven't wanted to. I've been saving them for you. I love you." She groaned and shook her head, but he cupped her face. "I love you," he whispered, "so...damn...much...." Then Trace licked into her mouth. "Let me show you...." He spoke softly against her lips.

Phoebe started to shake her head, but then groaned, suddenly blurting, "Show me." She sounded anxious, as if she didn't want to give herself time to change her mind. "Right now," she gasped. "Don't wait."

But she wasn't acting right. He didn't want her desperate like this. "Shh," he quieted her, uneasy with all she wasn't saying. "There's no rush...I'm going to show you over, and over, and over," he chanted, punctuating each declaration with a long drugging kiss. Tonight was about her. He'd use every skill on Phoebe's body he'd wasted his time perfecting with other women. He'd worship her, drown her in pleasure, until nothing existed except them, together. One person. Because for him, nothing else mattered.

PHOEBE PANTED through her mouth, her throat and eyes burning. His words echoed through her mind. He loved her, he loved her.... But he didn't know her. Not really. The woman Trace believed he'd fallen in love with didn't even exist. Some brave and wild alter ego. Ready to live life for the moment and damn the consequences. But that was all an act. She'd only been able to pull this off because she'd known that eventually she'd go back to the same boring old Phoebe she was at home.

"Don't cry," Trace whispered.

She ducked her chin, and clung tightly to his chest. Phoebe knew that he believed they were going to be together, but knowing he loved her only made her more determined to end this now before it was too late. Dragging the pain out to the bitter end would be cruel to them both. Already she'd allowed herself to become too attached, their relationship no longer about some stupid plan to change herself and live wildly, but about love. The kind of love that could take over until nothing else mattered.

"Please don't cry." He kissed her eyes, her nose, her chin. Frowning, he reached over to turn off the water. "Come on, let's dry you off." He took her hand and began to lead her from the shower, when he glanced down at himself. Grinning, he said, "You and this room are a deadly combination for my clothes." He kicked off his shoes. The rest soon followed, pushed aside into a wet clump on the tile.

As he walked her to the towels, she devoured every inch of his damp skin with her gaze. This was their last time and she felt an almost frantic need to commit the tiniest of details to memory so she could pull the images out later when she was alone.

While he dried her off, their eyes met. He tapped her nose. "If I see one more tear, I'll bite you," he said, easily reading her.

And Phoebe realized that she needed to get a grip on her emotions. Any second, he'd start questioning her, probing her for the truth behind why she was so upset, and she couldn't let that happen. She needed this last time with him too much. Phoebe took a shaky breath before turning for the bedroom. Over her shoulder, she taunted him, "And that's supposed to make me stop, right? Pretty poor incentive, McGraw. Why don't you come and make me...."

"How about I just make you come?" was his quick response as he followed her to bed.

11

TRACE PRESSED his lips to the button of flesh between her legs. His fingers dug into her thighs while she strained against his mouth, and with infinite care he bit down on her hood. "Damn, you're sweet."

Panting, Phoebe gasped for breath. "Okay, I'm sorry I teased you. You were right. Your bite is torture."

He laughed then nipped her again before licking away the sting, and she groaned. "I think I've proved my point," he said, chuckling softly. He slid up her body, catching his elbows beneath her knees.

"Yes," she panted, "you certainly did. Four times over by my last count."

Trace grunted. "Five," he said, thinking a certain amount of smugness on his part was deserved.

She wrapped her arms around his neck and tried to tug his weight down on top of her. "Only if you count that last one as two."

"Cripes, woman. That two-for-one deal was nothing short of heroic. I deserve a medal for time and effort given in the line of duty."

She shivered and licked his lower lip. "You certainly do. As a matter of fact, I'm done with keeping score. I'll never catch up."

Laughing, he capped himself in her heat and her eyes flared. He gritted his teeth as her tight sheath trembled around the head of his arousal. "Now, let's see if we can try to end this together." And Trace slid so deep, he swore he could touch her heart. They moved and strained together for what could have been minutes but felt like hours until he knew he'd burst. A tear trembled on her lashes and right when it spilled over she arched her back and cried out, "I love you," and Trace swallowed her words with his mouth as if he could trap them inside him. Then he felt his own body tense in release, and reality simply fell away.

Moments later, he panted for air, his head hanging between his shoulders as he slowly returned to earth. He told himself this was the right time, yet his pulse bolted like a runaway horse. *Do it. Do it. While you're still buried deep inside her and her scream is ringing in your ear....*

"Marry me," Trace blurted, then held his breath. All right. So that proposal probably wouldn't go down in the annals of history as the most romantic or well thought out. But he'd meant it. Forget the wine and the flowers. The fancy jewelry box in his coat. He didn't want it choreographed, didn't want to churn out some contrived declaration. He wanted her to agree to be his wife while the sweat dried on their skin from the most incredible experience of their lives. It sure as hell had been for him and he refused to believe it had been anything less for her.

She mumbled something indecipherable from beneath him.

Trace lifted his head and flicked his hair from his eyes. "Was that a yes?" He tried to laugh. "Because I should probably tell you that it's the only answer I'm willing to except."

"Thank you," she said through her yawn. "You're heavy, hon. Do you mind moving?"

He gritted his teeth. "You're welcome. Yes, I'll move. And answer my question."

She blinked sleepily. "Hmm? What are you talking about?"

Anxiety and the sheer terror of rejection made him abrupt. "I just proposed. You slept through it. You're a woman and probably wouldn't have thought much of my delivery anyway, so I won't bother repeating it. But the deal's still on the table. What'll it be?"

Her eyes snapped open. "You proposed?"

His shoulders tensed and any lethargy that might have remained from his phenomenal orgasm flew out the window.

She gave him a funny smile while her hands fluttered at his shoulders. Her laugh sounded forced. "I'm a little confused here. Are you saying that you asked me to marry you and that if I was a man I'd find your proposal acceptable?"

Trace scowled. "Not funny. Unless you turn me down." His entire nervous system went haywire waiting for her response, and as he stared down at Phoebe, her bottom lip began to tremble. Then quiver. Then shake out of control. And before he could convince himself that this was a good thing and what every woman probably does before saying, *yes, darling, of course I'll marry you. You've made me the happiest woman in the world,* she burst into tears. Big noisy sobs that shattered any illusions he'd had left.

"Why do I get the feeling these aren't tears of joy?" he asked flatly. Probably because he'd been dumped on his whole life and by this point was pretty well able to gauge the signs. He rolled off her, wincing as he pulled out. Hands shaking, he removed his condom and walked into the bathroom. His lungs wouldn't expand. She was going to say no and he could hardly fathom the reality of it. He ground the heels of his palms into his eyes. Why? Why would she do this?

Anger was his only defense, a relief from the betrayal searing his chest. When he got back to her, he tossed a wad of toilet paper on the sheets. "Blow your nose and tell me what the hell is going on."

"Oh, Trace, I can't marry you." She sat up and wiped her eyes.

Hearing her come out and say it was like getting punched

in the stomach. His knees felt ready to give out and he couldn't seem to breathe past the lump in his throat. He slumped down on the side of the bed, his elbows on his knees, his head heavy between his shoulders. He had to clear his throat twice. "Why not?"

"I should have talked to you earlier," she choked out. "Let me clean up. I'll be right back." And there was nothing for him to say to that.

When Phoebe returned, she'd brushed her hair and put on a thick chenille robe. He snorted. As if he didn't know exactly what she looked like down to the tiniest detail under that mountain of bulk. Her eyes were even puffier than before and she kept sniffing into her tissue. She cast him a quick glance. "This would probably be a bit easier if you'd put on some clothes."

He didn't sound very nice when he answered her, but then, at the moment, he didn't feel very nice. "I ruined mine back in the shower. I'm down another pair of shoes, too."

Her voice was hoarse. "I'm sorry."

He rubbed his hands over his face and laughed. If he didn't, he was afraid he'd cry even harder than Phoebe. "I'm out another heart, too. This is the second time you've stomped mine into the ground."

"Oh, Trace. You don't understand."

"*There's* a news flash." A muscle ticked in his jaw and then he rose to his feet and began pacing the length of the room. "Explain to me what the hell is going on here, kitten, because I'm jumping to conclusions and none of them are pretty." He wasn't, but that was only because he was incapable of thought.

She twisted her hands together and gave him a pleading look.

Trace had to turn away from her. "Save the puppy-dog eyes. I may be a lot of things but I don't screw with people's heads. Stop messing with mine." His voice caught and he swallowed before going on. "Do you enjoy this? Is this some kind of payback for whatever you think I did to you in college?"

"No." She sucked in her breath. "It's nothing like that. Oh, Tr—"

"If you say 'oh, Trace' one more time..."

Phoebe's hand brushed his back. She'd sneaked up on him unnoticed and he turned and pulled her into his arms. He buried his face in her neck. "Why are you doing this to me? To yourself? Hell, kitten, even I can see you're miserable. What do you want me to do? What can I say?"

Gently she twisted free. She walked to the dresser where the roses sat wilting in the crisp florist paper. When he'd seen the blooms they'd immediately brought to mind a little girl's ballet slippers, the same subtle yet pure shade of pink, and he'd bought every stem.

Phoebe shook her head. "The woman you love doesn't exist," she said, and though he had no idea where she was going with this crazy line of thought, he was afraid to interrupt.

Clearly agitated, she tugged and twisted with the belt on her robe as she spoke. "I pretended to be so different than I was in college, you know—" she waved her hand "—wild and impulsive. That's why I let Tiffany talk me into this whole mess. Helping out with the police and everything because the idea sounded kind of exciting. But after this is all over, I'll go back to being the same old Phoebe." She laughed hoarsely. "Maybe not so uptight and nervous, but still pretty unexciting. Normally I'm a ballet teacher, nowhere close to the showgirl I've been these past few days. You probably wouldn't even like me, really."

"Of course I would, kitten." Trace raised his hands to his hair, all but tugging the stuff out at the roots as he roughly ran his fingers through. "I've all but begged you to stop dancing on that damn ship. I'm thrilled that you don't want to be a showgirl. You're not making sense."

Phoebe groaned and turned away. "I'm not saying this right. It's not just the dancing, it's who I really am. You'd hate me within a week. Your feelings are based on a person who doesn't exist. I mean, come on, Trace—" she faced him, her eyes pleading with his "—you know how much I drove you crazy when we were in college. My idea of a fun Saturday night is renting a movie and eating too much chocolate. Yours involves multiple women and undercover writing."

She scowled at her *multiple women* accusation, then looked away, rubbing her forehead. "I didn't mean for this to happen. I didn't know I'd fall so hard or so fast." She turned toward him, her gaze imploring him to understand. "Don't you see? Eventually it won't work. I want a family. Kids. A husband who'll be around all the time. You know, fight over *Wheel of Fortune* with me or rent stupid movies at the video store. These last few days aside, I'm basically a very boring person. You're not." She laughed helplessly and shrugged. "I don't even know why you're with me in the first place. You could have any woman you want."

A muscle ticked in his jaw. "Apparently not. And how do you know that I don't want the same things from marriage?"

Phoebe sighed. "Give me a break, Trace. How many boring men do you know who'd take off their clothes in front of hundreds of women for a story? Being a showgirl was different for me. At least I was already a dancer and used to performing in front of an audience."

Trace stood perfectly still. This was too much. Phoebe was rejecting him for supposedly not wanting the very things he'd dreamed of all his life. He scowled and held out his arms. "This is ridiculous. I'm the most boring guy I know. I haven't even been on a date for almost half a year."

Phoebe pursed her lips. "Hmm? I guess that would have been back around the holidays, right? Back when you so boringly copulated with your editor's daughter on top of a copy machine. During the Christmas party, I believe." She nodded sarcastically. "You're right. It's hard to find a man much tamer than that."

Trace narrowed his eyes. Pressure rose through him from his feet to the top of his head with enough force to make his hair blow off. "I did not have sex with that woman. Yes, I was drunk. Yes, she attacked me. Yes, I didn't feel I could fend her off by winding up and punching my editor's daughter." He turned away, unable to look at Phoebe without shaking her. Or begging. That was a big possibility, too.

Phoebe lifted her hands to her head. "You can't just change who you are at the drop of a hat because you stick a ring on some woman's finger and say I do. Or decide to have a few Trace juniors running around." Her words stopped her and she blinked then looked away. "And then where would I be? The woman holding you back. Keeping you from being happy and fulfilled. Besides, you may want me now, but the feeling will go away. That's how it is with men. Especially men like you."

He stilled and slowly turned his head toward her. No. *Please, God, tell me I'm not hearing this,* he thought. It would be too priceless that after all this time he was still being hung with the same frigging rope he'd been twisting from since he was old enough to know the difference between boys and girls. "What kind of man am I, Phoebe?" he asked softly.

She waved her hand and looked away. "Please don't make me spell this out. You know you're every woman's fantasy come to life." Her cheeks flooded with color. "Jeesh, when you performed tonight, those screaming females all but rushed the stage. I've never seen so much cash all in one place. Heck, bank robbers don't even see that much cash in one place. And it was all being thrown at you. Keep dancing for a few more weeks and you'll be able to finance your own newspaper."

Trace stared hard at a point over her shoulder. "I told you, I love you. I would never cheat on the person I love."

"You love me now, but what about five years from now? Ten? Feelings are different for men. They fade over time and just go away...." Phoebe's mouth twisted bitterly. "A man can love his children one day and then, poof, he's got a blonde with boobs and now she's getting the bedtime stories, but not the kind he told to his little girls." Her movements jerky, she wiped the back of her hand across her eyes. "A decade from now you'll look even better than you do today while my backside will be down around my ankles. Trust me on this. I know. My father makes Cary Grant look like he didn't age well. He's just like you. Witty and charming. So handsome you could cry—and if you're part of his family, you will. I can't go through that again."

Trace rubbed his jaw. His nostrils flared as he tried to slow his breathing. "Do you know why I became a reporter?"

His question took her off guard. "No," she said hesitantly. "Not really. I guess because you like to write."

"No." He narrowed his eyes and shook his head slowly. "I like the truth. Not what people want to hear, not what they want to believe, but cold, hard reality. Do you know why?" he bit out.

Her expression leery, Phoebe shook her head.

"You weren't the only kid with a father who screwed around. Except I had to face up to that fact every day of my life." He laughed harshly. "I can remember the folks in my hometown. I'd walk down the street and the rumors would start flying. 'There goes Pat McGraw's kid,' they'd say. 'Takes after his old man. Wild. A heartbreaker.' Never mind that my own heart had been broken before I was old enough to understand that my dad wasn't coming back. It didn't matter that I'd never seen the son of a bitch since I could walk. They just believed what they wanted and nothing I did would convince them otherwise."

Trace made a harsh sound in his throat. "And sure enough, some girl would end up pregnant and the whispers would start. Of course, the kid was mine. It had to be. After all, my father nailed every willing female that came across his path. What did it matter that I was twelve years old the first time I was accused? Or fourteen? Or sixteen? Or every frigging year thereafter? That I had to work full-time because my mother slaved to take care of her six kids and she needed every scrap of money to help? That I'd rather die than leave a woman to face what my mother lived through? What I lived through. Hell, I'm handsome. I'll take whatever piece of tail I can get." He sneered, his anger ice cold. "The main reason I hated working at the *Intruder* wasn't just the stupid stories. What really ate at me was knowing that my hard work at the *Herald* went down the toilet because some woman decided she wanted to score. I never touched her, but what did that matter? Her daddy didn't care. Hell, she didn't care, either. And the whole load of garbage was swallowed by anyone who'd listen because of who I am. How I look."

Phoebe stood frozen, her eyes wide. He had no idea if his words had gotten through to her or not, but in this case the truth behind Phoebe's rejection disgusted him. Frankly, he would rather have faced a lie. He felt sick to his stomach and, turning away, went into the bathroom and got his wet pants from the floor of the shower. He forced his legs into the ice-cold fabric, ignoring the chills puckering his skin. Swiping his keys off the counter, he saw his jacket on the floor. He put it on then fingered the square box in the pocket. Hell, he still just might cry after all. She was determined to throw away the best thing that had ever happened to him.

On the way out, their eyes met one last time. Trace spoke softly, ignoring the tears streaming down her face. "I thought you were different. I thought you knew me. But then I guess I thought a lot of stupid things. Sorry to have wasted your time, kitten." Then he walked away and out of her life—for good this time.

PHOEBE STARED into the darkness as the phone rang in the background. She knew it was Tiffany checking to see if she'd learned anything important earlier tonight during the shipment. The answering machine picked up and Tiffany's voice filled the darkened bedroom.

"All right, Phoebe. Where the heck are you? I've called three times. If you're screening your calls this is your last chance. If you don't answer, I'll know you're either dead in a ditch somewhere or in the hospital, and I'm calling Mom."

Phoebe picked up the phone. "How about I don't feel like talking because I just ruined my life?"

"You *are* there."

Phoebe could hear the relief in Tiffany's voice and felt a moment's guilt.

"So what's Mr. V. doing down in that room?" Tiffany asked. "Wait, don't tell me. You found out he's growing petunias in his basement."

Phoebe blew her nose. "Not exactly. But I know for sure Mr. V. is growing plants. Plants that are being guarded twenty-four hours a day."

"Then what's the problem? You're on the final stretch here."

"Nothing," she said on a drawn-out sigh.

Tiffany gasped. "Wait a second. I recognize that melancholy sound. You've met a man. I'm right, aren't I?" Her voice practically quivered with excitement. "What did you do to ruin it?"

"Thanks for the vote of confidence."

"Don't pout. I'm just good at what I know, and I know men. I also know you. So how did you screw it up?"

Phoebe bit her lip. "I fell in love with him."

"Fell in love with him? That was fast. But in your case fast is good. Keeps you from having too much time to think. Now, you just tell Tiff all about it and we'll come up with a way to make Mr. Wonderful fall madly in love."

Sniffing, Phoebe ran her wadded tissue under her nose. "That's not the problem. He's already told me he loves me. He even asked me to marry him. It's the worst thing that's ever happened."

"All right. Back it up. If you love him and he loves you then what's the holdup? Marry him and live happily ever after. Get pregnant and have babies. Our children can play together. You are aware of the fact that you're rapidly approaching the big 3-0, right?"

Phoebe took a deep breath, ignoring the reference to her status as a fossil, and said, "Well, for one, he's fallen in love with the person I've been pretending to be, not the real me." When Tiffany didn't appear suitably impressed, Phoebe added, "And he's handsome," she made this pronouncement as if Trace suffered from a deadly disease.

Tiffany sucked in her breath. "What a jerk. The nerve of the man. Falling in love with you when obviously you deserve a hideous troll." After this sarcastic bit, she said pleadingly, "Tell me you really didn't tell this guy to hit the road because he's easy on the eyes."

"Apparently I didn't explain myself. He's not just attractive. He's a hunk. One hundred percent gorgeous. Testosterone on the hoof." When Tiffany still didn't respond, Phoebe sighed and said, "Let's put it this way. He's better-looking than Dad."

"Holy crap. It's a wonder the poor guy got as far with you as he did. Where did you meet this doomed man?"

"On the *Mirage*. But I know him from college. I sort of used to have a crush on him."

"Are we talking about that young god who for some reason ignored the fact that you're a lamebrain and chased you for four straight years?"

"No. The other guy I had a crush on," Phoebe said dryly.

Tiffany grunted. "This is no time for jokes unless I'm telling them. What was he doing on the *Mirage*?"

"Trace is a reporter. He's trying to get information for a story on Mr. V. Sort of like me, except Trace is actually good at his cover."

"Which is?"

"He's one of the male strippers."

Tiffany choked. "No way. Tell me he's not this Sea Stud person the girls keep talking about."

"All right, I won't."

Tiffany huffed. "I swear, Phoebes, sometimes you make me so mad I could kill you. Why on earth are you home crying when you could be in bed with this guy?"

"I was the first two times you called. Then he asked me to marry him. I said no and he left."

Her little sister groaned. "Phoebe, Phoebe...what am I going to do with you?"

"Eat chocolate with me. You're pregnant and I'm depressed. For the first time in our lives we should be in complete munchy agreement."

"I was thinking something more along the lines of a good swift kick in the butt."

"I'd prefer the chocolate."

"I'm sure you would. Then you could go on pretending that you're not a walking case study of the Oedipus complex."

Phoebe stiffened. "What on earth are you talking about?"

"I assume you gave this Trace person some cock-and-bull line about how you don't want to end up with a man like Dad."

Phoebe's lips parted. "How did you know that?"

"Oh, please. You're painfully predictable on this. Your only relationships have been with men who could've served as founding members of Middle-Aged Dorks Anonymous. Meanwhile, you're beautiful and funny. A bit of a dork yourself, but nothing that the right man wouldn't overlook. Phoebe, you don't want a husband, you want a father. But that will never work because eventually you'll take what you need, mature and grow, then wish you had a mate, not a parent."

Phoebe pulled the phone away from her ear then stared at it. When she brought it back to her mouth, she said, "Who the hell is this I'm talking to?"

Tiffany ignored her. "The fact is, Phoebe, you've been hiding your head in the sand over Mom and Dad for a long time and I haven't bothered to correct you because I know how upset you get. But Dad loves us and would be a completely different person if Mom wasn't insanely jealous of her own daughters. Why do you think Dad was always so scared to pay any attention to us? Still is, for that matter?"

Phoebe opened her mouth then closed it. After a moment she said, "But that's not right. If he loves us he should stand up to her."

Tiffany sighed. "I didn't say that he isn't screwed up himself. In spite of what you may think, he loves her, too. Why else would he stay with her?"

"Mom's a convenience. A hostess for his parties—"

"Yeah, that's Mommie Dearest all right. So warm and approachable to her guests. Especially the female ones. Not!" Tiffany gave a frustrated growl. "The point of telling you all this is to make you realize that Mom and Dad have created their own mess. Not because Dad didn't love us but because Mom's a neurotic she-wolf who never should have reproduced."

"Well, thanks for clearing that up. I feel much better."

Tiffany snorted. "You'll feel much better when you realize that loving a man who has the ability to get a date other than yourself is a good thing. You wouldn't know since you haven't tried it but, believe me, it's not to be underestimated. And as far as this guy only being interested because you've become such a *wild woman*..." Tiffany said this last part with such disbelief there was no mistaking her meaning. "If I recall, he was crazy about you back in college when you were a confirmed loser. What did he say when you explained how boring you really are, and that he'd have to be an idiot not to despise you?"

Phoebe stared at her lap, worrying her bottom lip. "He claimed that he was boring, too. Something about not having a date in ages, and junk like that. But I think he knew it was what I wanted to hear."

"Oh, yeah. Men usually come up with all sorts of lies to get women to marry them. The needy fools, so anxious to settle down and give up their freedom. If this jerk is telling you that he wants you over all the other women that throw themselves at him, then don't listen. It's the oldest line in the book."

Stunned, Phoebe could only gape silently. Then finally, no longer able to hide or avoid the truth, Phoebe groaned, her eyes stinging painfully. "Oh, Tiffany, how'd you get so smart? And why aren't you locked up in a rubber room somewhere after the childhood from hell?"

"Because of you, Phoebe. All because of you. So if you love Trace then trust yourself."

Phoebe groaned. "I really think I blew it this time."

"Then fix it. Now. And for heaven's sake, do not wear your nerd clothes when you chase him down and beg his forgiveness. Look in my closet and wear the tightest thing you can find. Remember, nothing says I love you like a short spandex skirt."

"Last week you said that nothing says I love you like going without underwear."

Tiffany laughed. "Use the underwear trick with a spandex skirt and he'll be singing 'here comes the bride' before the poor man knows what hit him."

TWO DAYS LATER, Phoebe slammed down the phone. Trace was either dead or avoiding her. And after an unbearably long forty-eight hours she didn't know which possibility was worse. He'd tended bar again last night, but by the time she'd gotten off the stage he'd disappeared. Other than the plain envelope slipped under her door yesterday, containing the infamous leaf, Trace might as well have slipped off the face of the earth.

She'd taken the stupid piece of greenery to Alvarez this morning and should soon have some sort of results. Otherwise, the last two days had been painfully uneventful. Yes, Renaldo and Delefluente had arrived with their men, but like Mr. V., neither of the pair were the scariest of fellows. Both short and round with bushy mustaches, they more resembled a real-life Super Mario and his brother, Luigi.

Phoebe was tired of worrying about the whole mess, so, her stomach growling, she headed for the kitchen. She hadn't been to the grocery store recently, and rooted through Tiffany's cabinets hoping to find a can of soup or maybe some macaroni and cheese that she could whip up, boxed or canned foods being the extent of her culinary abilities.

Shoving packages aside, her hand landed on a mason jar of Mr. V.'s deep red sauce. Phoebe grinned and wrinkled her nose, the thought of another serving of Mr. V.'s homemade marinara more than she could stomach at the moment. Poor Bobby hadn't been the only one over the last two days who'd been forced to eat a few plates of spaghetti. Angelo Venzara cornered anyone and everyone who worked on his ship to try his latest recipe. But as she went to move the jar aside, her gaze landed on the paper label glued to the back of the glass, the words Filleto Di Pomodoro leaping out at her. *Filleto Di Pomodoro.* Phoebe's hands stilled and she shook her head.

"No, it couldn't be," she whispered. "Filleto Di Pomodoro...Isola Pomodoro..." The words, the names, were so similar. Inexplicably excited, Phoebe knew that she was on to something. Especially when she considered all the batches of homemade sauce Mr. V. had been so frantic to perfect.

A few minutes later, Phoebe sat in front of Tiffany's computer, staring at the screen. Her eyes were wide as she reread the words on the Italian vocabulary site she'd found on the Web. The pieces clicked together as Phoebe forced herself to acknowledge the truth. Slowly, her smile grew until her face actually hurt. And then she let herself laugh, a wave of relief sweeping through her. Halleluiah! Tiffany and Tony had been right. Go figure.

A few minutes later, her tears of laughter all but finally stopped, Phoebe picked up the phone. "Yes, could I please speak to Detective Alvarez?" she asked the dispatch operator. Alvarez was going to be livid when he heard her theory, but in her heart, she knew she was right.

Then she realized what this could mean for her and Trace, and a plan began to take shape in her mind. Maybe it was about time to acquaint herself with Tiffany's new sister-in-law. Strangely enough, Angie Venzara might be just the person to help Phoebe fix the mess she'd made of her life. The few times she'd spoken to Angie on the ship, the woman had actually been very nice. And she loved her brother Tony to distraction, that much was obvious. If Phoebe could enlist Angie's aid, then Trace would be forced to listen. After that, it would be up to God and Tiffany's miniskirt....

12

TRACE WALKED onto the cruise ship, and as usual, the first thing he noticed was the rich aroma of tomato sauce wafting through the hallways. It was enough to make his stomach turn. As far as he was concerned, he never wanted to see another damn noodle in his entire life. Mr. V. had had Trace eating more spaghetti in the last two days than any man should have to consume. And to think, he hadn't felt a single ounce of sympathy for that poor schmuck Bobby.

The second thing Trace noticed was Phoebe's presence. She was somewhere close by. He could sense it, and every hair on his body practically stood at the alert.

"Hey, Trace." Phoebe stepped into view, walking around the corner.

He took one look at how she was dressed and almost punched the wall. Forcing himself to study her, he tilted his head and tapped his finger against his bottom lip. "You know, I just can't tell. It looks like you're pretending to be the *exciting* Phoebe, but I could be wrong. You're so good hiding your many boring parts, and letting the wild ones all hang out." Here, he purposely stared at the *nonboring parts* that were spilling from the neckline of her microscopic top.

Phoebe's cheeks turned pink but her eyes sparkled and she appeared inordinately pleased to have him actively ogle her breasts, considering that the other night she'd all but implied he became a slathering idiot when any old pair was flashed his way. "I need to talk to you about that. It's really important. Did you get my messages?"

"No," he said, stepping around her. He didn't explain that he'd purposely ignored his answering machine. After all, what more could they possibly say. The only thing he cared about now was getting his damn career back.

Though he'd still hold off on his story until the cops made their arrest, it had been a stroke of luck that not only had the regular bartender gotten sick tonight, but Sonny had decided to use Trace as a replacement. His promise to Phoebe notwithstanding, Trace wasn't about to miss the opportunity.

Phoebe scurried around him, trying to keep up with his much faster pace. "I really need to talk to you as soon as possible."

His breath quickened but he tamped down the emotion. "Maybe later. I've gotta go make sure the bar is set up. Open the wine and stuff." He lengthened his strides, hoping to escape before falling to his knees and begging her to give them another chance. Damn he was pathetic.

Phoebe jogged to catch up, wobbling on her stilettos. "Didn't they tell you? There's been a change in plans. I'll be working the bar with you tonight. We'll be together the whole time...."

PHOEBE STOOD beside Trace, her eyebrows lowered. The showroom was empty except for the long mahogany table where Angie and Mr. V. sat with his new business associates and some of the showgirls like Daisy and Barbie who'd been sent to round out the numbers and provide the men with escorts for the meal.

So far, everything was going right on plan. Well, except for the part where Trace treated her as if she didn't exist. But other than that, she felt pretty good. Angie had easily worked it out so the other bartender, Brett, had been given the night off and Trace switched into his place, as Phoebe had asked. Not all that difficult in light of Mr. V.'s not-so-secret, not to mention anticlimactic mission.

It seemed that if you weren't a cop, Angelo Venzara was no longer quite the security freak he pretended. When Tiffany had said Mr. V. didn't like the police, she'd been making the understatement of the century. The man not only hated any lawmen, but had a rollicking good time driving them crazy with his suspicious behavior whenever he could. A hobby of sorts Mr. V. had taken up in his twilight years. And one that probably still had Alvarez cursing a blue streak as he'd done when the leaf Phoebe had brought him indeed turned out to be from…a tomato plant.

Grinning, Phoebe shook her head, and at just that moment Angie waved from her seat. Phoebe smiled and waved back, grateful for all the other woman's help. Poor Angie was actually very nice, even if she did have a voice like nails on a chalkboard. And she was well informed about the activities on Isola Pomodoro much to Phoebe's delight. Any gaps she hadn't been able to jump herself, had been filled in by Angie during their enlightening conversation last night. Apparently, there was a brawny gardener or two to whom Angie had taken a fancy, and she made regular trips to the island whenever she could get away. The agreement with her uncle—who indulged his niece in all her romantic endeavors—being, she'd tell no one, not even Tony or the rest of the family, what was really taking place on the island until Mr. V. was ready to make his big announcement tonight. *Big* being a relative term after everything the police had suspected, but still the dream of a lifetime for Mr. V.

And hopefully it was an announcement that as of yet, Trace still didn't know about…. Phoebe just prayed that the massive amounts of groveling she planned to do would soften him up when he discovered that Mr. V. was not smuggling drugs, but growing tomatoes. Of course, according to Mr. V., these weren't just any tomatoes. These were a special produce grown from the ancient Venzara family vines originating in Italy and transplanted to Isola Pomodoro. The highly valuable offspring was to be used as the secret ingredient for Mr. V.'s homemade sauce, which he planned to mass-produce and sell. With Renaldo and Delefluente's help.

That is, assuming these men's own homegrown tomatoes or personal sauce recipes didn't win what amounted to be the giant cook-off taking place here on board the *Mirage* tonight. The final product, if indeed Venzara, Renaldo and Delefluente decided to pool together their considerable cooking talents, was to be called Three Dons' Spaghetti Sauce.

That was the actual reason for the guarded rooms, Angie had explained, claiming each of the three families' tomato plants—the parent vines and seeds originating from the old country, aka Italy, and dating back to the late 1800s—to be more valuable than any street drug could ever dream of being. In her uncle's opinion, even the Ragu family would kill for one of these babies. Especially the Venzara plants, as these tomatoes were by far the best-tasting. And flourishing in the fertile soil indigenous to Isola Pomodoro, almost as if their happy little roots were back in Sicily. And if Delefluente's and Renaldo's tomatoes took to the island even half as well, their company was sure to be a success.

As Phoebe snickered to herself, a clang sounded by the side doors, jarring her from her thoughts. Sonny Martorelli had just carried in the first platter of food with all the pomp and circumstance of a royal banquet. He stopped next to Mr. V. and lifted the shiny dome lid. Steam billowed from the dish and Mr. V. nodded then motioned to Trace.

Trace took the bottle of wine he'd opened earlier and served the guests. As Mr. V. looked up, he spotted Phoebe and smiled. She smiled back and dropped him a secret wink, which made him chuckle.

Mr. V. was apparently a romantic at heart, and had willingly agreed to help Phoebe after Angie had explained the situation—minus the part about the cops, Phoebe's real reason for taking Tiffany's place as a showgirl, or Trace being a reporter. Meaning girl meets boy, girl loses boy, girl wants to lock boy up in one of the staterooms to get him back, what do you say? Fortunately, Mr. V. had said yes.

While Sonny portioned out the servings of pasta, Trace returned and stepped behind the bar, still depressingly successful at pretending she'd turned invisible. Phoebe scowled at his back as the noise from Vincent Delefluente's servers came into the room and the process was repeated in much the same way Sonny had just finished. Robert Renaldo's men came last.

"I didn't realize Mr. V. and his friends were so formal," she commented inanely, desperate for an icebreaker.

"Me neither." Arms crossed over his chest, Trace appeared intent on the men's conversation over the pros and cons of each sauce.

Deciding to use her time wisely, she edged closer to Trace. Her lips were dry and she moistened them with her tongue. "I've been thinking about a lot of things since we last talked."

Trace gave her a strange look then combed his fingers through his hair. "Good for you. That ought to keep you busy," he said, as he moved farther away.

Phoebe frowned. So far, every time she'd tried to move in, he'd moved back, and she decided it was time to put phase two into action. Taking hold of Trace's arm so he couldn't get away, she leaned across the bar. "While everyone's busy, I thought maybe we could slip away. There's something I need to show you in Mr. V.'s stateroom," she said, glancing over her shoulder. "It'll definitely be worth your while."

He raised his eyebrows. "I thought we were done. You're breaking a lot of your own rules here tonight, kitten. No talking to me. No meeting with me. No sharing information on the case," he taunted, his voice low.

Phoebe licked her lips. "I was wrong. About a lot of things. I think this will help me make it up to you."

Trace looked skeptical, but his unquenchable curiosity eventually won out. "What's in the stateroom and who told you about it?"

"Angie. And I can't tell you any more down here," she said, talking from the corner of her mouth, playing the game as if it were vital they not be overheard.

He looked over her shoulder at the group at the table. A loud argument had just broken out between Mr. V. and Robert Renaldo over which of their tomatoes had produced the zestiest flavor. "And what will be our excuse if we're discovered missing?" Trace asked.

She smiled slowly and walked her fingers up his arm. "I'll just tell them that I can't keep my hands off you."

His eyes widened almost imperceptibly and he coughed into his hand. "I guess that'll work," he said, smirking. "You sure fooled me."

Phoebe scowled, but Trace wasn't looking at her. He was checking his watch. "Slip away as soon as you can," he said. "I'll meet you outside the Moonlight Casino." And with a last quick glance, he turned his back as if they'd never spoken.

Phoebe narrowed her eyes. He wasn't giving an inch, and while she may deserve the cold-shoulder treatment, he wasn't making this any easier. It was time for a quick trip to the bathroom before they got together. She'd worn underwear under her skirt, but after this latest brush-off she decided to up the stakes. When she was finished with Trace he'd be begging. Guaranteed.

Less than five minutes later, Phoebe stood outside the empty casino tapping her heels.

"You ready?" he asked, quickly scanning the hallway.

She was more than ready, champing at the bit actually. "Yep. Let's go. Follow me."

"So how did you get Angie to talk?" he asked as she led him toward one of the upper berths in Mr. V.'s private portion of the ship.

"There's a tentative relationship between us, since I'm Tiffany's sister and she's Tony's. So I called and we went out to dinner. I really didn't need to do much. Just steer the conversation in the right direction." And so far, everything Phoebe had said was true.

Trace snorted. "Yeah, if you can listen to her voice. The sound makes my teeth ache. It's like two blocks of Styrofoam rubbing against each other."

Phoebe laughed then stopped outside the room Angie had told her to use.

Hands on his hips, Trace stared at the door. "Well, this is your show. Is the door locked?"

Phoebe forced a worried expression. "I don't know," she said, pretending. Her hand had just touched the doorknob when she heard a faint noise. A tapping sound, and Phoebe smiled to herself. She purposely widened her eyes and said, "Hurry. Sonny's coming," then grabbed Trace's hand and pulled him into the dark room.

Silently, Trace brushed past her the second they got inside. The next thing she knew, his lips were at her ear, whispering so softly she could barely hear him. "Come here," he said, tugging her into another room in the cabin then closing the door.

Ridiculously, Phoebe's heart pounded, caught up in the moment as if she were really in danger. Blindly she reached for Trace. He pulled her into his arms and hugged her tight. His chest was hard with muscle and felt so good she could have wept with relief. Then she noticed the taps had grown louder, steadily coming closer. Her decoy, the big jerk, was supposed to have locked the outside door, but he'd followed them into the cabin. *What the hell is Sonny doing?*

"If he comes in here, just go with whatever I do. Like last

time, when we were in the hold. Okay?'' Trace whispered and Phoebe changed her mind. *Thank you, Sonny.*

A lamp clicked on in the outer room, a sliver of light creeping under the door. Staring at the glowing band, they waited. And then the taps were right outside their room and the light dimmed beneath Sonny's shadow. And just when Phoebe was about to get pissed off again at Sonny for laying it on too thick, Trace breathed in her ear, ''Here we go.'' And then he consumed her in one move.

Trace licked into her mouth and slid his hands beneath her short skirt. He flinched as he encountered her naked skin, then his hands flexed, gripping her bottom, and moving her against the throbbing length stretching the front of his pants. Their bodies pressed together. The need to be absolutely silent, as Trace believed, made her even crazier as she played along.

Guilt about deceiving Trace threatened to steal her pleasure, but she couldn't stop now. Not when he was between her legs, his middle finger sliding deep then pulling out, before thrusting two fingers back in. Her spine arched and desperately she moved against his hand. She could feel her essence leaking into his palm, the sounds of him pleasuring her the only noise in the room. His thumb flicked across her clitoris once, twice, and Phoebe jerked in surprise, suddenly coming in a rush of heat.

Her nails dug into his shoulders and her mouth had the metallic taste of blood from where she must have bitten her lip to keep from crying out.

''Damn, I'm sorry, I'm sorry,'' he chanted in her ear, his voice no louder than a breath. ''I didn't know you were so close.''

''Not a problem,'' Phoebe whispered, causing Trace to actually laugh, though very quietly. Then the light clicked off in the main room and Phoebe suddenly remembered about

Sonny. They could hear the outer door shut then the clear slide of a dead bolt locking.

Trace spoke quietly. "I'm sorry, I didn't mean to do that to you." He started to step back. "I guess I got a little out of control."

Though she had until they docked before Angie unlocked them from the room, she needed to do this now. "No, you were perfect. You *are* perfect, at least to me." Phoebe wished she could see him, but what she had to say seemed easier to say in the dark. "We need to talk, Trace. Right now. I've been going crazy since you left. I'm so sorry. I was wrong. Really, really wrong." She hugged him tight, yet he held himself stiff in her arms. "Please forgive me. I know I hurt you. A lot. But I was so scared and stupid." A shaky laugh broke from her throat. "Mostly stupid, and I want another chance. Not at being stupid, of course, but at doing this right," she blathered nervously. "Being together, you and me. I mean, if you can forgive me and still want me..." Her heart pounded in jumpy quivers, her breath panting as she waited for him to say something, anything.

His voice sounded hoarse. "Really. What about all my women? Aren't you afraid that I'll run right out of this room and screw Barbie? Or Angie? Or whoever the hell female I see first—"

"No," she interrupted, shaking her head though he couldn't see. "It was me who I didn't trust. That I wouldn't be able to keep you happy. I was just so scared that I'd love you too much. I had some childish image of what I wanted in a husband, but I realized that what I need is to have those things from my father. But they're things he's incapable of giving—like safety and trust. Pretty stupid, huh? Thirty years old and still wanting my daddy." Pressure swelled in her throat and she could barely speak. She blinked rapidly, staring up into the darkness. "I know you weren't lying. You haven't lied to me once." She stopped, then laughed. "Other than telling me you were a stripper, but even that was partially true." She shook her head. "Please forgive me. I know I screwed up, but I love you. You're the only man I've ever loved." Her voice broke. "Y-you're the only man wh-who's ever loved me. P-p-please don't stop now. I couldn't bear it."

Phoebe waited, her body tense as tears silently dropped from her chin. She dropped her head down, the seconds dragging over her heart, each one feeling like a thousand. Well, that was that. She'd tried, but it was too late. She'd hurt him too badly and he couldn't forgive her. And as she started to turn away, she felt his hand on her arm. And then he was pulling her against him and hugging her tight.

He groaned into her neck. "Oh, God, kitten. I love you. I've never stopped. Not for nine years. Nothing matters without you. Nothing. I'm the one who should be scared of losing you. I'm a total screw-up. This is all my fault—"

She pressed her fingers to his lips then kissed him long and hard. When they finally broke apart, she whispered against his mouth, "You are not a screw-up and you'll never lose me. Never. And I'll never lose you. If you say that again I'll, well, I'll *bite you*."

Trace laughed and swooped her around in a circle. "Anytime, kitten. Anytime."

Then Phoebe hesitated, knowing that there was one more thing Trace needed to know. "There's something else I have to tell you. It's sort of funny really, but you know Mr. V.'s island? Well…

THE NEXT DAY, Trace lay back against the pillows stacked beneath his head. He held Phoebe's left hand to the light. Absently, he twisted her finger this way and that, catching the sun filtering through the blinds and sending a sparkle of rainbow prisms dancing across the wall from the big white stone. "Sauce," he muttered. "All this hassle for a big exposé on three old guys making spaghetti sauce."

She squeezed his hand and brought it to her mouth, kissing the back of his palm. "Look at it this way. If you or the police hadn't suspected them of more, we never would have seen each other again."

Trace grunted. "That part I like." Then he groaned. "But a tomato farm. And a sauce company..."

"You've got to give them credit. It's a catchy name. Three Dons' Spaghetti Sauce. I like it." She giggled. "I can understand why they were worried about the plants enough to guard them. They're original vines from Italy. Mr. V. said they were very valuable. And he certainly couldn't expect Renaldo and Delefluente to invest without seeing how well their own tomatoes grew in Isola Pomodoro's lush soil." She laughed harder. "Hey, Mr. V. can hardly be blamed if the cops misunderstood."

"Ha, ha," Trace grouched. "Well, at least Alvarez is even more pissed off than I am."

"Good point. Knowing that someone else is suffering more than yourself always tends to have a cheering effect," she teased primly.

"And some private cruise. Cripes, the whole thing was pathetic. Three old farts deciding which recipe's the best and whose tomatoes are the plumpest. Mr. V. foisted off pounds of spaghetti on poor bums like us, the entire crew becoming one massive taste-test group, just so he could beat out his friends." Trace scowled. "At the least, we deserve extra pay."

Chuckling softly, Phoebe rolled over and rested her head on his shoulder. Indulging himself, he ran his fingers through the cool weight of her hair. "Don't laugh," he said. "I have no job. We're going to need all the money we can get."

Phoebe sighed and held out her hand. "You shouldn't have spent so much on my ring. But I love it. And I love you. I don't care about the money."

Trace smirked. "Thus says the woman who's never been poor a day in her life. We'll see what you think of being flat broke when we have nothing to eat and are reduced to living out of my car."

"I think I know where we might be able to get a meal or two. I hear they're always looking for taste testers."

He pinched her. "I'd rather starve, thanks."

Phoebe folded both her hands on his chest then propped up her chin. "I was wondering. Why does your story have to be some big article that sends people to jail? Why not just write about this?"

He stared into her big gray eyes as she talked and felt his chest tighten. Damn, he loved her. Loved touching her whenever he wanted. Lying around in bed. Laughing, and bickering, and making up. He'd never get used to this. Never.

Phoebe had pulled back and was looking at him expectantly. "So what do you think?" she asked.

He shook his head and grinned. "About what?"

"About my idea. I know there are a lot of papers out there that would be interested in running this as a human-interest story. Come on, just picture it. Three ex-Mafia dons, retired and in the spaghetti sauce business? People will love it. You might even be syndicated."

His smile grew wider.

She rolled her eyes and moved up to kiss him hard. "So, what do you think?"

Damn, he loved her. They were going to make it this time. He knew it, and he lowered his voice. "You know what I think, kitten?" he crooned in her ear. "I think you're going to come again. Right—" he slid his hand under the sheet "—about—" and he found her core, silky and wet and slid his fingers deep "—now..."

And what d'ya know, Trace thought smugly. He was right.

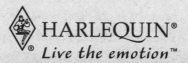

If you enjoyed what you just read,
then we've got an offer you can't resist!

Take 2 bestselling love stories FREE!

Plus get a FREE surprise gift!

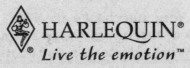

HARLEQUIN® *Blaze*™

Look for more

men to do!

...before you say "I do."

#126 TAKE ME TWICE
Isabel Sharpe (March 2004)
&
#134 THE ONE WHO GOT AWAY
Jo Leigh (May 2004)

*Enjoy the latest sexual escapades
in the hottest miniseries.*

Only from Blaze

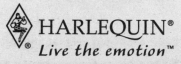

HARLEQUIN®
® *Live the emotion*™

Visit us at www.eHarlequin.com   HBMTD2

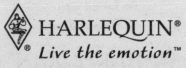